Broken Surface

Seth Garner

HALE
CRIME

ROBERT HALE · LONDON

ISBN-10: 0-7090-8147-2
ISBN-13: 978-0-7090-8147-0

Robert Hale Limited
Clerkenwell House
Clerkenwell Green
London EC1R 0HT

2 4 6 8 10 9 7 5 3 1

Typeset in 10/12pt Palatino
Printed in Great Britain by St Edmundsbury Press,
Bury St Edmunds, Suffolk
Bound by Woolnough Bookbinding Limited

the supporting cast

The indefatigable Joan Deitch for believing in this book from the beginning and never letting up.

Lesley Pollinger for enthusiasm and dedication right from the word go.

Joanna Devereux, Ruth Needham and all at Pollinger for just being great in general.

John Hale, Gill Jackson, Sarah Patel, Shirley Day and my editors at Robert Hale for their unequivocal diligence and professionalism.

Steve Humphreys for the nth degree discussions.

John Blithell for the perspicacious observations.

Shaun Varga for the helpful suggestions.

Howard Roughan for the spark.

And Midori for everything.

Also thanks to Jon Garner, Paul Knott, Sandy Morton, Cordelia Feldman, Andrew Pogson, Tom Hardwidge, Lynnette Knox, Simon Lovejoy, Sarah Harvison, Dan Vaughan, Ella Cope, Belle Briggs, Cat Pitts-Tucker, Jennifer Lewis, Larissa Bannister, Albert Seleznyov, Tim Bax and Rachel Kelley.

For my Mother and Father

When it comes to forbearance you wrote the book

one

I stood outside the boardroom and ran my mind over the situation again.

Holt Fulton Powell & Kelly, the advertising agency I had co-founded, had failed to meet its overheads for the last three months.

I knew that this meeting would be used by Rod Russell – managing director of MediaWide, the holding company that had purchased a controlling stake in our business a year ago – to set an ultimatum. I had a sickening feeling that the word 'redundancies' was going to be used. And as the 'K' of HFPK, and holder of the title of new business director, much of the responsibility was going to rest with me.

I took a deep breath and began to push the boardroom door open, but was stopped by my mobile ringing in my pocket.

It was a voicemail call. 'Duncan, I hope I'm not bothering you,' said my mother, who sounded as if she hadn't stopped worrying in years. 'Just wanted to let you know that your father was asking again about the money for the retirement home for Gran. I don't want to put you under pressure, but I called The Acorns, and they can only hold the place until the middle of next week. And you know what Gran's like about going into a home without Auntie Beryl—'

I raised a weary finger to the phone and cut the voicemail call. I cursed myself for the umpteenth time for promising to lend my grandmother a small fortune to reserve a place at the same luxury old people's home as her sister, Beryl. But I was still determined to see it through.

I put the phone away and entered the room. Two of the four founding partners were already there. Jared Holt and Nigel Powell; our creative director and client services director respectively.

As usual, Jared was leaning back in his chair chewing gum,

chunky trainers lolling atop the polished elm boardroom table, with one hand across his mouth, stifling a yawn.

Nigel was looking straight at me with the kind of pearly razzle that only a client services director who camps-it-up for England and spends two grand a year on dental hygiene can. 'And how is Duncan today, Duncan?' he said.

'Fine, thanks, Nige. Apart from feeling completely knackered from being terrorized all night by a 2-month-old yobbo with a fixation for expressed milk.'

Nigel clicked his fingers and threw an index finger at me. 'Up all night again with the 2-month-old yobbo? Sympathy vote not given,' he said. 'You're the responsible father of two, that's what you always say isn't it? So you're just going to have to live with the consequences.'

'You're all heart, Nige.'

'Steady on the flattery, Duncan, steady.'

'Boring,' muttered Jared, just loud enough for us to hear. 'Been waiting here for ten minutes already. I hope this meeting's as important as Rod says it is.'

'Something tells me it will be,' I said.

He snorted, and his trainers began twitching back and forth as he scanned the room for something to divert his attention. He was wearing a padded black PVC jacket that creaked whenever he moved. He ran a hand through his wild, peroxide blonde hair and let out a falsetto bored-to-tears sigh.

I rested my laptop case on the table and unpacked my computer. God, I needed a coffee. Truth be told, I was tired because I had stayed up until 3 a.m. carving together a PowerPoint presentation in a desperate attempt to convince Rod of the healthy state of our new business prospects.

'Has anybody seen Anne?' I said. 'We really need her to be here. Shall I give her a call?'

Anne Fulton was the fourth partner in the business. She was the brand strategist. Or, to put it into plain English, the person responsible for making sure that Jared's creative ideas matched the personality and style of our clients. It was a difficult job, but one which Anne did brilliantly.

I looked impatiently towards the door. With her sharp mind and level-headedness, it was imperative that Anne attended our management meetings. But I knew I shouldn't worry. Anne would rather die than not turn up to a high-priority meeting with

Rod Russell. Maintaining a grip on company matters meant everything to her.

'No! Don't call her,' barked Jared, flinching as if I'd spat at him. 'She knows what time the meeting is; she knows how important it is. She shouldn't need reminding.'

I let it pass.

A few seconds later, the door swung open nearly shaking the plate glass panelling from its fixings. A waft of whisky mixed with stale cigarette smoke danced past my nose. Jared swung his feet off the table. Nigel's grin puckered at the edges. Rod had arrived. The meeting was officially in progress.

'Where the hell is Anne?' he growled. 'Why are you people always late for my meetings?'

I watched him drop three sugar lumps into his black coffee and wished I had made myself a cup as soon as I had arrived. It was too late now. And Rod was in a far worse mood than expected.

'I'll just get right down to it,' he said, breaking the no-smoking rule and gluing a Marlboro to his cracked lips. 'Your business is struggling. You haven't been meeting your targets for the past three months. This is unacceptable and it's giving MediaWide a major problem.'

Jared stared down at the table, smiled bitterly, and shook his head. Nigel puffed out his cheeks, as he often did when he didn't know what to say. I rested one foot on top of my knee, and fixed my gaze squarely on Rod, trying to guess how far into doomland he would be taking us.

'Creative work's been first class,' sneered Jared. 'Nothing wrong with my department.'

Tiny bombs of spittle machine-gunned from Rod's mouth as he bellowed, 'Don't interrupt me, Jared. You're all equal partners. The responsibility lies with all of you.'

The creative director sat looking at him. Rod tapped on his notepad three times to break the spell.

'Now,' continued Rod. 'I'll just recap on the deal. MediaWide upped its holding in your company just under a year ago, from thirty-three to fifty-one per cent. In other words, majority control. In turn, each of you relinquished just over four per cent from your sixteen per cent holding in the company.'

He held up a grizzled palm spangled with mouldy yellow fingers.

'Yes, yes, gentlemen. I know you've heard it all before. But this is important. I should remind you that MediaWide paid you each a considerable sum for that four per cent, amounting to some one hundred and thirty thousand shares each....'

It was my turn to flinch. This was painful territory. At the time of the sale, MediaWide shares had been hovering around the 190p mark. To take the payment as shares had seemed like a good idea as the group was performing well. Unfortunately, MediaWide had still not managed to reduce their debt. This, plus the catastrophic news that they had lost several of their flagship group clients meant the share price lay bloodied and broken at just 30p. You do the maths; I'd prefer not to if you don't mind.

Rod grabbed hold of his coffee cup, guzzled down the contents, brought it down hard against the tea tray, and turned to us with a turkey-like wobble of his jowls. 'And so to the nitty-gritty,' he said. 'It's written into the sale agreement that MediaWide must purchase the remaining forty-nine per cent of the company in two years from now. But I'll tell you what, gentlemen, I've got Sir bloody Geoff Deacon on my back every day asking about you lot. As one of the most recent purchases of the group, it's up to you lot to perform. And you haven't been doing.'

Jared leaned forward. 'Sorry to interrupt, Rod, but we *have* been performing. We're shortlisted for three awards this week.'

Rod looked him in the eye. 'What good are awards if the company isn't around to receive them, Jared?' He watched the creative director slink back into the safety of his chair.

It was my turn to speak. Jared would only screw things up even more, and Nigel was useless in confrontations. 'Let's look at the bigger picture for a minute,' I said. 'Our new business list is in excellent shape. In fact, I have prepared a—'

'It had *better* be in excellent shape,' countered Rod. 'Because if you can't find a fifty thousand pound retainer client in the next ten days, Sir Geoff has decided that we have no other option but to close you down.'

'You can't,' I said, trying to keep calm. 'You would get no return on your investment.'

'Oh, we can and we will,' said Rod. 'Fifty thousand pounds a month retainer, minimum.'

'That's ludicrous!'

'Ten days, Duncan, nothing more. You've got until just after the MediaWide AGM next week. And there's absolutely—'

He was cut short by a knock on the door. Carol, his secretary, craned her head into the room and whispered curtly, 'Sorry to interrupt, but there's an important call for you.'

Rod didn't try and hide his irritation. 'I don't suppose it's about our missing attendee?'

'Yes, it is. You'd better take it.' She seemed anxious.

'You lot stay here,' said Rod. 'I'll go and find out what's going on.'

After he had left the room, I frantically ran my hands through my hair, searching for answers that simply weren't there. Eventually I said, 'Fifty thousand a month. He's a lunatic! Where the hell are we going to find a client like that in ten days?'

'Don't look at me,' said Jared, placing his boots back on the table. 'You're meant to be the new business guy. I just crack the briefs, come up with the ideas, win awards, establish our reputation....'

'For God's sake, Jared, can you just forget about your ego for one minute? Rod's right – if we don't turn things around, we could be collecting our P45s by the middle of next week. Any ideas, Nige?'

'I think Anne mentioned that Hi-ren Finance may be up for rolling out their poster campaign in Europe. Could be some extra revenue there,' he mused.

'I only wish it were that simple. The last I heard was they were considering slashing their outdoor budgets and concentrating on PR. Same old story. Anyway, it would never bring in an extra fifty grand a month. No way.' I rubbed my temples in frustration. 'Damn it, where is Anne when you need her? She always has an idea in a crisis.' I suddenly found myself hammering the table with my fists. 'I *can't* lose this company, I can't! I'll lose everything. I'll have to sell my house! I need the money—'

Then the door opened slowly. Rod took three steps forward into the room and slumped into the nearest chair. He struggled to raise his head to look at us, as if a heavy weight had been tied to his chin.

'That was the police on the phone,' he said slowly. 'I'm afraid I have some bad news. It's about Anne.' He pressed his lips together as if holding his breath, and for a few seconds all I could hear was the whirr of the air-conditioning.

'What's happened?' asked Jared.

'She's dead.'

two

No one said anything.

A torrent of pain, panic and confusion began welling up in my brain, but I couldn't find any words to let it out.

I looked at Nigel. His bottom lip was moving, but it seemed he was also too stunned to speak. Jared's head was facing the floor, leaving an incessant bunch of unruly peroxide curls spilling on to the table, the artificial colour of which seemed grotesque in the presence of such devastating news.

'I'm sorry,' said Rod.

This seemed to yield the finality, the grim confirmation we were waiting for, and Nigel and I both spoke at once.

'Poor, poor Anne,' croaked Nigel. 'I can't believe it.'

'Do they know what happened?' I asked.

'Apparently, she was discovered by her cleaning lady this morning. The police said they have other statements to take today, but they'll be coming in to talk to us tomorrow.'

Jared shook his head slowly. 'It could have been a robbery gone wrong.'

'We shouldn't start speculating,' said Rod. 'The police didn't tell me anything more than what I just said.'

'I can't believe it,' said Nigel again. 'I can't believe it's true.' His face was completely white, and he covered it with a shaking hand.

'I'm afraid it is true,' said Rod. 'And it's an appalling shock for everyone. Did anyone see her over the weekend?'

We shook our heads. Then I said, 'I worked late with her on Friday evening.' The news still hadn't sunk in yet. It was as if we were being quizzed about our timesheets.

'How late?'

'About 8.30.'

'Did you leave the office after her?'

'We both left at the same time. But we went our separate ways outside. I walked to Covent Garden tube, she went to Holborn.' I suddenly felt uncomfortable. 'Look, what is this, Rod, some kind of interrogation?'

Rod shook his head. 'I'm sorry, Duncan. We're all as shocked as you are. It's just that the police will probably want to talk to you first, as you were the last to see her on Friday.'

Jared glanced at me then turned away. I could sense Nigel looking at me from behind his hand.

There followed a heavy silence. After a few moments, I said, 'I guess it puts this meeting into context, doesn't it?'

'Yeah, bloody inconsiderate of her. Leaving it for us to sort out the mess.' It was Jared, of course. But the comment didn't seem entirely callous. It was the kind of tension-breaking joke that Anne would have approved of.

Rod stood up. 'We should leave it here,' he said. 'I'm sorry to end the meeting like this, but I have to get a report to Sir Geoff. You gentlemen should do some talking amongst yourselves. I'm sorry about Anne.'

As he was leaving, Jared said, 'Ten days to find that client? Surely you won't hold us to that? Not now?'

'Sorry, but what has happened to Anne doesn't change the state of your business. If anything, it's more desperate. The situation remains. Ten days to find the client, or we'll have to wind up the company.'

three

Half an hour had passed. I was sitting alone in my office, thinking.

I was devastated. But I still had a business to run – or to save, as seemed to be the case now. Feeling an overwhelming sense of trepidation swimming beneath my skin, I let my eyes wander around the room as I tried to come to terms with what had happened.

The office was spacious, with whitewashed walls and a black leather two-seater. My desk was fashioned from three planks of thick unvarnished pine, so typical of an ad agency spending beyond its means.

Behind me was a floor-to-ceiling window overlooking the beer garden of the Albert Arms pub on Covent Garden's Endell Street. Today the tables were smattered with a few intrepid drinkers trying to squeeze the last drops of sun from a mild British autumn. Usually I enjoyed the faint background noise created by their hubbub, but now it only made me feel more depressed.

I walked over to the bookcase and took out the company press-cuttings book. I flipped through the pages until I came to a sizeable story taken from *Campaign* magazine, featuring a black and white picture of the four partners standing with Sir Geoff Deacon of MediaWide in the foreground.

The headline said, 'Hotshop HFPK snapped up by MediaWide'. Myself, Jared and Nigel were all grinning inanely. But Anne was donning the kind of smile she always wore in publicity shots. The kind of smile that says, 'Thanks for the attention, but I'd really like to get back to work if you don't mind.'

Whilst looking at the photo, it dawned on me just how different Anne was from the rest of us. Whilst Nigel and I were wearing suits, and Jared was over-playing it in a black tank top and T-shirt, Anne was dressed in a nondescript baggy sweater and jeans. She wore her jet-black hair tied up so it fell in unruly wisps around her neck and face. But the exterior hid a sharp intelligence that would be impossible to replace.

Although I felt guilty for doing so, I thought of what Rod had said about Anne's death putting us in a more desperate position. I wondered whether her passing would hasten our demise.

'I'm so sorry, Duncan,' said a female voice behind me, as I felt a pair of slender arms creeping around my shoulders. 'It's terrible. Awful. I've just heard the news from Jared. How are you coping?'

'Just trying to make sense of it all, I guess,' I said, carefully slipping away and placing the press-cuttings book back on the shelf. Those arms had been responsible for nearly ruining my marriage on one occasion during the past year, and I wasn't going to make the same mistake again, whatever the circumstances.

Although Karen Bennington enjoyed a high-powered position as group client services director for MediaWide, she shared office space with us here at HFPK. We often worked together on new business pitches, and to say she was ambitious would be an understatement. When you're the daughter of a certain news correspondent whose face was virtually burnt into the screen of every television in the country throughout the 1980s, you have a lot to live up to I suppose.

'Nigel's really in a bad way,' she sighed. 'He seems intent on chucking it all in.'

'He's in shock,' I said. 'We all are. I need to have a serious talk with him and Jared.'

Karen watched me intently. I avoided her gaze, but – to my annoyance – still found myself considering her appearance.

She had the kind of eyes that moved urgently, yet gave away a hint of fun at your expense. Her mouth was always in the shape of a quarter smile, and bordered by medium-length, wavy blonde hair. It was the kind of face you would remember if you saw it on public transport. A face that would make you look twice, before spending the rest of the journey wondering whether she was mocking you or flirting with you, or both. Not that Karen would ever be seen dead on public transport, of course. Not when she had a BMW Z4 to break the balls off.

'You're planning on having a talk with them at the bench?'

'Where else?'

The bench in question was located on Embankment, just down

from Cleopatra's Needle, next to the Savoy Pier. It was on that bench that the four of us had first agreed on the idea of launching our own advertising agency. Difficult to believe that it was only three years ago. We'd achieved so much so quickly, and now it was all falling apart.

'I'd like to come too, Duncan, if you don't mind.'

'It's a crisis meeting.'

'I know. That's why I want to come along. I can help.'

'How?'

'I have an idea, that's all. I'll tell you about it at the bench.'

'Thanks, Karen. But I'm pretty sure we can manage.'

I walked over to my computer and fired off a short email to Jared and Nigel, suggesting we meet as soon as possible.

Karen continued watching me. She was dressed in a formal dark-blue business suit which, although not figure-hugging, was diverting all the same. I hated it when she stared at me like this. But she knew how to get a reaction, and I knew she wouldn't move until she did.

Finally, I gave up. 'OK, OK. You win,' I said, running a hand over my face again. 'I'll need all the help I can get persuading Nigel to stay.'

She loosened up a little. 'Good,' she said. 'You need some moral support.'

The inbox on my screen pinged with Jared and Nigel's instantly returned messages. Both were in agreement.

I closed my laptop, and leaned forward against my desk. 'It just doesn't make sense.'

Karen said, 'It must be very hard. I know you were the closest to her.'

She was right. I had known Anne ever since I had joined my first agency on a graduate trainee scheme in the early nineties, and we were indeed very close. Not in any romantic way, of course, and we never had been.

Anne had always been the typical single professional, whilst I was a married man with two young children.

My relationship with Anne was based on a kind of silent understanding; a mutual respect. We were both dedicated to the success of the company, and knew we couldn't make it without each other's help. That was why I would have to give Karen the benefit of the doubt. Like Anne, she was an experienced brand strategist and, in Anne's absence, would be able to offer vital help.

I thought back to the last time I had seen Anne. Last Friday, due to a rare disagreement between us, we had verbally torn into one another in my office.

She had accused me of spending too much time concentrating on the smaller project-by-project clients and letting the new business stream dry up. She had insisted that we needed a single, large, retainer-based client to survive – exactly, ironically enough, as Rod and Sir Geoff Deacon had done.

'Do you know the most difficult part?' I asked Karen.

'What?'

'I had an argument with her on Friday afternoon. We'd straightened things out by the time we left the office, but….'

'Duncan, what's happened is not your fault,' she said, giving me a pat on the back as we walked out of my office. 'You can't go through life regretting everything you do. You have to be strong. Nigel's near breaking point, and it's up to you to convince him to carry on. Think about Anne. That's what she would have wanted, right?'

four

London has a warped sense of humour.

There we were, stuffed up in raincoats and macs in early November, sitting facing the Thames, mourning the death of a close colleague and friend, eager to press on with a thoroughly depressing conversation – and was it drizzly, dark and wet?

Of course it wasn't. It was a bright, blue-skied, spring-like day.

We sat in silence for a while. Nigel began sobbing and had to be comforted by Karen. I experienced a wave of relief that she was there, as I suspected both myself and Jared would have been useless at the task.

I looked upriver towards the London Eye. From this angle you could actually see it moving. I turned my attention to the never-ending stream of traffic passing over Waterloo Bridge to the east. A train passing over Hungerford Bridge sounded its horn to the west. This was the perfect vantage point to witness the capital's blood flow firsthand. Everywhere I looked I saw cars, buses, trains, boats, people. The life, the energy, the sheer confidence of it all was in stark contrast to my feelings of guilt and inadequacy generated by the death of someone close.

'When are we going to get back to work?' said Jared, inserting a rectangle of Juicy Fruit into his mouth. He screwed up the foil wrapper and lobbed it over the wall into the river.

Nigel leaned his face against one hand, and rubbed his eyes vigorously with the other. 'Where's your tact?' he hissed at Jared. 'You're so insensitive. Didn't Anne mean anything to you? *This* is why I'm quitting, Duncan.' He got up to leave. 'I've had three years of this and I can't hack it any more.'

'I'm just being realistic,' said Jared. 'There's no point drowning in self-pity.'

I said, 'Calm down, Nigel. Think about it for a minute. We have to keep going. We will find that client. We owe it to Anne.

Think about how much she put into getting this company off the ground. Our prospects will pick up soon—'

'No one doubts you're the world's greatest optimist,' said Jared. 'But the only reason you're so set on keeping this company afloat is you want to sell your shares for that posh old people's home for your grandmother.'

'I don't deny it,' I said. 'The share price is so bad at the moment that if I do sell, I'll only just about cover the costs. But if we can keep the company going, at least I'll still have an income and a chance for MediaWide to buy out the remaining shares in two years. That goes for you, Jared, and you, Nigel. Anyway, I'm *proud* of what we've achieved. There's absolutely no sense in throwing it all away. Don't you see? Somehow, we have to keep going. Our prospects will pick up—'

'Yeah, that's the second time you've said that,' moaned Jared. 'But like Rod said, we haven't been hitting our targets for the past three months. And we were barely hitting them before that. What makes you think you can suddenly find a big retainer client in – what was it Rod said? Ten days? Are you mad?'

'I'll find one,' I insisted. 'I have to.'

Karen was giving me that look again. 'Duncan, why do you have to sell your shares to pay for your grandmother? Hasn't she got a house to sell? What about your parents? Can't they help?'

'It's the wrong time to talk about this,' I said. 'I haven't got time to explain it all now. I promised my grandmother I'd give her the money, and that's that. It's important to me. End of story.'

'I'm touched,' said Jared, sensing an opportunity for his favourite argument. 'But what's important to *me* is that we're the most creative agency on the planet. *That's* why *I* started this company. And, correct me if I'm wrong, that's why Anne started it too.'

'Stop it!' said Nigel, with a hysterical edge to his voice that made us all silent. 'She's been murdered. Do you hear me? Murdered! And you – you're talking about company politics? Anne was a human being. Not some piece of machinery to make your company tick.' He swallowed hard and wiped his eyes again. 'Bloody cruel bastards! If I ever catch who was responsible I'll … I'll …'

'Oh, yeah,' sneered Jared. 'Of course you will.'

'Shut up, both of you!' It was Karen, her voice hoarse and raspy, and more terrifying than Nigel's. 'You'd better get this thing sorted. By all means grieve, but don't go at each other's throats. What's happened *is* terrible. But you've got almost thirty staff whose livelihoods depend on you getting this company working again. Duncan's right, you know. Anne lived for this company. If her work's going to mean anything, you've got to get through this.'

'But Rod said she was murdered,' insisted Nigel. 'Who could do such a thing?'

Karen didn't answer. Instead, she squeezed in between Jared and I on the bench, and hunched her hands into the pockets on her heavy sheepskin coat. 'OK, speech over. Sorry, but I can't stand watching you lot argue it all away when there's so much to be done.'

'So where do you fit in?' I asked her.

'Simple. As the head of brand strategy.'

'You're replacing Anne?'

'Try not to think of it in those terms. There's another planner who's joining my department tomorrow, working for MediaWide Corporate. He's an assistant to me, really. If you can find that big client and get the company back on course within ten days, then perhaps he could work with you full time.' She saw the look on my face and said, 'Don't worry, he's not going to cost you money. I'll make sure Rod keeps him on the payroll of MediaWide, and not HFPK.'

'Who is he?' asked Jared.

'Oh, I think you know him already,' replied Karen. 'His name is Richard Regan.'

As soon as I heard that name, I felt ill. I turned to look up the Embankment, so as to keep my reaction hidden from the others. I loosened my tie. I desperately wanted to scream out in dismay.

Richard Regan.

The only person in the world who knew the truth about The Accident.

A bad day had just become a great deal worse.

five

I opened the front door of the house and saw my young daughter, Lily, running towards me. She jumped into my arms and I hoisted her into the air.

'How are you, Lily?'

She looked down from her elevated position with a sly, mischievous smile. I noticed – too late – that she was gripping a small pot of something, and that the top was open and pointing downwards towards me. Something sticky dropped out of it and hit me in the face.

'Honey! This is from bees, Daddy.'

I put her down, and she hurried away brandishing the pot in front of her, eager to try the game on someone else. I wiped my face with my tie.

Welcome home.

I entered the kitchen and found Silvie standing over the worktop and eating a plate of stir-fry noodles, with baby Giles sleeping across her shoulder. 'Oh, Duncan. Did you manage to get to Tesco?'

'One nipple pump, as ordered,' I said, kissing her on the cheek and accepting Giles who woke up and began wriggling. 'I think the check-out lady thought I was buying it for myself.'

'What a typical middle-class, middle-England, male thing to assume,' she said, popping a forkful of noodles into her mouth. She studied me for a second or two as she chewed the food. 'It conjures up an amusing image nonetheless.'

'Yes. Let's just leave it at that.'

Silvie leaned against the worktop, observing me. 'Well, it sounds like you've had a quiet day. Usually you can't wait to tell us what you've been up to.'

I looked back at my wife. After all these years, she could still set the pulse racing. She wore her blonde hair fashionably straight and medium length, and had an attractive oval-shaped face with large, deep-set turquoise eyes.

That was all on a good day, however. Today, she just looked tired and in need of a decent sleep.

It was tough on Silvie, having her parents live down on the south coast when she had two small children to take care of in Cambridgeshire. Although, as she herself insisted, it was much better to have a spacious, detached timber-framed four-bedroom cottage to become exhausted in, rather than a tiny flat in the middle of London.

I shrugged. She was right. Usually I did tell her everything about my day. But today was different. I couldn't bring myself to tell her about either Anne's death or Rod's ultimatum.

'Are you all right, Duncan?' my wife asked. 'You're thinking about something. What's wrong?'

I managed a smile. 'I'm fine. I was just thinking that I should be on night duty with Giles tonight. You get a decent sleep.'

'Thank you.' She gave me a hug. Lily ran over to join in. 'But don't look too worried about it,' she laughed.

'Do I look worried?'

'You did when you walked in! Oh, I forgot to mention that your mum called,' said Silvie. 'It was about the retirement home again.'

'Yes, she left me a message. It sounds as if we need to get her in there as soon as possible.'

I couldn't miss the sarcasm in Silvie's voice as she said, 'It's nice you're able to pay for your grandmother to go in that expensive home.'

'Well, I did promise her,' I said, not wanting to get drawn into this conversation.

'Why does she have to go into The Acorns? It's so expensive. Why can't she go into a normal one?'

'Silvie, we've been over it many times. It's because her sister Beryl is there. Anyway, I'm not giving her the money. I'm just lending it to her while the commotion about selling her house is sorted out. Once that's finished she'll be able to pay me back.'

'Story!' said Lily. 'I want *Where the Wild Things Are*.'

'OK, Duncan,' said Silvie. 'I know you made up your mind a long time ago.'

'Yes, I did. I'm sorry.'

Silvie brightened and said, 'Well, at least there's only a couple more years until you sell the rest of your share in the business. Then we'll have some money for ourselves.'

I felt my insides perform a somersault. 'Sounds great.'

She quickly kissed me and walked out of the kitchen holding Giles.

Lily marched over and looked up at me with her arms tightly folded.

'Daddy, *Where the Wild Things Are* – NOW!'

SIX

I was on my third cup of black coffee and it wasn't even eight o'clock in the morning.

This was going it some, even for me. I'd been arriving at the office a good two hours before everybody else recently in order to give myself a head start on my presentations and proposal documents. And last night's feeding duties, coupled with a barrage of never-ending worries and thinking about Anne, ensured that a decent sleep was out of the question.

Giles had woken at 12.30 a.m. and 5.30 a.m. I had managed to get a couple of hours' kip in between the feeds out of sheer exhaustion, but after the last feed I had lain in the bed for an hour or so thinking about what had happened, before getting up to come into work on the early train from St Neots to King's Cross.

I had the shakes. I knew full well that several cups of black coffee after only a couple of hours of sleep were a mistake, but I couldn't help it. The company was facing closure, and I didn't have my best colleague around to help me. It was shit or bust, now. The faster I worked, the more chance I had of keeping it afloat.

By ten o'clock, I had completed a ring-round of half the names in my business card file, but hadn't found any good leads.

I did have some cause for hope when a soft drinks brand for whom we had once done a one-off poster campaign told me they might need someone to help them with a 'new and exciting project'. But my disappointment returned when they mentioned that it wouldn't be advertising at all, but events management – an area in which we had absolutely no expertise – and did we know of any good PR agencies that might be worth talking to?

A couple of dozen business cards later and still no luck. I pushed the phone away and drained some treacle-like coffee from my mug. It tasted disgusting. I coughed and whispered a stream of obscenities under my breath.

'You look like death, if you don't mind me saying so, Duncan.' It was Dan Hitchin, one of our copywriters. I continued sorting through my card box with one hand, and took another slug of the black stuff with the other. 'Sorry, unsuitable comment,' he said. Dan, together with the rest of the staff, had been told what had happened to Anne yesterday afternoon. Not surprisingly, several of them had called in sick this morning.

'Accidental,' I replied. 'But thanks for the compliment all the same. 'You're looking pretty sharp, yourself.'

He was wearing a knitted jumper that looked as if it would fall apart at any minute, and drainpipe jeans with small patches of dried paint on them. He had about four days of stubble growth on his shaven head.

'I don't feel like working anymore,' he said glumly. 'It doesn't seem worth it.'

'We're all upset,' I replied. 'We all feel guilty, but we've all got a job to do.' I slapped him on the shoulder.

'Do you know if they've arrested anyone yet?'

'I don't think so. It's probably too early. They think it was druggies breaking in, so hopefully they might have an idea who it was.'

'Why did they have to *murder* her?'

'Who knows what goes on in peoples' minds,' I said.

'Scumbags.' Dan thought for a moment. 'Was this what you were meeting Rod about yesterday? Or was it about us being closed down?'

I glared at him. If a rumour like that got out it would be the lead story in the trade press in milliseconds. 'Who told you that?'

Dan held up his hands defensively. 'It was just something someone was talking about in the tearoom. I can't remember who it was.'

'Well, it's not true,' I said, immediately wanting to bite off my tongue. But I knew I had no choice but to lie to him. If I told the truth, morale amongst our staff would drop like a stone. They'd spend the entire week bunking off work and visiting head-hunters, and from there recovery would be impossible. 'We're just going through a rocky patch at the moment, that's all. Look, I'm sorry Dan, but I'm kind of busy. I'll have to talk to you later.'

As if to prove the point, the phone began ringing on my desk. Dan sauntered off, and I let it ring twice before picking it up so as not to appear too desperate.

'Duncan Kelly,' I said.

'Hi, Duncan. It's Jane Markham, marketing director from the Tea Society. You made a presentation to us a couple of months back.'

The Tea Society was an independent organization that promoted the consumption of tea in the UK. They did exactly what it said on the tin: they encouraged sales of tea by promoting it through advertising, PR and sponsorship. They made their money from subscription fees from the major tea brands.

But why would something as deeply ingrained in British culture as tea need any promoting? The answer is the high-street coffee outlets. When these shops had first started appearing on the high-streets, the industry had regarded them as a bit of a joke. Now, a dozen or so years down the line, brands such as Starbucks and Costa were ubiquitous, and had changed people's beverage-guzzling habits. This was a big worry for the Tea Society.

These days, young people thought of coffee as the 'top-of-mind' beverage – in exactly the same way as when they wanted a soft drink they thought of Coke, and when they wanted a burger they thought of McDonalds. The Tea Society was worried that, as the armies of time-starved young latte and mocha drinkers grew older, they would habitually turn their noses up at the good old Great British Beverage.

And if they wished to spend money on advertising in an attempt to shift perceptions and alter habits, who was I to turn their business away?

'Jane, it's great to hear from you,' I said. 'How is Derek?' Thank God I managed to remember her husband's name.

'Derek's good,' she said. 'He's just had a promotion to the board at AMV.' It was all right for some, I thought. AMV was one of the biggest ad agencies in the country. No money worries for him.

'That's great news,' I said. 'So what can I do for you, Jane?'

Jane described how they had been impressed with my speculative new business presentation, and especially interested in the award-winning creative campaigns for Froopz, our soft drinks account and flagship client. So impressed, in fact, they wanted to invite us to pitch for the Tea Society account, which was currently up for review. And furthermore, we were the only agency on the list.

I took copious notes as I listened. This situation, by no means unheard of, was a new business director's dream: to be pre-chosen by a client on the strength of your creative work, with a pitch presentation being a mere formality. Not only that, but I knew the Tea Society was a major operation and would be easily capable of paying the kind of retainer fee Rod was demanding.

Jane said, 'Sorry for the short notice, Duncan, but we do like to work to tight deadlines. If I email the brief over to you today, how soon do you think you can get back to us with a full presentation of strategy and creative?'

I grabbed my calendar. Part of me desperately wanted to say: *tomorrow*. But that would appear ludicrously unrealistic. At least a week was needed for us to make a proper go of it. And as this would probably be our only chance of staying alive, we had to do it properly.

'A week today,' I answered. 'Next Monday.'

I agreed an exact time for the meeting, and assured Jane that I was looking forward to it already.

'So am I,' she said.

I put the phone down and punched my fist into the air with joy and relief – and immediately felt consumed by guilt. It was as if Anne was watching me with a distasteful look on her face.

After a few minutes, I heard my email alert sound. I fixed my eyes on the screen. Jane Markham's message lit up my Outlook Express.

I downloaded the attached brief, and had a cursory skim through it before forwarding it on to Jared, Nigel and Karen with a note of the presentation date, and a message that we should all get together and discuss it as soon as possible.

Time for a cup of tea.

seven

I walked into the agency tearoom on the first floor. Karen was rummaging through the cupboard searching for one of her herbal sachets.

'At least there is some good news,' I said. 'The Tea Society. It's looking promising. Full pitch presentation next Monday at their offices.'

Karen raised her eyebrows in surprise. 'Who are we up against?'

'No one. We're the only agency on the shortlist.'

She raised her eyebrows again, even higher. 'Amazing,' she said. 'You *have* pulled a rabbit out of the hat, Duncan.' She prepared two mugs. One with a ginseng and blackcurrant infusion sachet inside, and the other furnished with a standard tea-bag.

'It only took an amount of caffeine that's guaranteed to do permanent damage to my nervous system,' I said. 'The things we do for advertising. I just wish I didn't feel so bad about it. If Anne were here, she—'

'Don't,' interrupted Karen. 'Embarking on a guilt trip won't do you any good. Try to think about something else. Tell me about this thing with your grandmother.' She emptied the kettle into the waiting mugs.

'It's no big deal. She needs someone to lend her some money urgently and I volunteered. She needs to reserve her place in an old folks' home.'

'It's an expensive one, I take it?'

'Costs an arm and a leg.'

'Can't she just go in a local one instead?'

'No, she won't hear of it.'

'What about getting someone to help her out around the house? Meal deliveries, that sort of thing?'

'It's the same home as her sister Beryl or nothing. That's what she says.'

'Understandable.'

'Yes, but the thing is Beryl's living in one of those retirement complexes where buying a house is part of the deal. It was easy for Beryl: she was able to use the funds from her detached five-bedroom Victorian house after her husband died.'

'So?'

'There's a problem. My grandmother's house is next to some disused farmland that has just been given planning permission for a big new asylum centre to be built on it. It means she'll have no chance of selling the house to raise the money. At least, not until the fuss has all died down in the village. It's scared all the buyers away. The government reckon they'll make a decision at the end of January, but that's far too long to wait.'

Karen took a sip from her drink. 'Tricky.'

'This retirement home – it's called The Acorns – will only hold her place until the middle of next week. They've got a huge waiting list. And I can't sell my shares to raise the money for the deposit until the one-year no-sell period has passed, which is Monday.'

Karen grimaced. 'I suppose you've seen the share price over the last few months?'

'Have I ever!' I said. 'I check it several times a day, not that it does any good. The price is around eighty per cent down from when we got them. It's painful, but that's just the way it is.'

'Surely a bank can help? Give your grandmother a loan on the basis that the house will get sold sooner or later?'

'They might, but I've already promised to lend her the money. I'm not going to start messing my family around now.'

'A man of his word,' said Karen, resting her mug on the microwave. 'A rare thing these days in London. In the advertising industry, too.'

'Apparently so.'

There was an impatient knock at the door and Rod came in. 'How are you bearing up, Duncan?'

'I'm all right. I'm trying not to think about it.'

'Very wise. Doom and gloom is the worst way of dealing with it.' He turned to Karen. 'Have you told him yet?'

'I was just about to,' she said. 'Duncan, tomorrow is Richard Regan's first day. How about having a catch-up with him first thing in the morning?'

Again, I experienced the unpleasant churning sensation in my stomach. 'Sounds perfect,' I managed to say.

'You don't feel uncomfortable about it, do you, Duncan?' asked Rod. 'After all, Richard was almost the fourth partner in your company, wasn't he?'

I could feel my chest tightening up. Whenever I heard that name, I always felt as if I was having the life squeezed out of me.

'He and I may have some history,' I admitted. History? Is that how I was referring to my past association to Richard Regan and The Accident these days? Not as the single, secret event that nearly ruined my life, and actually ended someone else's? 'But that's all over with now. We're on good terms. I think even Richard himself admits that not being the fourth partner was a blessing in disguise.'

'I suppose you know about his illness?' asked Karen.

'Yes, I heard he had some problems a few years ago. Depression, and so forth.'

As if I didn't know. He had spent six months in a hospital for the mentally ill on twenty-four-hour suicide watch. Although I suspected that was nothing to do with losing out on the fourth partnership position to Anne – and everything to do with The Accident.

Rod said, 'There's no need to feel any blame about it, Duncan. Whatever happened with the set-up of your company in the past, Richard is fine now. In fact, he's an excellent brand strategist. He did a first-rate job at Jamison Mendell, his previous agency.' Rod chuckled to himself and said, 'You'd better watch your back.'

My thoughts exactly.

Rod slunk away, and I heard him a few seconds later shouting at someone in the stairwell for walking too slowly.

Karen said, 'Going to the awards ceremony on Thursday night, Duncan?'

I rested a hand against the sink and let out a deep breath. 'I don't know if I can make it. My in-laws are coming up from Dorset on their way to Norfolk.' Awards night? I'd forgotten about that.

'I'll rephrase that,' said Karen. 'I'll see you at the awards night, tomorrow, won't I, Duncan? If you're not there it will look bad. How can a new business director miss an awards show? Think of the networking to be done. The amount of clients there, the agencies....'

'Yes, I know. I'm aware of the hob-nobbing potential.'

'We're shortlisted for three gongs. But remember it's not all down to Jared and his brilliant ideas. If you hadn't secured him the clients in the first place his campaigns wouldn't even exist.'

But I was miles away.

At a disused railway line somewhere near the A428 in Bedfordshire. Two airguns, three boys and five tin cans. The scene of The Accident.

Not that I needed reminding of the memory, of course.

It had been responsible for me waking up in the middle of the night on at least four occasions during the past year alone.

'Have the police talked to you yet, Duncan?'

I turned to see Rod standing in the doorway again. His cheeks were an angry shade of red, which seemed to indicate he had been waiting there for some time. 'There's a policeman here, Duncan. He wants to see you about Anne. It's a Detective Sergeant Tomkins. He's waiting in your office.'

'Thank you.'

'Before you go, Duncan, I've scheduled in your meeting with Richard tomorrow morning at 9.30. Think you can make that?'

'I was here before seven this morning, so I think—'

'Good. You'd better not keep Tomkins waiting. Remember: chin up. See you tomorrow.'

eight

I imagined Detective Sergeant Tomkins to be bald, squat, dressed in a cheap nylon suit, and armed with a Bob Hoskins London accent.

But stereotypes are best left to London gangland Brit flicks.

This guy was about 6' 4" and as thin as a rake. He dressed smartly, in a dark blue suit and overcoat, and had a friendly face with an easy smile.

He was examining the creative awards that stood on top of the bookcase in my office.

'How do you do?' he said, with a firm handshake. 'Detective Sergeant Tomkins from the Met.'

'Duncan Kelly. Pleased to meet you.'

'Are they gold?' he asked, pointing at one of the trophies.

'I wish they were,' I said. 'I'd be able to melt them down and retire. There's another fifteen in the cupboard over there.'

'Interesting idea,' he said. 'They for adverts, these trophies?'

'Yes. TV commercials, posters, press ads, various forms of marketing,' I replied, wondering if I sounded like a pompous fool.

Tomkins removed his overcoat and hung it on the coat rail. 'They'll be giving out trophies for lollipop ladies next.'

I nodded with a polite laugh. 'Well, stranger things have happened. Are you here about Anne?'

'Yes, I'm sorry about her death,' he said. 'She was young and, I gather, very good at her job. Don't worry, Mr Kelly, we'll catch those who did it.' He paused. 'Now all I need to do is ask a few simple questions to determine her movements before the crime.'

I noticed that he didn't have a notebook.

'Go ahead.'

'When was the last time you saw Anne Fulton?'

'Last Friday, in the office.'

'Time? Approximately?'

'About 8.30.'

'About 8.30,' Tomkins repeated. 'And were you two the last people to leave the building?'

'Yes,' I said. 'I locked the front doors.'

'And did you then spend time together?'

'No,' I said. 'We didn't need to continue our discussions after work. It had been a busy week, and we were both keen to get home.'

'You say "discussions". What were you discussing, exactly?'

'Clients. How to increase our revenues. Nothing out of the ordinary.'

Tomkins clapped his palms together softly. 'I've heard your company has a cash flow problem.'

'Who told you that?'

'Rod Russell. Your boss. I've already had a chat with him this morning. He said your part of the group is struggling. Losing money. Is that true?'

'We're going through a difficult phase. But we're not losing huge amounts of money. It's a temporary problem.'

'I understand,' he said, blinking slowly as if I were boring him. 'Tell me, Mr Kelly, can you think of anyone who would have had a grudge against Anne Fulton?'

'No. I can't think of anybody. I can't imagine her crossing swords with anyone.'

'I see,' he said. 'Can I have a look at her office?'

'Of course.'

I led him down the short corridor to where Anne used to work.

'This is – was – her room,' I said. This was the first time I had entered her room since I'd heard the news, and I immediately felt that I was intruding somehow. I decided to wait at the door.

Tomkins took it all in. 'A bit different to your office, isn't it?'

Anne had been a cat enthusiast. There were endless amounts of feline-themed bric-à-brac dotted around the room: carved wooden cats, metal cats, stone cats, glass cats. There was a cat-shaped clock hanging on the wall made out of terracotta tiles, with two hands – shaped as fish – positioned in the middle of its belly.

'She had a thing about cats,' I said. 'She even wanted to get an office cat, but Rod wouldn't allow it.'

'I don't blame him. Spread fleas, they do. Dirty animals, licking themselves all the time. Who are the photos of?' He pointed at the half dozen frames positioned on the desk.

'Family,' I think. 'But mostly of cats. She had about ten cats at home, as I understand.'

'Strange, we didn't see any.'

'Not in her flat, I meant at her family home in Essex. Rural Essex. She grew up on a farm there.'

'Why was she so obsessed about cats?'

'I once asked her the same thing. She told me it was because she could trust them more than people.'

'She was probably right,' muttered Tomkins. 'Has anyone been in this room since Friday?'

'I doubt it,' I said. 'No one would have needed to. Except the cleaners.'

The detective glanced at the photo frames again, and gave a final nod, as if he'd seen all he wanted to. 'That her computer?' he asked. 'She didn't use a laptop like you?'

'No, she tried to avoid taking work home. Plus, she didn't need to make as many presentations as I do, so when she needed a laptop she used one of the spare machines. Don't you need to check her emails or anything like that?'

'No need at this stage,' he said. 'Unless you think there's a need to.'

'No, I don't,' I said. 'I was just trying to help.'

He smiled. 'Thank you. Checking the emails won't be necessary.'

'Have you got any suspects?' I asked.

Tomkins bowed his tall frame and furrowed his brow. 'Suspects?'

'Yes. Have you got any idea who did it?'

'Far too early,' he said. 'Our scene of crime guys are still at the flat.'

'What do you think happened?'

'Sorry, Mr Kelly, but I can't discuss exact details. Not yet. But I will say this: for all its trendy image, Camden is still home to a lot of hard drug addicts, a lot of desperate people. Break-ins, many with violent consequences, are a common occurrence. As I said, it's early days, but the evidence so far points to a break-in, most probably by addicts looking for money, or things to sell. It seems Ms Fulton was hit on the head. Either that or she fell and hit her head on something sharp.'

For a few moments, I imagined Anne returning home from an off-licence with a bottle of wine under her arm, to find her front door broken in. Being the type of person she was, she would have marched inside to challenge the intruders, and then....

'Have you got a business card I can have?' Tomkins asked. 'In case I need to contact you?'

'Yes.' I took out my cardholder, and handed him one. He looked at it with interest.

'Partner, new business,' he read. 'Nice title. Now, if you think of anything I should know, please be sure to ring me.' He scribbled a number on a piece of paper and handed it to me. Then he sniffed, took one last look around the room, and shook my hand. 'Thank you, Mr Kelly. I don't know whether we'll be meeting each other again, but if we don't, good luck with the company.'

nine

Maybe it was because he was from the police, but after Tomkins had left it wasn't long before I was reliving The Accident in my mind again.

9:20 p.m., 23 April 1987. Just a few weeks to go until my O level exams.

Richard and I were fooling around near the disused railway line that ran through our village of Great Trenton in Bedfordshire. Even today, I still live only ten or so miles from the spot. Why I didn't put as much distance as possible between it and myself over the years would have criminal psychologists salivating at the mouth.

Richard and I were at a secluded part of the track. We had pushed and scrambled our way through undergrowth and trees until we had come to a muddy, seemingly long-forgotten millpond. As good a spot as any, we thought, and proceeded to line up the five empty baked-bean cans we had brought with us against a fallen tree, and loaded our air pistols.

We'd been firing them for less than fifteen minutes when we heard someone approaching. Richard ordered me to stay still.

A grinning face came into view on the track behind the branches. It was Doofy Gordon, a boy from the outskirts of the village.

Doofy, to put it in politically incorrect terminology, was five sandwiches short of a picnic. Not only that, but he was a bit of a lunatic as well. I can well remember the occasion when he had carried a large cardboard box to the A428, and insisted he was going to 'sleep' in it for a while in the middle of the traffic. This he had proceeded to do, with the box slap bang in the middle of the two lanes for almost ten minutes, while cars travelling in both directions tried to avoid it frantically. When somebody did finally stop to move it, Doofy jumped out of the box and ran around waving his arms in the air and laughing hysterically. You should have seen the driver's face.

Doofy lived with his mother in a dilapidated caravan. As far as I could see, she made a living from collecting pieces of metal from the refuse tip. No one knew who his father was.

'What you up to?' said Doofy in a guttural voice from behind the trees. 'What's them bloody guns?'

Richard explained that we were doing a bit of target practice. Doofy was intrigued, and scuttled forwards to join us, scratching his face on wild brambles (not that he seemed to notice). When he emerged from the undergrowth, I noticed his clothes were the same as ever; speckled in what looked to be a mixture of engine oil and hardened tomato sauce. I also noticed that he was carrying a dustbin liner across his back.

'What's in the bag, Doofy?'

'Food,' he replied, keeping his eyes peeled on the tin cans as Richard outstretched his gun-toting arm and peered down the barrel with an expert squint of his right eye. 'Hitchhiking up to Scotland to find my dad. Glasgow.'

'You're hitching all the way up to Scotland?' I said. 'How long will it take? Isn't it dangerous?'

'Ready,' said Richard.

Doofy belched loudly and said, 'Dangerous? Nah! You daft? I hitched up there, what, four month ago. It took six days. Was really cold and all, but I didn't find my dad.'

'Aim.'

'This time is different. I'm going up there forever. Met someone last time who said they'd give us a job. A farmer, not in Glasgow but not in England, neither. So going up there again. Stay there till I find my dad. Mammy not that happy about it, but that's—'

'Fire.'

Crack! went the gun as the pellet exited the extra-long barrel that had been styled by Richard using a piece of copper pipe for increased accuracy.

There was a loud pinging noise, and a blur as the pellet came zinging back towards us. There was then a tiny thudding noise.

Doofy fell backwards into the mud and lay there with his mouth wide open.

Motionless.

His left eye was in a terrible mess.

Richard and I stared at each other. I tried to find the pulse on

Doofy's wrist, but wasn't sure I was doing it correctly. Richard told me to stand aside.

After a short period of trying to revive him, Richard set the agenda. I was so frightened and confused, I didn't know whether to run away and hide, or run to find help. Richard, however, wasted no time in ordering me to help him push Doofy and the dustbin liner down into the mud of the old millpond.

It made a sickening gurgling sound as we used our feet to push the body under the surface. Richard snapped a branch off a nearby tree, pressed it against Doofy and, with much sweating and grunting, pushed him down to a depth of another three feet or so.

We paused for breath, staring at the line of bubbles that ran across the filmy surface of the mud. Suddenly there was a noise that sounded like air being let out of a whoopee cushion, and Doofy's face broke the surface. His mouth was wide open and completely filled with mud. His eyes, hair and nose were also covered in the stuff.

I closed my eyes tightly and looked away. I heard Richard laugh and say, 'Bastard just doesn't sink. We're going to have to weigh him down. Go and find something heavy.'

'But what if—'

'Now,' hissed Richard through gritted teeth, shoving me backwards.

I ran to the old railway line and began searching around for something to use. I desperately wanted to leave, to run away, to run home and admit everything. But I couldn't. Fear made me incapable of doing anything except what Richard told me to do.

Eventually I discovered a pile of rusty bolts and several large brackets that must have been used to fasten the original sleepers in place. I dragged two of the brackets back to the millpond, and then went back for the other one.

'Wrap them up in his shirt,' said Richard. 'Come on, move!' He pointed his gun at me menacingly.

Holding my breath and trying not to look at Doofy's face, I knelt down beside the millpond and grabbed hold of one of his arms. With much effort I managed to pull him towards the bank. Richard pushed the brackets towards me, and I lugged them one by one on to Doofy's chest, and stretched his shirt over them.

When I fastened the third bracket on top of the other two, the weight took its effect and the body began to sink beneath the surface. Richard jabbed the branch against Doofy's chest and pushed him away from the bank and down into the mud. It gurgled as it slopped over the ends of his old Dr Marten boots, which were the last part of him to go under.

I hardly knew what was happening. I just watched, and helped, and nodded, and listened. I even heard myself suggesting that we should sprinkle leaves and some old, sun-bleached crisp packets over the top of the disturbed mud to help conceal it.

We walked home in silence, pausing only to throw our air pistols and the five empty cans into the river. It was then that Richard laid into me.

He slapped me round the face, hard. 'Never, *never* tell anyone about this,' he growled. 'Tell a single soul and your life won't be worth living. Understand? See you tomorrow, call for me as normal on the way to school.'

He walked away.

I ran into my house, bolted up the stairs, and took refuge in my bedroom.

My parents were out at a careers evening at the local school with my sister Julia, and I paced around the room in tears, desperately wanting them to return so I could say what had happened.

After half an hour had passed, I couldn't bear to wait any longer, so I rushed out to my grandmother's house to tell her what I had done. I had to tell *someone*.

It usually took fifteen minutes' walk to make it round to Gran's house, but I ran the distance in three minutes flat. I promised myself I would divulge the truth the instant she opened the door.

As it happened, however, I did nothing of the sort. Gran hugged me, waved me in, and insisted on making me a cup of tea. When she saw that I'd been crying, she said, 'Pull yourself together, lad. You're just covered in a little mud, that's all. It'll all come off in the wash.'

After that, she wouldn't let me talk about anything other than how I was getting on at school.

Later she called my parents to ask them to collect me. When my father arrived, he demanded to know how I'd gotten into such a state, but Gran insisted to him that I'd been helping her in the garden. Every time I tried to speak she told me to be quiet.

I didn't have the courage to tell my parents what happened that night. Anyway, I was convinced that, come the next day, the police would arrive to arrest me.

But they never did.

Gradually, after a few weeks, rumours began to filter around the school that Doofy had gone missing in the north of England. There had been, as I recall, a half-hearted police search in the Glasgow area, but Doofy's mother had been convinced that her son had ran off to start a new life in Scotland and would never return.

The effect on me of all this over the next six weeks was immeasurable. Whereas before I couldn't have cared less about my exams, now I just studied, studied, studied. The more I worked, the less time I had for thinking about The Accident. I also became obsessed with the notion that the more exams I passed, the further I would escape from the killer-incarnation of myself.

I still saw Richard at school, of course. When I told him I was concentrating on my exams in the evenings he seemed satisfied.

My parents – both teachers themselves – just assumed I had seen sense, and provided me with as much support as they could to help me pass my O levels, which I did comfortably.

I worked just as hard on my A levels and, although I found a place at university studying English, The Accident continued to hold me under its spell.

I found the further away I was from Doofy and the millpond, the more unbearable the guilt became. I realized that putting physical distance between myself and The Accident was never going to work.

Perhaps that's why, at the earliest opportunity, I persuaded Silvie that we should move out of London to rural Cambridgeshire.

Being near the scene of The Accident was my way of dealing with the secret that always threatened to tear me apart.

ten

'You're a monster, Daddy!'

My family and I were sitting in the car on the way to visit my parents. Silvie was looking pensive with her arms crossed. Giles was sleeping in his baby seat. I was entertaining Lily by pulling a selection of faces in the rear-view mirror.

Silvie turned her gaze out of the passenger side window and said, 'I take it you're not feeling stressed anymore, then, Duncan?'

'Yes, I do feel a bit better.'

'I wonder what was getting you all worked up? Is work becoming a nightmare again?'

'No, it's definitely not work. I'm not sure what caused it. Maybe I'm just apprehensive about Gran.'

I took a left at the junction, drove at a steady thirty past the supermarket, and entered the housing estate where my parents lived.

It was a new estate, not more than two years old. My parents occupied a tasteful three-bedroom detached bungalow with a short driveway and detached garage.

'Looks like Julia is here,' said Silvie, noting the old red Citröen parked behind my parents' VW Golf in the driveway. 'This should be fun.'

I swung the BMW next to the kerb. 'They didn't tell me Julia was coming. Maybe they forgot. It must be the first time in weeks that Gran has been able to come round for dinner.'

My mother gave us all a hug and welcomed us in. 'It's rabbit with juniper berries,' she announced, fussing us out of our coats, and kissing the little ones rapid-fire. She quick-stepped down the hall, and we followed her into the large kitchen-cum-dining room.

Dad was standing in front of the huge bookshelf. He looked every inch the scholar with his half-moon glasses, tweed jacket, and shiny bald head with wiry grey hair sticking out each side just above the ears. We exchanged greetings.

My sister, Julia, was already at the dining-table. She waved a hand to Silvie and the kids. 'Hi to the Kelly family,' she said. 'So they give you evenings off in the advertising business, then, Duncan?'

'Yes, Julia, I get evenings off. And weekends too, as a matter of fact.'

My sister adjusted the knitted purple shawl that was draped across her shoulders. 'Lucky for some,' she said. 'I thought I'd have to bring my marking along with me.' Julia taught at a high school in Letchworth, and she hated it; most of all the endless marking of coursework she had to do in the evenings.

'Where's Gran?' I asked.

'She's by herself in the front room,' said my mother, carrying the plates to the table. 'She didn't want to be disturbed until the food is ready.'

My father tweaked Lily's cheek and slapped me on the back. 'So! How are things in the fascinating world of marketing?' A good three inches shorter than me, he looked up and waited for a challenging riposte.

I managed a fond smile, as if recalling some particularly remarkable occurrence in the office. 'Crazy,' I said.

The others took their places at the table, and Silvie began chatting to my mother about Giles's feeding habits. My father lowered his chin, and stared at me over his spectacles intently. Then, with two fingers on each hand bobbing up and down twice to denote quotation marks, he said, 'Quote, "Crazy", unquote, from the man who narrowly missed a first in his degree.'

'I wish you'd stop saying that, Dad. I didn't *narrowly* miss a first. I only *just* avoided a 2:2.'

'If you say so, Duncan.'

Mum intervened and guided us to our places at the table. 'Come on, stop arguing, you two. Sit down, that's right. Are we all ready? Good. I'll go and fetch Mother.'

I was keen to change the subject. I didn't enjoy discussing my academic history – or lack of it – at the best of times and now, with Richard Regan about to appear back on the scene, I wanted the subject out of my head. 'How's Gran been?' I asked.

My father sighed and scraped away the juniper berries to the side of his plate.

Julia said, 'Not too good today, unfortunately. She's not stopped talking about Kenneth since she arrived. If anything, she seems worse than last weekend.'

Kenneth was Gran's older brother. He had been killed in Egypt during the war.

My mother helped my grandmother into the room. I jumped out of my chair and went over to see her.

As I approached, Gran stopped in her tracks and said to me accusingly, 'Kenneth? No, you're not Kenneth. Kenneth has a wooden leg, you know.'

Shooing my mother's hands away irritably, Gran negotiated her way into the chair and looked in horror at the stew on the plate. 'I can't eat this,' she said. 'Beryl would never have served me this!'

I heard my father sigh unnecessarily loudly, and knew it wasn't going to be an uncomplicated mealtime.

Fifty minutes later, we were ready for dessert. We had spent the entire meal convincing Gran that Beryl wasn't hiding upstairs. Now she was sipping a cup of orange juice through a straw and gazing out of the window, murmuring the word 'Kenneth' occasionally.

Lily was sitting quietly and eating the soft middle bit out of a chunk of French bread. Giles was snoozing in his recliner, having guzzled 4oz of milk. Silvie was nodding sagely as she listened to Julia's tales about a particularly rowdy 14-year-old in one of her classes named Cameron, and his attempts to set another boy's hair on fire with a magnifying glass the previous June.

'So, Duncan,' said Dad, pleased that Gran was quiet at last, 'which products have you coaxed the public into buying today then, hm? Hamburgers? Shampoo?' He finished the sentence with a soft humming noise. If you were to do an impersonation of my dad, this is the mannerism you would probably choose as the key facet of your act.

'Oh stop it, Michael,' said my mother, emerging from the kitchen with a tray of puddings. 'He's done very well for himself. We all know that.'

'I'm only pulling his leg, Christine!' He peered over his half-moons and chuckled. 'You know I'm only joking don't you, Duncan? It's only a bit of banter.'

'Of course I do, Dad.'

'So how's the company doing?' he said.

'Well, one of the founding partners is dead, there's every chance we might close if I can't secure a major client before the end of next week, and tomorrow we've got someone joining whom I once helped dispose of a body with at school,' I almost said. Although, luckily for everyone present, what I actually said was: 'We're really busy, and on Monday I have a big client whose business I'm convinced we can win. Oh, my favourite,' I added, glancing at the desserts.

Mother said, 'Well done, Duncan. That's wonderful news.'

'That is good news indeed,' said Dad. 'Now, how are you doing with the funds for The Acorns? Not sure we can wait much longer. Even the GP's been asking what kind of care arrangements we've got.'

My mother gave him a warning look as if to say, 'Gran's listening, you know'.

Dad scooped a layer of caramelized sugar from the crème brûlée. 'Sorry if I sound pushy.'

I was aware that both Julia and Silvie had allowed their conversation to trail off, and were half watching me as they sank their spoons into their desserts.

'You're not being pushy, Dad. After all, I did make a promise, didn't I? The funds should be ready next week. I can't sell the shares until then because I was under a one year no-sell clause.'

'That's good to hear, Duncan,' Dad said, 'because The Acorns have contacted us to let us know they can only hold the place for another few days—'

'Michael, I've already told him,' interrupted my mother, dropping a grateful nod in my direction. 'Duncan already knows the situation. As does Gran. Now, how's dessert?'

'Absolutely lovely,' said Silvie, looking at Lily who had almost finished hers.

'Beryl,' said Gran. She raised a spoon to her mouth and said to no one in particular, 'Where's Beryl? Is she coming back soon? I hope she's not out dancing with Kenneth's friends. I want Beryl. I want my sister!'

Mum rushed over to her. 'You can be with Beryl soon, Mother, very soon. I promise. Now, let's get you home.'

After Mum and Gran had left, Dad made us all a cup of tea. Lily went into the back garden with Silvie to see if there were any frogs in the pond. Giles sat quietly in his reclining chair and, after a few minutes of listening to his Aunty Julia quizzing me on her favourite subject, dropped off to sleep.

'Oh, come on, Duncan,' she persisted. 'How much do you earn? Go on, it must be a fair bit if you're willing to give up your windfall for Gran.'

'It's not a windfall, and I'm not giving it up.' Julia made one of those long whistling noises, the same as she always had done when I got flustered at the dinner table. I continued, 'I'm only lending it to her until her house can be sold. Anyway, what happened to the good old British reluctance to discuss wages? It's not anyone's business what I earn.'

'Oh, come on, Duncan,' said Julia. 'Spill the beans.'

'Can we stop talking about my job?' I said. 'I'm up to my ears in it all day. I don't want to talk about it in the evenings as well.'

To my surprise I realized that I'd been banging my fists on the table. My father was glaring at me in a way that suggested that I'd never really stopped acting like a belligerent oaf after all. Giles woke up and burst into tears.

Julia seemed wounded. 'I didn't think you'd be so touchy, I—'

'Sorry, I'm just under a bit of pressure at the moment, that's all.'

Silvie entered the room holding Lily's hand. Silvie threw me a suspicious look and swiped Giles out of the baby chair. She screwed up her nose and said, 'Needs his nappy changing.'

'I'm not surprised,' said my father, picking up the sauce bottles that had fallen over. 'Being witness to an outburst like that.'

Without saying anything I wandered over to the sideboard and took out Giles's Winnie-the-Pooh mat. Silvie laid the baby down and unfastened his nappy. Julia made a show of grimacing into her tea. While Silvie and I fiddled around with wipes and nappy bags, Dad decided to carry some plates into the kitchen.

It was probably around then that I decided we'd best be getting home for Lily's bedtime.

eleven

That night, I couldn't sleep for hours. When Silvie had got out of bed at half past two to feed Giles, I had continued to lay awake beneath the duvet, thinking, before finally falling asleep.

When I woke up in the morning, I looked at the alarm clock in disbelief. I realized it had not gone off at 7.30, and now it was almost five to eight. Silvie was still sleeping, which meant that Lily and Giles must be too.

If I moved incredibly quickly, I would have a chance of making it into the office by ten.

Meaning I would be, at best, thirty minutes late for the meeting with Richard Regan.

I made a frantic dash for the bathroom.

Four minutes later I was out the shower and dressed. I made a few instant calculations in my head. It was now 8.15. It would take me twenty minutes to reach the station if I drove extremely fast; just in time for the 8.37 to King's Cross.

Into the car. Forget breakfast.

And drive like a maniac.

Despite accelerating away with a spin of the tyres around the blind-bend between our driveway and the road, I couldn't resist stealing a glance at the house.

'Impressive', 'Delightful', 'Imposing' were some of the words used in the estate agent literature, and for once they hadn't been taking liberties with the truth.

A Georgian farmhouse. The real thing, mind you. Not any of that neo-mock stuff. Five good-size bedrooms, all literally creaking with beams. Three reception rooms, two with original stone floors. Inglenook-fireplaces big enough to lose yourself in. Half an acre of land. A selection of outbuildings, one of which I had turned into a snooker room. Impressive indeed. No wonder my finances would be so desperate if the company closed down.

I checked the clock. It was 8.30 exactly. Seven more minutes to go. I pushed the accelerator down and the car surged forward. The needle nudged eighty.

Luckily, I didn't need to worry about speed cameras. There were none around these parts, just endless green fields and the odd pocket of woodland. It was about as far away from the London advertising industry as you could get.

My choice of abode was a constant source of amusement to Nigel, and especially Jared. But I had always aspired to country living, just as many of my peers in adland dreamed of living in one of those all-white, all-minimalism, no-soul open-plan studio get-ups in Old Street or Hoxton Square. Anne, however, had known exactly where I was coming from.

Five minutes later I turned into the St Neots station car-park and threw the car in the nearest available space.

I was in luck – the 8.37 was still at the platform. So I made a dash for it, deciding to take my chances with the parking ticket.

But the train began pulling away, and I knew there was no point in running. I stood in the car-park and watched the train disappear into the distance, knowing that any chance I had of a good day had been taken away with it.

I arrived in Covent Garden forty-five minutes late for the meeting with Richard Regan.

On the train, I realized I'd committed the worst crime in the new business director's rulebook: I'd forgotten to charge my mobile and the battery was stone dead. This meant I couldn't call *en route* to say I was running late.

When I finally arrived at the office, I heard Rod's voice wafting out from the meeting room.

'Don't worry, Richard. Duncan isn't really the most useless person on the planet. He's usually rather resourceful.'

'Yes, I already know that,' agreed Richard, as I walked in. He stood and gripped my hand. I greeted him as warmly as I could manage. It was hard, but I think I did a pretty convincing job.

It was more than three years since I'd last seen him, back before we'd launched the company. As I recalled, Nigel, Jared and I had been all set to begin, but then Sir Geoff Deacon at MediaWide insisted that we needed a head of strategy. As MediaWide had taken a thirty-three per cent stake in the business and were providing us with valuable introductions to their clients, his idea couldn't be ignored.

Jared had worked with Richard for several years in his previous agency, so the name was among those put forward as a possible candidate during one of our conversations at the bench. Unfortunately, Jared had foolishly promised the position to Richard without consulting the rest of us.

I was horrified. It was bad enough that Richard had managed to enter the advertising industry by blagging a trainee position in some start-up or other in the mid-nineties, but the idea that I might end up working with him was impossible to contemplate.

And it got worse: Jared threatened to pull out completely if Richard didn't come on board.

That's when I mentioned Anne's name. As I had worked with her at a previous agency, I knew she was a brilliant strategist. I took Nigel out for a drink to persuade him that Anne was the best person for the job.

So with Jared outvoted 2:1, all that remained was for Anne to agree to come on board. And, to my absolute amazement, she did. HFPK was officially launched three months later.

I only met Richard again once in the run-up to the launch. It was in a pub in Victoria called The Trees. I had been dragged along by Jared who insisted I tell Richard in person why he was not going to be the fourth partner.

Richard had taken it badly. In the pub, he had tried to attack me with a beer bottle, and Jared had managed to pull him off. Somehow, a story got passed around for weeks afterwards that it was really I who lunged at him – perhaps because Richard was discovered the following morning curled up in a shop doorway near his flat, shaking and screaming, and the industry felt obliged to give him the sympathy vote. He was taken to a psychiatric hospital where he had stayed for the next six months, before being released and – somehow – blagging a job at our competitor Jamison Mendell.

And now he was standing opposite me in the meeting room of my agency.

He had changed a lot over the last few years. His hair had been shaved off, accentuating the orb-like appearance of his small head.

His face was peppered with tiny shaving scabs, and his skin seemed almost colourless, with a taut quality about it, as if it had been grafted from another part of his body to repair a burn injury.

But his eyes were what unnerved me the most. Whereas before they had been constantly darting in different directions, unceasingly calculating, assessing – now they just remained dead still.

Richard always had the kind of appearance that made people step out of his way, but now it was the kind of look that made you want to cross the street. He looked mentally damaged. Destructive. I wondered what Rod hoped to achieve by employing him. Maybe he wanted to scare some of the clients into increasing their budgets.

'Traffic bad?' asked Richard, grinning. It was obvious he was putting on a show of affability for Rod's benefit.

'Yes. I commute in from Cambridgeshire. Have you had far to come in?'

Richard appeared amused by this and said, 'No, not at all. EC1. I live just past Old Street tube.'

I was beginning to burble. 'Unfortunately, I missed the train, I—'

Rod raised a hand. 'Save it, Duncan. We're pushed for time enough as it is. Richard, I'll leave you in the capable hands of Duncan here, and we'll have another chat later.'

Rod left the room.

Richard watched me unpack my laptop and pens and lay them on the table. Neither of us said anything. He scratched his arm vigorously through his white nylon shirt.

After a couple of minutes he said, 'I know HFPK is on the verge of folding. Rod told me everything. Looks like you're up against it, old pal.'

I continued booting up the computer, although it was difficult because my hands were beginning to shake. 'We'll be fine,' I said, opening a Word file and turning the screen to show him. 'Now, here is a list of our current clients. The Tea Society is the hottest prospect.'

Richard ignored the computer and began a leisurely stroll around the room, his eyes remaining fixed on mine.

'I see you're still the same as you always were, Duncan,' he said. 'In denial.'

'Currently, the Tea Society is doing some heavy spending in PR. But following a creds presentation I made to them a few weeks ago, they've decided to get back to traditional advertising. Posters and press. And perhaps some online stuff too.'

He stopped next to a window overlooking the coffee bars and

boutiques of Endell Street and leaned against it. 'You see? In denial. You're a sad case, Duncan.'

'Can you look at the screen, please, Richard? I haven't got much time.'

'You haven't got much time?' he repeated. *'You haven't got much time*? You try to ruin my life by cutting me out of this company, and you say you haven't got much time?'

'That's all in the past. Can we move on?'

Richard didn't seem to hear. 'I was willing to forget about The Accident, you know, once and for all. I never told anyone about it in hospital, and I—'

'Please don't mention The Accident, Richard.'

He pointed at me. 'Shut up! Fucking scum! I'm doing the talking here, not you.' He pulled his lips back to expose gritted teeth, and for a moment I thought he was going to really lose it. He scratched the side of his neck, dry skin flaking off, and said, 'You cheated me out of a place in your company. All because you thought I'd tell someone about The Accident. Am I right?'

'Of course not! I believed Anne's skills and experience matched our—'

Richard stepped forward to the table. I flinched backwards in my chair. 'You say any more of that smarmy corporate crap and I'll kick your bollocks in.' The whites of his eyes sizzled.

'I could just walk away,' I said.

There was a pause. 'What did you say?'

'I said I could just walk away. From this job. This company. Leave it all to crash, and wait for my redundancy pay from MediaWide. Anything to avoid working with you.'

Richard chuckled to himself. 'That's not going to happen. You could never do that. I've been doing my research, Duncan. The shares you got when you sold out, you're selling them for your grandmother. You've got to keep the company going so you can cash out in two years' time. You've got a lot to lose if you pull out now.' He leaned forward. 'And you've got a lot *more* to lose if the truth about The Accident ever comes out.'

'Make your point.'

'Listen, you piece of shit. I've been waiting years for this. Here's what's going to happen. On Monday next week, you will sign over the 130,000 shares you own in MediaWide to me. I have the paperwork ready. Totally legit, drawn up by a solicitor.'

What was this? Blackmail? Was he blackmailing me?

'I don't understand,' I said. 'Why should I give them to you?'

'I can see you don't understand,' he replied. 'It's quite simple. You owe me those shares. It's what I would have got if I were the fourth partner. It's what I would have got if you hadn't cut me out of the deal. The way I see it, you stole those shares from me.'

I struggled for something to say, but Richard was too quick.

'This is the bit when you ask me: "what if I refuse",' he said. 'Well, I can see you're preoccupied with the problem of how to break the news to your grandmother, so I'll just come right out and tell you. If you don't sign those shares over to me on Monday, I will tell everyone, and I mean everyone – Rod, MediaWide, the trade press, the police, your wife, and your grandmother – about what really happened to Doofy Gordon. I'll tell them where the body is – and, yes, it's still there in the same place.'

This had to be a joke. It had to be. I spoke quietly, lest someone should hear. 'You can't be serious. This would be suicide. I wish to God that we'd told the truth about The Accident when it had happened, I really do. But telling people now would be stupid. Too much time has gone by. You'd ruin not only my life, but yours as well.'

'Oh yeah? What have I got to lose? I told you already, cutting me out of that deal messed up everything for me, so I don't give a shit anymore. I could tell the police about The Accident tomorrow if I wanted and not care.'

'But what about your career? What about your family?'

'I haven't got any family now,' he sneered. 'Just my brother, Mick – you remember him? He lives in Australia now. And what was the other thing? My career? I haven't got a *career*. All I ever wanted was to run my own company, to be in charge. And you made sure I didn't get the chance.'

I slammed a hand down on the table. 'Will you stop blaming me! It's not my fault. It's nobody's fault.'

Richard wasn't interested in getting sidetracked. 'Duncan,' he said. 'Your life would be destroyed if the news about The Accident got out. Think about how the industry would take it. Think about how your family would take it. It would be everywhere. Front-page news. The police would be on your back. Your life would be a living hell.'

'I didn't shoot Doofy,' I said. 'You did.'

Richard threw his head back and laughed heartily. I noticed for the first time how incredibly thin he was. I could almost see the pattern of his ribs through his shirt. 'Oh, you crack me up,' he said. 'I shot him, sure, and by accident, but you're the one who helped me hide the body. Which, as I said before, is still in the millpond. It would be devastating if such news got out. *Devastating*.'

He was right about that: it would ruin my life. Whatever the outcome of any investigation, my existence would be reduced to tatters. Allowing Richard to go round shooting his mouth off about The Accident was not an option.

'In a bit of a fix, aren't you, scumbag?' said Richard. He had his eyes fixed on me again.

Part of me longed to attack him, but that would be stupid for several reasons. Firstly, he could go through with his threat. I didn't doubt he was merciless enough. Secondly, a fight in an advertising agency? In a time of company crisis? The agency would be closed down by MediaWide before I knew it.

Blackmail, I was learning, was a game of chicken. The player with the biggest balls wins.

'Why are you doing this?' I asked.

'Why the hell do you think I'm doing it? I've told you already. Those shares should have been mine. You should have treated me with more respect.'

'And *this* is how you think you can earn my respect?'

'No, Duncan, I'm not interested in your respect any more. It's too late for that. I just want what's mine. Those 130,000 shares.'

I tried one last gambit. 'They're not worth having,' I said. 'The price is a fraction of what it was.'

'If they're not worth having then you should have no problems about giving them to me. Christ, I should have brought the paper-work with me today! I'm fully aware of what the share price is, Duncan. It'll go up again, it always does. It may take three, five or even ten years, but the price will go up again. And when it does, I'll take full advantage. You, on the other hand, will remain thankful that I kept my word and never told anyone about The Accident.'

'This is ridiculous,' I said. 'I can't agree to anything right now. I need time to think.'

'I know you do, Duncan. That's why I'm giving you until Monday. So you can prepare the necessary excuses to your family. I'm being *nice* to you.'

'What the hell do you expect me to tell them?'

He shrugged. 'I don't care. Just make sure you're ready to sign on Monday. Otherwise you know what will happen on Tuesday. Understand?'

I nodded. 'I understand.'

Richard moved towards the door. 'Monday,' he said. 'Oh, and about your clients? Wasn't that the real reason for this meeting today? Send me an email with the details. I understand there's a review tomorrow for the Tea Society, which I'll take the liberty of inviting myself to. See you later.' He waved goodbye and left the room.

I remained seated at the head of the boardroom table. Part of me wanted to go after Richard and give him a good beating ... but I couldn't risk it.

I thought of Gran, of Doofy, of Mum and Dad. And then of Silvie, Lily and Giles, and knew that, either way, my life was about to be ruined.

Then, as if to hammer the final nail of hatred into me, Richard suddenly stuck his head back into the room, and said, 'By the way, sorry to hear about Anne. It must have been a real shock for you.'

And with that, he was gone.

twelve

I was sitting at the desk in my office. It had been almost an hour since my meeting with Richard, and I still hadn't decided what to do.

I ran a hand through my hair and found that my brow was covered in sweat. I would have to go to the washroom and splash my face with cold water. Again.

'Found that all-important client yet?'

It wasn't a voice I immediately recognized. I glanced up from my laptop screen and saw Sir Geoff Deacon with Rod. Behind them was the man I recognized as his chauffeur, Andy Flanagan.

Sir Geoff cut a cartoon-like figure in a dark navy blazer and satin polka dot cravat. He was very much 'old school' advertising. He believed to be successful in the business, one had to make a statement every step of the way. Which was presumably why, judging from the few times I had met him, he seemed to have such an appalling taste in clothes. That being said, today's attire was positively mild compared to the usual cream-coloured linen suits he wore in summer, and khaki safari outfits he sometimes sported in autumn.

But, *haute couture* aside, he was the chief executive of MediaWide, and you couldn't help but feel humbled and not a little daunted whenever you came face to face with him.

I immediately stood up. 'I'm working on it,' I exclaimed, taking care not to overdo the enthusiasm.

Sir Geoff shook my hand. I asked them if they wanted to sit down to hear the details about the Tea Society.

'No, thank you,' replied Sir Geoff. 'We have some important business to do.'

'Other than drinking my whisky,' said Rod.

All three of them roared with laughter, even Flanagan. He was 6' 6" of pure brawn, and was rumoured to be ex-army. He wore a dark, expensive suit that contrasted with his shaven head and goatee beard. From what I could see, he didn't appear to have any neck at all; his tie seemed to disappear into his chin.

I waited for them to stop laughing and said, 'We're working hard to find the big client, Sir Geoff. You certainly won't need to close us down.'

It was clear from his response that Sir Geoff thought I was being confrontational. 'Really? Well, if you and your colleagues can prove to me exactly why I should *not* close you down, then I won't do so. But as it is, you are causing me nothing but problems – very *big* problems.'

The chairman of MediaWide waited for my apology. Flanagan tilted his head back, and gave me a condescending, threatening look.

'I'm sorry,' I said.

'Just find that client,' said Sir Geoff.

Rod ushered them towards the door and, before I could say anything else, they had gone. No goodbye, no condolences about Anne, nothing.

I crashed back into the chair again, deep in thought.

'Daydreaming on the job? Don't you have a company to save?'

At first I thought it was Sir Geoff again, but then I saw Jared standing opposite my desk. I saw the clock and realized I had been sitting thinking for over thirty minutes.

The more I turned it over in my mind, the more it became clear that Richard had me in a tight corner.

But the ultimatum set by Rod remained. I had to win us the Tea Society account. I took a long, deep breath and tried to push Richard Regan out of my head.

'There's an excellent new business prospect,' I said. 'Did you see my email?'

'The Tea Society? Do you really think they could bring in the kind of money that Rod's after?'

He was chewing gum again, smacking his lips incessantly.

'Without a doubt,' I said. 'They're currently spending more than fifty thousand a month on PR alone. But they want to move back to advertising because they've found PR hasn't been working as well as they'd liked. When they saw the campaigns for Froopz and Jackmann Fitness I showed them last month, they decided that we're the agency for the job.'

Jared grinned as he let his pride get the better of him. The ideas behind those campaigns had been his. In the case of the Jackmann Fitness brief, the creative teams had scribbled for an entire week on their layout pads trying to crack the brief – until Jared had turned up on a Friday morning with a brilliant concept fully mocked up. We had all been amazed, but not entirely surprised. Our two creative teams seemed more and more to be a token department. It was Jared who came up with all the big ideas.

The Jackmann Fitness campaign had gone on to win major awards at four of the world's leading shows: gold at Cannes, a silver pencil at D&AD in London, and bronzes at Clio and The One Show in the US. MediaWide had done very well out of the publicity, and Sir Geoff Deacon had insisted that duplicates of the trophies be displayed in their reception area.

Most importantly for Jared, it had been one in the eye for his father who was a co-founder of one of the country's largest ad agencies and an advocate of the view that his son never had what it took to pass O level English, let alone be a creative director.

The comment about Froopz and Jackmann Fitness seemed to do the trick. Jared warmed to the idea of the Tea Society, and he agreed enthusiastically to my suggestion of an impromptu briefing.

'I'll go and fetch Nigel and Karen,' he said. 'Also, I've been told that Richard will be working with us.' I could see he was trying not to make it a big deal. 'Have you debriefed him on the client list?'

'Yes, I met with him about an hour ago.'

'Productive meeting?'

'Yeah ... it seemed to go pretty well. He's eager to get started.' I was keen to get back to the Tea Society, but I didn't want to appear flustered. 'How do you feel about working with him again?'

'Can't say I'm crazy about it. And it's worse after what happened to Anne. I suppose it's just the way things have turned out. Shall I ask Richard to come along too?'

'He's probably busy swotting up on the client lists. I sent him an email containing a list of new business prospects. Let's not ask him unless Karen specifically requests it.'

Jared resumed smacking his lips, and I detected a sense of relief in his eyes. 'Good idea,' he said.

A few minutes later, he returned with Nigel and Karen. They all had mugs of coffee in their hands. Nigel was holding two, and handed me one.

'Black, two sugars,' he said.

'Godsend,' I replied. 'Feeling any better, Nige?'

He thought for a moment and nodded.

'So. The Tea Society,' announced Karen. 'It looks promising. Do you want to fill us in on the story so far, Duncan?'

Karen, Jared and Nigel sat down and began making notes as I recapped on how the business lead had been generated.

All we needed to do, I told the three of them, was turn up at the presentation, shake hands, tell a few jokes (only Karen smiled at this), present a solid marketing strategy and some great creative ideas – and we'd be home and dry.

HFPK would be saved.

And, I thought to myself, Duncan Kelly and extended family would be very relieved indeed.

All I'd have to face then would be Richard Regan....

'It's there for the taking,' I said. 'It's easily worth fifty grand a month. What do you think a fee like that would buy them, Nige?'

He wrote some numbers on his jotter. 'I think we can put together a dedicated team for them. Fifty grand is a hefty retainer for a company of our size, so it will swallow up a fair amount of resources.'

'It's worth it,' chipped in Karen. 'For fifty grand and the guaranteed survival of the company, they can use as many resources as they like.'

Nigel continued. 'The team would comprise an art director and copywriter, two account execs, one planner and a project manager or two. The fee could also buy the undivided attention of yours truly for at least half the week, and eight hours a week of Jared's time.'

'Bargain,' said the creative director.

'It's serious money,' countered Nigel.

'Good,' Karen said. 'That's the money out of the way. Let's go through the brief. That OK with you, Duncan?'

I waved a hand in agreement. 'Fine with me. You're the new temporary head of strategy.'

'Thank you.' She switched her attention back to the printout. 'It all looks pretty straightforward. It's not so much a brand-building campaign as a reinvention exercise. They're keen to counteract the rising sales of coffee, particularly amongst the youth market, and want a campaign to challenge current perceptions. Any comments so far?'

'Yes,' I said. 'Just playing devil's advocate for a second, isn't such a strategy hugely risky?'

The truth was, I still felt full of anxiety, and I hoped that talking would help take my mind off The Accident and calm me down.

'As in?'

'Well, they run the risk of alienating their core market. The great tea-drinking British public. If we go out there with one of Jared's funky, award-winning ideas, isn't there a chance of the product becoming too niche?'

'Not the slightest chance,' said Karen. 'Tea drinking is too deeply ingrained in the cultural psyche of this country. All we're going to do is target a small segment of the public, and challenge *their* perceptions. The great untargeted will never know.' She flicked a renegade curl from one of her eyes. 'Besides, the media budget will be nowhere near large enough to shift perceptions amongst the wider public. That would require a spend of gargantuan proportions, and it would be silly anyway.'

'Point taken,' I said. 'Anyway, as long as they spend their money with us, I don't really mind what they do.'

Karen nodded. 'Exactly. Now, according to the brief, they want the tone to be edgy and challenging.'

'Tea is about as edgy as a freshly ironed sock,' warbled Nigel. It was the first time I had seen him smile since he had heard the news about Anne.

'That may be true,' said Karen. 'But there's nothing wrong with shaking things up a bit. It's a brand-repositioning job, after all. Look at Super Noodles, and what a bit of brave reinvention advertising did for their sales.'

'Yes, I suppose so. Do the tea brands have any say in the marketing campaign?'

Karen looked over to me. 'Duncan?'

'Jane Markham said they're not too bothered about it. They each have their own established brands, their different positions in the market. As far as I can gather, they agree with the Tea Society about the need to fight the rising trend in coffee sales. That's all she said. Which probably means she forgot to ask them.'

'I'll buy that for fifty grand,' said Karen.

Jared was unusually quiet. He was sitting patiently, biding his time. Normally by this stage he would have taunted Nigel something rotten, and would have offended everyone else at least once with his sarcastic comments. But, in this meeting at least, he seemed unnervingly reserved.

I noticed he was clutching some folded-up sheets of A3 paper. That must mean he had some ideas already. He was sipping a fizzy raspberry drink from a plastic bottle through a straw, and kept pausing to bulge out his cheeks and slosh the liquid around his mouth before swallowing it. And, as always, he had a piece of chewing gum stuffed in there somewhere.

'Moving to the proposition,' Karen continued, 'which is, "refreshingly healthy", I kid you not.'

I laughed. 'Healthy? On what grounds?'

'The positive qualities are detailed in the support section at the bottom of the page,' she said. 'Quote, "Tea is rich in polyphenols, including catechin flavonoids, which are potent antioxidants that protect cells from damage. Tea is the best source of this type of active flavonoids", unquote.'

'What does that mean?'

'I think it means it's good for you, Duncan. Drink a lot of it. Green tea's the best.'

'OK, but let's not allow any of those words to find their way on to the ads. Keep it quick and simple. Remember the target market. They get very bored, very quickly. What do you think, Jared?' I asked. 'You're strangely quiet.'

'I think the proposition's a good one,' mused the creative director. 'It conjures up good images.' He unfolded the sheets of A3 paper. 'I've scamped up a couple of rough ideas, as it happens.'

He fished a piece of bright orange chewing gum out of his mouth and threw it into the bin by my desk. I noticed that the fingernails on each of his hands were crowned with dried blood where they had been bitten down to the quick.

'Let's hear it,' said Karen.

'This might raise a smile,' he said, holding up the first sketch for us to see.

It was a large picture of the recently disgraced Home Secretary, whose son had been arrested for drunk and disorderly behaviour outside a football ground a few days before. The man looked terrible. He had been photographed standing by the front door of his Chelsea home, looking as if he had been subjected to three rounds with a heavyweight boxer. He looked thoroughly tormented by the pressure of being the high-profile father of a mindless thug with a penchant for jabbing people with broken bottles.

However, in true Jared style, a negative image had been turned on its head to create a superb creative idea. Above the politician's head was a headline in a subtle typeface, which said simply: 'Someone give him a cup of tea'. The small type – the bodycopy – spelt out the invigorating health benefits of a single cup of tea in plain English.

Simple, striking, memorable and the kind of idea you wished you had come up with yourself. All the winning ingredients were there. It felt good to be talking about good advertising again. I was beginning to feel a lot better.

'As you can see,' said Jared, 'it's a tactical campaign. Highly visual and immediate. Ideal for those with attention spans of less than three nanoseconds, otherwise known as our target audience. We can run it off the back of daily news.'

I wanted to be the first to voice my support. 'I like it. I think it's strong. And it's definitely edgy.'

'There's a lot more where that came from,' added Jared. He then went on to reel off a list of recent scandals that we could use. Anything too edgy or tragic was left out. Anything that had whipped the middle-England readers of the *Daily Mail* or the *Telegraph* into a frenzy was most definitely in.

'It works, it answers the brief. It's fresh. What's the turnaround time for something like this?' asked Karen.

'It's not a problem,' revealed Nigel. 'There have been tactical press ads that have run on the same day in the past. And TV space – provided it's on the satellite channels, which I gather will probably be in the media plan – can be booked with as little as a single day's lead time. I think we could just book the media space and wait for the scandals to present themselves.'

'The turnaround time is no problem,' I agreed. 'Tell me, is this one of your own ideas, Jared, or one of the team's?' I didn't really need to ask, but it was worth giving Jared his moment of glory. A bit of ego massaging in these times of crisis wouldn't do any harm.

'I haven't told the team about this job yet,' he said. 'They're busy on the bread-and-butter projects like Puppie-Snoops and Hi-ren Finance. I did it myself.'

'Well, judging by the strength of this first idea, you won't need to tell them,' I replied. 'I think you've cracked it, kid. What's the other idea?'

He placed the first piece of paper on the coffee table and held the other piece towards his chest. 'This is more controversial,' he said, 'but interesting.'

Nigel edged forward in his chair. 'Controversial is good.'

'We create our own reality TV show,' Jared continued, turning round the A3 sheet to show a photocopy of a well-endowed naked man.

Karen laughed saucily.

Nigel said, 'Impressive. But how did you manage to acquire a nude photograph of me, exactly?' He was really lightening up.

'Listen,' said Jared, brushing the interruptions aside, and waving his hands excitedly. 'We create our own reality TV show but, of course, we don't show it on TV. That *would* cost loads of money, unless the client could sort out a hefty sponsorship deal, which we don't have the time for. What we will do is show it on the Internet instead. We create a website that features a webcam showing the room where this guy lives. Easy, cheap, and bang-on as far as the target audience goes.'

Karen: 'So what happens?'

Jared ran his tongue over his lips. It was bright orange. 'It's cool,' he said. 'There's this small white room, right? There's a camera in the wall, a webcam. And what we do is put a guy in there for six months with nothing. No food, no clothes, no TV, nothing to read. Zilch. The only way he can get hold of things is to enter mail-order competitions, scratchcards and the like. We send him a bunch of junkmail; a certain amount a day. Anything he wins is listed on the webpage, and he can use it to help make his life more bearable. It's like an ongoing one-man endurance extravaganza. It's naked survival!'

Karen again: 'And we promote this website – this one-man web comedy-drama – with press, posters and TV?'

'Got it,' said Jared. He started biting his fingernails, and then pulled his hand away and buried it in his pocket. With his other hand, he produced a stick of chewing gum from somewhere, pulled off the foil and pushed it into his mouth. He seemed nervous. I presumed he was getting worked up about whether we liked the concept or not.

'It's intriguing, but where does the Tea Society come in?' I asked.

'Simple,' he said, 'and this is the clever bit. The only thing he's allowed to drink for the whole six months is tea.'

'So he's able to keep healthy, right?' commented Nigel.

'Yep,' agreed Jared. 'Although, in reality, the guy will probably turn into a hyperactive, malnourished, caffeine-addled lunatic. But that doesn't matter. What *does* matter is that kids will love it and the press will love it.'

'It's not half an idea,' I said. 'It's big. It's got the word "PR" plastered all over it. It's cult enough. It's bizarre. Did you say six months?'

'Yeah, six months. Anything shorter, and there won't be enough time for it to build into a media event. The guy will be really tormented by the time he's been in there for a few months, and kids will be fascinated by it, trying to guess what he's going to do next, hoping to see him top himself.' The creative director laughed nervously.

'What will he eat?' Nigel asked.

'Only what he wins,' replied Jared. 'A year's supply of baked beans, that kind of thing. Whatever prizes he can score from the junkmail.'

Nigel rubbed his chin. 'Sounds a bit extreme. We can't deprive him of food. It's inhumane.'

'Inhumane?' spluttered Jared. 'It's *entertainment*. It's what the public wants to see.'

'Is he allowed to clean his teeth?' I asked, trying to lighten the mood. 'They'll turn a disgusting shade of yellow otherwise.'

'No! That's cheating.'

'It might not reflect well on the product if the guy's teeth go bad and fall out.'

'No,' said Jared again. 'The idea is set in stone. It's a guaranteed award winner. I'm not changing any aspect of it.'

'Fair enough. Nigel? Your thoughts?'

The client services director clapped his hands excitedly. 'I think it's a rather wonderful idea, as long as I get to choose the talent. Someone who looks like Richard Gere, but who's hung like a donkey. Let's get Michael Portillo!' He blushed at his own joke, and I realized he was pushing himself to be jovial.

'Who says it has to be a man?' I shrugged, and turned towards Karen.

'Sexist pig. You couldn't afford six months of my time.' She smiled a kooky smile. Damn! She had taken it as some kind of come-on. If there was one thing I didn't need it was Karen thinking I was making a pass at her. 'This reality show is a great idea,' she said enthusiastically. 'It's fantastic, in fact. It's just ... it's just that it seems slightly familiar. Haven't I seen it somewhere before?'

'No,' said Jared. 'It's totally original. Unless you can see into here.' He tapped the side of his head.

'Well, I've never seen it before,' I offered.

'Me neither,' added Nigel. 'And I think I would remember if I had done.'

'OK then,' said Karen. 'Outvoted. I must be getting confused with something else.' She closed her notebook. 'Let's leave it there for now. I think both ideas are worth pursuing. Jared, you can start working them both up on the Mac. We'll have another internal review tomorrow. Maybe I'll ask Richard if he wants to come along.'

I could feel myself shaking my head. 'No!'

Everyone looked at me. I had reacted a little too loudly, a little too urgently.

'What do you mean "no"?' asked Karen.

'What I meant was ... I don't think I can make it tomorrow. I might be out at another meeting.'

Karen looked confused. 'I already checked your diary, Duncan. I didn't see any time booked out for tomorrow.'

I knew I was digging myself into a hole. 'Yes,' I said, 'you're right. I think I got confused with something else.' I silently cursed Richard Regan.

'Good,' said Karen, eyeing me suspiciously.

Jared began nibbling on his fingernails again and wandered back to his desk. Nigel stopped by the door. 'Going to the awards show tomorrow night, Duncan? I am. You know, to help get over the bad news and all that. We can have a few drinks and a good chat.'

I was just about to tell him I couldn't as Silvie's parents were coming to visit, when Karen said, 'Yes, he is. Aren't you, Duncan?'

Unfortunately, I knew she was right. Any awards ceremony was a crucial date in the social calendar. I couldn't afford not to go. Reluctantly, I said, 'Yes, I am.'

'Great,' said Karen. 'Richard will be there too.'

thirteen

I never really expected to get much work done that afternoon, as I was preoccupied with considering Richard's threat.

Thank God the Tea Society meeting had been a productive one, I thought, as I could now leave the others alone to get on with putting the presentation boards together.

Towards the middle of the afternoon I decided to get out of the office for some fresh air.

I grabbed my coat and left without anyone noticing. I informed Hilary I was going out to meet a new business contact, and that I would be away from the office for the rest of the day.

I felt better as soon as I emerged from the stainless steel revolving door on to the street. I took a sharp breath of ice-edged November air, subtly flavoured with petrol fumes and burnt toast courtesy of the taxis and greasy spoons, and walked in the direction of Global Coffee, an Internet café near Covent Garden tube station.

The tourists and street performers had greatly diminished since the warmer months, but there was still a buzz about the place. Shivering olive-skinned girls with European accents waved into camera lenses. Mime artists entertained passers-by generous enough to drop a few coins into their collection boxes. Street traders stood behind boxes of cheap novelty toys. There was even a tramp who had hit on the notion of collecting money by blowing loud noises through an old traffic cone.

I reached Global, found a spare terminal, and began thinking. Richard Regan. The Accident....

Two things were clear. First, there was absolutely no way I was handing my shares over to him. I had been through a lot to get my hands on them, and I was determined to fulfil my promise to my grandmother. No one would stop me from doing that.

The other was that Richard's freakish behaviour had unnerved me. He had been impulsive, unstable, and obviously past the point of caring any more. I strongly believed that he would go through with his threat.

I considered the options.

Telling Karen, Rod or even Sir Geoff Deacon that Richard was not suitable for the job would have dire consequences. And what would I tell them anyway? That we didn't require Richard's help – when we needed all the help we could get?

Going to the police was also a strict no-no. In fact, that was probably the worst option of all. I would be a fool to even entertain the idea.

No, Richard may have developed into the psycho I always suspected him to be, but he'd certainly made sure his scam was airtight. He had me over a barrel.

I suddenly had a brainwave. How about if I contacted the doctors at the hospital where Richard had been treated, and told them he was trying to blackmail me with fictitious claims?

The notion disappeared as quickly as it had arrived. Even if the doctors did believe me, I would still be risking my reputation if Richard's claim got out. And at this point in time, with Rod's ultimatum hanging over the company, that would prove fatal.

Besides, if Doofy's body was still in the same place as Richard claimed it to be, then all it would take was one curious journalist or detective.

It was useless. There was no way out.

I checked my watch. I had been sitting thinking for almost twenty minutes, and I still hadn't typed in a single web address.

So I entered the same one I always did when I was in need of a little diversion.

Ad-versity.com.

It was a website dedicated to the hardships suffered by the advertising industry. There were news stories about companies in trouble, agencies losing accounts, clients pulling budgets, and key figures who had lost their jobs. The site was run by a group of industry journalists as a side project. At least, that's what everyone believed. In reality, no one really knew who wrote the site, and the web domain was registered to an address in Brighton. And no one cared. The fact that it was an interesting and revealing read was what mattered.

As the homepage loaded up, I suddenly experienced a sickening premonition that the main headline would be, 'Duncan Kelly of HFPK investigated for 1987 murder'.

But that's what a guilty conscience is all about. You are convinced you will be exposed at any moment. It was at times like these I wished I had confessed all on the evening of The Accident. My life would have been hell, sure, but it would all be in the past now, and I would be on a level footing with society – and what remained of Doofy's family – again.

When the homepage appeared, I immediately noticed a headline of one of the smaller news stories. I tensed and clicked on it.

TOP AD EXEC MURDERED IN SUSPECTED BOTCHED BREAK-IN

Metropolitan police today confirmed that Anne Fulton, 32, co-founder and planning director at leading creative hotshop HFPK had died as a result of a serious head wound, following a break-in at her home in Camden. She was discovered two days later by a cleaning lady.

Fulton was widely known as one of the best strategists on the London advertising scene. She had helped mastermind the relaunch of several major brands including Froopz and Jackmann Fitness Clubs at the agency she co-founded three years ago.

In recent months, however, the agency has suffered a general downturn in business, and it is believed that Fulton had been growing increasingly depressed and disillusioned with her job.

She will be remembered by her friends and colleagues for her wit, easy sense of humour and dedication to a profession that she loved.

A private funeral service will be held next Tuesday in the village of Little Hayford, Essex.

I sighed heavily. Head wound? Break-in? I wondered again how something like this could happen to Anne of all people. I clicked the back button on the browser to exit the story.

But I couldn't stop thinking about the third-from-last paragraph. Where had they got that piece of information? I had never seen Anne depressed. She had been worried about the company, sure. We all were. But depressed?

A sudden feeling of shame washed over me. What if she had been feeling depressed for weeks and she never told me? What kind of friend had I been to her? Was I so focused on keeping the company alive that Anne felt she couldn't even ask me for help?

And so what if she was depressed? What did that have to do with drug addicts breaking into her flat?

Glumly, I ran my eyes over the homepage. Surely it couldn't be all terrible news today.

Then I saw it:

COMMUNICATIONS GIANT JENROL EYES UP MEDIAWIDE

Not content with owning two of the UK's top ten ad agencies, Philip Hammond of Jenrol is rumoured to be considering a purchase of Sir Geoff Deacon's MediaWide mini-empire.

Jenrol already owns 20.5% of the struggling communications group. After losing several of its largest clients this year, MediaWide is considered ripe for a takeover bid.

Sir Geoff Deacon, MediaWide's founder and chairman is understood to be contemplating selling the group after undergoing heart surgery earlier in the year and considering an earlier than planned retirement.

I considered the implications of the story. If MediaWide did sell, what would happen to us?

I cast my mind back to our acquisition deal, and remembered a clause in the contract that protected us against an eventuality such as this. The deal that required MediaWide to buy back the remaining 49% within the next two years would still be legally binding if the group was purchased by a third party.

I considered the long game. If MediaWide was acquired by Jenrol, the future could be good for HFPK – providing we survived. Philip Hammond was one of the advertising world's biggest hitters. And, bearing in mind that Rod Russell had only a couple of years' work left in him at most before he retired, if I could manage to prove myself to Hammond the opportunities could be immense.

However, I knew that if we didn't win the Tea Society account, then I might as well throw in the towel right now.

And as for Richard exposing the truth about The Accident ...

Time to go home. I paid for my untouched coffee and the Internet time, and left.

fourteen

On the train home I called Detective Sergeant Tomkins on my mobile to ask him if there was any progress on catching Anne's killer.

'We've made some inroads,' he told me. 'There was definitely a break-in, but not of the type we imagined. The scene of crime guys checked for prints, but found something we didn't expect: glove prints. That means it probably wasn't addicts breaking in looking for money for their next hit. We think her credit cards have been taken. We also think she may have disturbed the intruders, as there is evidence of a scuffle, and her injuries could be the result of a fall rather than an attack. I can't tell you any more than that at the present time.'

'Any leads?'

'I really don't want to go into details,' he said. 'I couldn't even if I wanted to. However, I'll need to call by your office again some time in the next couple of days. I need to have a look through Ms Fulton's possessions there. Can you make sure no one goes into her office?'

I assured him that I would.

Within half an hour of arriving home I was leaning on my elbows, lost in thought at the dinner table.

'Are you sure you don't fancy any Singapore noodles?' asked my wife.

I nodded.

'Well, that's fine by us.' She located a particularly choice shrimp with her chopsticks, and popped it into her mouth. 'That's all the more for Lily and me, isn't it, darling?'

Lily sat in the wooden antique high-chair that she insisted on using from time-to-time, and smiled contentedly, masses of yellow noodles hanging from her mouth.

'Seriously,' said Silvie, 'are you feeling all right? It's not at all like you to turn down Singapore noodles. Is it because there's no chilli in it? I know you like it extra spicy, but we have to make it safe for Lily.'

I shook my head. 'No, it's fine.'

'You can't fool me,' she said. 'Something's definitely up. You've been acting weird since Monday, and whatever it is you're worked up about seems to be getting worse. Tonight when you came home you looked as if you'd been told the world was going to end.'

'Did I?'

'Yes! You looked terrible. I know you well enough to tell when something's up. Are you going to tell me what it is?'

I sighed. There was never any hoodwinking Silvie, but I wasn't ready to tell her the whole story.

'OK, then. We've got a few problems at work,' I began. 'Jared's playing up again and Nigel's threatening to leave.'

'Nigel's threatening to leave? Why on earth would he want to leave? Surely if he leaves he loses everything? He can't take his shares in the company with him if he goes, can he?'

'No, he'll have to give them up.'

'So why would he want to leave when MediaWide have already agreed to buy the rest of the company in two years?'

'I don't know,' I said. 'Maybe the stress is getting on top of him. You know what Nigel's like.'

'I'm not sure I do,' said Silvie. 'You always used to talk about how much he enjoyed his work.'

'Yes, but he's a sensitive lad. He's over it now, anyway. He's decided not to leave after all.'

My wife helped Lily gather up the remaining noodles from her special little plate, and then poured some more milk into her beaker. 'Very strange,' she said. 'What does Jared think about it? What does Anne think?'

I couldn't let it go a step further. I had to come clean with her about Anne – right now. Not telling her the truth in the hope of avoiding unnecessary worry would only backfire drastically later. I had already learned that the hard way. She would find out soon enough.

I flopped back in my chair and put my hands flat on the table. 'I haven't been entirely honest, Silvie. I'm afraid I know exactly what Nigel's problem is.'

'What are you talking about?'

'It's really bad. I haven't mentioned it to you yet because I didn't want to worry or upset you.'

Silvie became flustered. 'Just tell me, will you, Duncan.'

'It looks like Anne was murdered at the weekend.'

What an awful way of putting it. Anne watched a movie at the weekend. Anne went out for a pub lunch at the weekend. Anne was murdered at the weekend.

My wife raised both hands to her mouth in shock. 'No,' she whispered. 'No! That's terrible.'

Lily took a sip of milk and looked at her mother.

'It was a huge shock to us all,' I said. 'I didn't know how to tell you.'

'Poor Anne, poor girl,' she said. 'What happened?'

'It appears as if it was a break-in gone wrong,' I said. 'At first, they thought it was people after money for drugs, but now it seems like some kind of professional robbery.'

'How do you know that?'

I told Silvie about Detective Sergeant Tomkins and the discovery of the glove prints.

She shook her head again, not wanting to believe what I was telling her. 'My God,' she said.

'What makes me feel really terrible,' I said, 'is that I read on a trade website today that Anne had become depressed and disillusioned recently. That's what really hurts. Perhaps if I'd noticed, and spoke to her about it, this would never have happened.'

Silvie reached out and held my wrist. 'Oh, Duncan, it's not your fault. How could have talking to her prevented a break-in?'

'I don't know. Maybe if she had been happier, she wouldn't have been spending so much time at home, and maybe—'

She squeezed my wrist. 'Duncan, stop torturing yourself. It wouldn't have made any difference at all. If anyone needs warning about the stresses of work, it's you, Duncan. I'd say you've been suffering from nervous tension from the very first day I met you, which is over eight years ago now. All that waking up in the night you used to do, all those nightmares … it's always because of the pressure, isn't it?'

'No, of course it isn't. It's … look, I'm fine, OK?'

If only.

'I'm sorry about Anne.'

I nudged my head towards Lily. 'Maybe we should talk about it later.'

Silvie wiped her eyes with a tissue. 'Yes, I'm sorry,' she said. 'Lily, let's go and watch some TV before Giles wakes up.'

Silvie smiled and took Lily in her arms. She gave her a needful hug and carried her out of the kitchen into the living-room.

I followed them. It was actually too late for *Cbeebies*, so Silvie put a *Fimbles* video on and Lily began to dance joyfully to the music.

Suddenly, I experienced an overwhelming need to hold my family. I scooped Lily into my arms, took Silvie's hand, and we all fell backwards on to the sofa. Silvie and I sat there smiling for a while as Lily nearly cried with laughter.

At that moment in time, I felt as happy as I'd ever been. I watched Lily chortling and didn't want the moment to end.

After a while, Silvie took Lily off for a bath, and I waited on the sofa in case Giles woke up in the nursery upstairs. I switched the television off and raised my eyes towards the old oak beams of my living-room, as if believing they would yield answers.

OK.

So Richard thought he could just turn up and destroy all this?

I felt a surge of anger buzz through my veins.

I couldn't hand over the shares. And there wasn't the slightest chance I would allow him to reveal the truth about The Accident.

What could I possibly do?

I thought back to when he had first threatened me in the meeting room at work. If only I had turned round and battered him. Yeah, if only.

The truth was, I was scared of Richard Regan.

Who wouldn't be? He had killed another human being, and seemed to have no remorse whatsoever. I wondered again what the hell Rod was doing hiring him? Rod was a law unto himself at the best of times, but I still couldn't fathom it out.

It wasn't over yet. The jury was still out. There was still time. There must be something I could do. But what?

I was going to have to play for time.

I didn't have any alternative.

Did I?

fifteen

The phone rang on my desk and I picked it up quickly.

It was Karen. 'Ready?' she asked. 'We're going to do the review now in the main meeting room.'

'OK,' I told her. 'I'll see you there in a few moments.'

'Oh, I'm not going,' she said. 'I've got to make a new business presentation with Rod and Sir Geoff Deacon, over at MediaWide. Don't worry, the stuff for the Tea Society looks to be in pretty good shape. Remember Richard will be there. He should be able to offer his opinion.'

I sighed, but I knew I was going to have to face him sooner or later. Try to relax, I told myself; he's not going to tell anyone about The Accident just yet. He promised Monday was the deadline. In the meantime I would have to try my luck calling his bluff.

'I'll see you later,' I said.

'Yes,' replied Karen. 'Tonight, at the advertising awards. Royal Lancaster Hotel.'

'See you then.'

I drank my tea slowly. Then I ate a couple of the biscuits, and finished with a few mouthfuls from a bottle of spring water.

I went to the meeting room and found that Richard was already there with Nigel.

Our client services director was talking about Anne, and Richard was listening charitably. He was dressed in a grey pullover and blue jacket, and was holding a Biro pen which he rolled idly between his thumb and forefinger. He had a sympathetic, oh-life's-just-so-cruel-isn't-it? expression on his face, and he kept nodding slowly at everything Nigel said.

So now he's attempting to manipulate Nigel? Richard Regan was no fool. He knew that recruiting allies was always a wise move in such politically charged workplaces as advertising agencies.

Richard turned to me, and with all the concern in the world, said: 'Nigel was just telling me that Anne's funeral is on Tuesday morning.'

'OK. We'd all better meet at Liverpool Street station and travel up together.'

'No, no,' said Nigel. 'I can't handle funerals. Jared and I have decided that you should go on your own, on behalf of all us.'

'Nigel's been telling me about Anne,' said Richard. 'It sounds as if she would have preferred it that way.'

'Oh, she would have, would she?' I felt my blood boiling but was keen to avoid an argument.

'She sounded a very pragmatic lady,' he added.

Nigel nodded in agreement, as if Richard had spoken for him, and waited for me to say something.

'OK, I'll go up by myself then.'

'Thank you,' said Nigel.

Jared entered the room and pulled out a spare chair. He was clutching a bunch of A3 boards, and placed them on the table. 'Is everyone here?' he said. 'Where's Karen?'

'She can't make it,' said Richard. 'I'm standing in for her.'

Jared stood motionless for a moment. 'Is that a good idea?' he said finally. 'Shouldn't we wait until she gets back?'

'We *can't* wait,' insisted Richard. He motioned for the creative director to sit down. 'I understand there's no time left to spend on this client. Today is Thursday, and the presentation itself is on Monday. I think we'd better get on with it, don't you?' His voice sounded hard-edged again.

Nigel said, 'Yes, time isn't on our side with this one. Why don't I kick things off?'

Everyone seemed to agree except Jared, who slumped in his chair and eyed the presentation boards anxiously. He bit at one of his fingernails, but then stopped himself and folded his arms tightly.

'Go ahead,' said Richard, scratching the underside of his chin.

'OK,' began Nigel. 'I've been thinking about the two campaigns Jared presented to us in the last meeting, and the numbers seem to add up nicely. For the "Someone give him a cup of tea" concept, we might need to do a deal with the photo agencies, but we'll definitely be able to use pictures of politicians as they're public domain, so to speak. Naturally, a campaign such as this will be very high maintenance and would demand the scale of resources I described in the last meeting.'

'Which was?' said Richard.

'A task force that would comprise an art director and copy-writer creative team, two account execs, one planner and a project manager. Plus my time for half the week, and one day a week of Jared's time.'

'What's the media spend?'

I said, 'It could be as much as five or six million a year.'

Richard puffed his cheeks out. For the first time I could see how dry and chapped they actually were. 'Not bad,' he said. 'So for that team, our all-in costs to the client would be about half a mill annually?'

'Six hundred thousand,' confirmed Nigel. 'Don't forget that we'll propose that this tactical campaign is only the beginning. An "attack" strategy, being the first stage of a three-pronged approach. That is: attack the rising sales of coffee amongst the target audience by challenging perceptions. And, second, shift the positioning of where tea, as an umbrella brand, stands within the market right now. Finally: acquisition, which will consist of money-off coupons, directing consumers to the Tea Society's website and suchlike.'

'Who devised that strategy?' asked Richard. 'You?'

'The three-pronged strategy was put together by Karen after the last meeting,' said Nigel. 'It's a tall order, this brief. It needs an aggressive, brand-launch type campaign.'

Richard scratched his head. A shower of small white flakes settled on the collar of his jacket. 'OK. That all sounds pretty plausible,' he said. 'Karen knows what she's doing, and I trust her. Let's see the creative work, then.'

For the first time that I could remember, Jared appeared reluctant to stand up and talk about his concepts. He flicked through the boards and scrunched his lips together, as if he had suddenly taken distaste towards the concepts.

'Cat got your tongue, Jarry?' Richard curled a lip. 'Come on! We haven't got all day.'

The creative director arranged the boards into two piles on the meeting room table. 'There are two different ideas,' he said.

'I think we can see that,' sneered Richard. 'Tell us something we don't know. Who came up with these ideas? One of the creative teams?'

'No,' said Nigel. 'It was Jared himself.'

Richard was suddenly amused. 'Oh, I see! What inspired you to come up with these particular ideas, then, Jarry?'

The creative director shrugged. 'After an initial brainstorming, I had four or five ideas, and these two were the best of the bunch. Although this one,' he indicated the man-stuck-in-a-room-for-six-months idea, 'was probably inspired by the current glut of reality TV programmes.'

'Explain it,' said Richard.

As Jared talked through the idea from start to finish, I noticed the other man's eyes narrowing towards him.

When Jared had finished, Nigel said, 'It's a brilliant idea, isn't it? A man trapped in a room for half a year just drinking tea. The PR will be superb! The newspapers won't be able to resist it.'

But Richard didn't seem to have heard. Instead he continued staring at Jared, and said, 'Very interesting, Jarry. What's the other idea?'

The creative director rattled off a bit of pre-rationale for the 'someone give him a cup of tea' route, and held up the boards one by one, each adorned with black-and-white photocopies of the current tabloid scandals.

Amongst the themes on offer were the football hooligan's MP father, a TV chat-show host who had been caught 'red-cheeked' at a Soho bum-beating club, and the high-profile chief executive of a major stock-broking firm who had been photographed at an exotic locale rubbing sun cream into the loins of two grinning ladyboys in their birthday suits (with their bits and pieces pixilated out).

'Dry, reportage-style,' said Richard. 'I like it. Edgy. I think you've done well, Jared. As always.'

Nigel slapped his colleague on the back and said, 'Well done.'

The creative director simply muttered something and smiled vaguely.

Richard said, 'Do you have a copy of these concepts on a CD-Rom you can give to me?'

Jared sprung into life as if Richard had prodded him with a sharpened stick. He pulled the boards towards him and said, 'These are only work-in-progress ideas. They're not final versions, by any means. I don't think it's a good idea to copy them on to CD-Rom.'

Richard was intrigued. 'Why not?'

'Because I might come up with another, better idea at the last minute, and it would be a waste of a CD, wouldn't it?'

'Oh, go on, Jarry,' insisted Richard, 'humour me.'

'Yes, why would you need to burn it on to CD at this early stage?' I asked. 'The concepts haven't been finalized.'

'Because,' he said, gritting his teeth, 'I might need to show it to someone who you lot should be trying to impress. Like Rod. Or Sir Geoff Deacon.'

'OK, OK. You can have the bloody CD-Rom. I really don't care,' spat Jared. For a second or two I thought he was going to storm out of the room: throwing a tantrum because others didn't see things from his point of view was an all too familiar side to him that we'd all gotten used to. I imagined Richard to be used to it too, having worked with him in the past – but judging from his reaction you'd never have guessed.

'You fucking trumped-up twatbag,' he barked. 'I think you'd better *start* caring. Otherwise I'll have words with Rod. Understand?'

I was expecting a full-scale war, but instead Jared said, 'OK, Richard, I'm sorry. I really didn't mean that. I'll do the CD-Rom for you this afternoon.'

The blackmailer sat back in his chair. The shouting had flushed his cheeks, and I could see several purple veins pulsing angrily beneath the surface of his colourless skin. 'Tell me, Jarry. How do you see the TV spots for the "someone give him a cup of tea" concept?'

Jared nervously twirled a strand of peroxide hair between his fingers and said, 'I imagined it to be a mix of animation and real film. Sort of like that ChocoStix ad that's on at the moment. Cut-out figures with filmic backgrounds. Funky, irreverent, and kind of dangerous.'

'Yes, I like that execution,' nodded Richard. His mouth puckered upwards at the corners, as the yelling had opened up two long cuts that ran back into his cheeks. '"Kind of dangerous." I like it.'

Nigel clapped his hands twice. 'Marvellous. So we're all in agreement. These are the two ideas we're going for, together with the three-pronged – sounds like some sort of rude toy – strategy devised by Karen.'

'Oh yes,' said Richard. 'There's mileage in these ideas, all right.'

Normally the wrapping-up of meetings and designation of duties for new business pitches was my bag, but I remained quiet. I was saving my energy for a confrontation with Richard that I knew would come at the end.

Nigel said, 'Jared, can you have the studio work the ideas into as highly a finished state as you can, and scan them in so I can put the presentation document together? Duncan – I can send you the cost projections for these campaigns. I take it you'll use our standard creds PowerPoint to open the meeting?'

'Yes. It's all ready.'

'Then I think we're in pretty good shape,' concluded Nigel. 'All that remains is to collect our tuxes for this evening's awards show, where we can get totally plastered. God, I need a drink. We all do.' He rubbed his eyes and said a little too enthusiastically, 'How many awards are we shortlisted for? Three? Ready with your acceptance speech, Jared?'

The creative director, who had been gazing at his shoes ever since Nigel had begun speaking, got to his feet and, without saying anything, put the boards under his arm and walked out of the door.

'Oh dear. I think I might have upset him,' said Richard.

'No, he's fine,' countered Nigel. 'He gets like this sometimes before big pitches. It's the pressure, you see. But don't worry. He always does the business as far as the big ideas are concerned. He'll come round.'

'Good. The last thing you need before a major pitch is the creative director acting like a 5-year-old.'

Nigel clapped his hands again in rapid succession like a school dinner-lady. 'Well, there's only one thing left to say. I'm having a party round my place on Saturday. I'd like you both to be there. I'm inviting Karen and Jared too. And anyone else from the agency that wants to come, for that matter.'

'A party?' I said.

'Yes,' said Nigel. 'It's where people drink, eat, and sway from side to side to music. People sometimes enjoy themselves at them. Apparently they're fun, so rumour has it.'

'All right, less of the sarcasm. I'm just surprised, that's all. I thought you were upset about Anne.'

'I *am* upset, but I've decided it does no good sitting around being depressed. That's why I'm having this party – to get over it. To help us all get over it. See where I'm coming from?'

'I guess so.'

'Don't bowl me over with your enthusiasm.' He studied me for a second as he fiddled with one of his Prada shoes. 'Look, I know what you're going to say. You're going to tell me you can't make it, because you'll get home too late. Well, just promise me that you'll consider it, OK? And you?' He pointed at Richard.

'Count me in,' said the blackmailer.

'Great. Well, I'd better be popping back to the day job.'

I watched Nigel leave. Richard got up and shut the meeting-room door gently. This is where it would get sticky, but I had to face up to him sooner or later. He sat back down and took a sip from a glass of water.

Just then my mobile went off, and I saw my mother's mobile number on the caller ID. My parents never normally called me in the daytime, not unless it was about Gran.

Richard watched with amused interest as I answered the call.

'Mum?' I said into the handset. 'Mum, is that you?'

Richard giggled and leaned forward, captivated.

There was crackling on the line and then my mother said, 'Yes, Duncan. It's about Gran. Can you talk?'

'Yes, yes, is she OK?'

An awful silence and then, 'She's been having another off-day, I'm afraid.'

'What's happened?'

I heard a noise that sounded like a row of pots and pans falling off a shelf, and concluded my mother must be rummaging around inside Gran's bric-á-brac littered kitchen. There were saucepans galore, many from what looked to be a pre-war era, all for servicing a gigantic hoard of baked beans and canned soup. Once, my mother had taken her a microwave ready-meal for a change, but Gran had taken one look at it and thrown it all over the kitchen window. I remember this because it was me who had cleaned it off.

There was another pause, then more clanking of saucepans. 'Gran's having a panic attack about Beryl. She wants to see her right now, but I've tried explaining that she only has to wait a few more days and she'll be in The Acorns. I'm trying to make her something to eat to calm her down.'

Oh, Christ.

'Where's Gran now?' I said.

'Sitting in the living-room. I'm sorry to disturb you like this, but I can't seem to locate your father or Julia. I just needed to tell someone. It's a bit difficult to cope alone, sometimes.'

'Mum, calm down.' I heard a sniffle on the other end of the line. 'Would it help if I drove round tonight?'

'Oh, Duncan. You're busy. I really don't expect you to....'

'It's no big deal. I've got to go to an awards show this evening, but I think I can get up to Gran's and still get back to London in time.'

'You're a real life-saver,' said my mother.

I would leave the office early, get up to Gran's, and catch the train back to London from St Neots when either my father or Julia showed up.

'I'm on my way,' I said.

After I cut the call, Richard laughed again and said, 'She reacting badly to the shares?'

It was nothing more than a game to him. Would he ever be aware of the self-loathing he'd made me feel over the past fifteen years? Would he ever understand how I could never escape from Doofy's look of blank, lifeless surprise invading my every hour of the day? Would he ever realize how he'd forced me to lie to those closest to me?

He probably gave it as much thought as he would to swatting a housefly with a magazine. I could see it written all over his face. He knew he had the upper hand. He expected me to give up my 130,000 shares as easily as a 50p charity donation outside a super-market. But this wasn't about money, and it wasn't about punishment. It was about power. You didn't have to be the sharpest tool in the box to work out that Richard was an insecure basket-case searching for a way to measure the worth of his existence.

Richard drummed his fingers on the table, grinning, as he waited for me to answer.

I was livid. 'I'm warning you, if you say one more thing—'

He held up a finger to stop me. Then, without saying a word, he came over and stood opposite me. His mouth was so tightly closed that the veins bulged out on his neck. He said, 'Yes? What will you do? Kill me as well?'

He stared me down and I walked towards the door. I'd had enough. As I was leaving the room he said, 'Murderer.'

I froze. 'What?'

'*Murderer.*'

'Christ, Richard, why did they ever let you into this place?'

But he wasn't interested in conversation. He kept repeating the word over and over again. '*Murderer, murderer, murderer.*' His voice turned shrill and sent a grotesque quiver to the base of my spine. '*Murderer, murderer, murderer ...*'

I left the room and quickly made my way down the stairs.

If Richard Regan was trying to spook me, he was doing a pretty good job.

sixteen

It took an hour and a half – including a hurried diversion to Suits Hugo on High Holborn to pick up, and change into, a tuxedo for the awards ceremony – to reach my grandmother's house on the outskirts of Bedford.

It was a terraced affair that formed part of a large brick building that was originally part of a Victorian workhouse.

A private road ran around the building in a semi-circle and through the disused farmland earmarked for the proposed asylum centre, before joining a new housing estate on the outskirts of town.

I parked the car outside Gran's front door and let myself in.

As I walked into the hall, the loose carpet wrapped itself under my feet, almost tripping me over. I flopped it back in place with my shoe, and tucked it back under the door. I went into the living room and found Gran sitting in an old armchair, sobbing.

'Gran,' I said, pulling a chair up next to her. 'It's OK.'

She suddenly became terrified and cowered away from me.

'Everything's all right,' I said. 'It's me.'

'Kenneth, is that you?'

'Kenneth? Er, no,' I replied. She looked as if she were about to scream so I changed tack and said, 'Yes, I'm Kenneth. Now, do you want a cup of tea?'

Gran nodded tentatively.

'Beryl's gone,' she told me.

'No, she's not gone. She's in a big house called The Acorns. You'll be able to stay with her soon.'

Gran appeared unconvinced. 'I thought she'd been taken away from me. Or attacked.' She started sobbing again, and said, 'Why can't people just leave other people alone?'

'Gran, Beryl's fine.'

'*That's* what Beryl always said: "Why can't people leave other people alone?" She used to get herself into a right state, did Beryl. Oh, as well you know, Kenneth, as well you know. Not least when she was courting Gerald, and he threw her knickers from the back window of the bus after that night at Jack Straw's Castle over at town. Don't tell father, Kenneth! Don't tell him the truth!'

I suddenly regretted donning the Kenneth guise. I felt I shouldn't be hearing this, and went upstairs to find out where my mother was.

She was in Gran's bedroom scraping something off the carpet. She glanced up as I walked in. 'Ah, almost finished, Duncan. She insisted on bringing her dinner up here and then threw it everywhere when I said she couldn't see Beryl.' She paused for breath. 'Well, don't you look smart? If only your father could see you in that!' She turned her attention back to the job in hand. 'Mother seems to have settled down now. Thank you so much for coming. I hope we didn't put you out too much.'

'It's no trouble at all. Just glad to help out.'

'Did you see her? I'm afraid I had to abandon her downstairs while I came back up here to clean up.'

Gran wailed in the distance. 'There's your answer,' I said. 'Maybe I'd better get back down. Will you be long?'

'Just a few minutes more. I'll be down before you know it.'

'She's convinced I'm Kenneth, you know.'

My mother was amused. 'That'll be the tuxedo! Apparently Kenneth often used to wear one, the dapper chap he was. I should show you the photos sometime.' She concentrated on wiping the blankets and said, 'Well, Duncan, if it makes her happy, it can't be a bad thing. Anyway, not long to wait for The Acorns now. Just as well. Every day seems to be an off-day at the moment.'

I gave her a reassuring smile.

After I had jogged down the stairs, I was shocked to find Gran standing in the corner of the room banging her fists on the walls. 'It was him, it was him,' she was mumbling to herself.

'Gran, take it easy. Come on, sit down. Look, I'll go and make that cup of tea, shall I?' I gently pulled her hands away from the wall.

'Kenneth! How *dare* you run away from me like that? Don't want any tea, Kenneth! Why does no one ever listen to me?'

'We do listen, Gran.'

'No!' she hissed. 'You've *never* listened, Kenneth. You just think I'm a mad old bat. Loopy! Sometimes I think you just want to shut me up like Michael. He *never* told the truth, you know, not before the children were born, nor after. Not even Christine knew about it. No one did, Kenneth, except you and me. And Michael, of course. But then, he's the one that did it, isn't he?'

Hang on just one second. Michael? Christine? Why was she talking about my parents?

I asked, 'What did Michael do?'

'You haven't forgotten already, have you, Kenneth?' said Gran. 'We're a right pair, aren't we? He ... he, you know, had that *messy* affair with old Gwennie from the woods.'

'Gwennie? Who's Gwennie?'

Quite unexpectedly, she started laughing.

'Who's Gwennie? Oh, give over! You know Gwennie! Old Gwennie from the woods. Michael had a bit of a *how do you do* with her. Went on for four months in her caravan, it did.'

Gwennie? Was she talking about Gwendoline, Doofy's mother?

Surely there had to be some mistake. My father having an affair with Gypsy Gwendoline, as we used to call her at school? I couldn't believe it. I couldn't believe he had it in him. As far as I was concerned, all he had a passion for was Dickens and Blake.

'When was this?'

'When was what?'

'The affair,' I said.

'The affair? Oh, just after Christine and Michael got married.'

'Why did it end?'

Gran looked at me, blankly. Then she suddenly became surprised and whispered, 'You didn't tell Beryl, did you, Kenneth?'

'No, I didn't.' This was getting more bizarre by the minute. Why was I impersonating someone who had died during World War II to find out answers to things that probably happened in the late 1960s? If they had happened at all.

'Oh! It ended because Gwennie got pregnant. Michael panicked; some say he tried to kill her. But he didn't do anything. Shouldn't have dipped his wick in the first place, should he?'

I ran my fingers through my hair. Oh, shit. Where the hell was this going? 'What happened in the end?'

'Oh, you could say it ended happily. Gwennie just went and had her baby, didn't she? That's what she wanted, and good luck to her. Wasn't anything Michael could do, except keep his mouth shut. But me, I always knew the truth, and I didn't tell. Didn't want to hurt little Christine, did we, Kenneth? Are you sure your leg's not playing up again?'

I heard my mother walking across the landing. 'The baby,' I said. 'What was its name?'

'Name?' My grandmother chuckled, 'Well, Gwennie had the cheek to take Michael's middle name, didn't she, Kenneth?' She smiled at the memory. 'Donald,' she said.

'Donald? Donald Gordon?'

I felt my pulse quicken.

'Yes – a real little chubby cheeks, he was. I think Gwennie used to call him *Doofy*.'

seventeen

I sat alone in the car, parked in a lay-by on the A428 somewhere between Bedford and Cambridge.

After leaving Gran's house, I had driven aimlessly for almost two hours. When I did finally decide to stop and collect my thoughts, it turned out that all I'd been doing was driving in a circle around Bedford.

Awards night could go to hell, I thought.

After all, that was where I was going.

Doofy ...

I felt beyond worthless. My whole body was alternating between absolute helplessness and numbing grief. My arteries were filled with such an incendiary mixture of emotions I feared they would burst.

Anger, resentment, self-loathing, shame. Added to grief, guilt and confusion. There were probably another few in there that the psychoanalysts hadn't even thought of yet.

Would I ever know for certain that Doofy was my half brother?

Unless I confronted my father, probably not. But I could start with examining what I already knew.

Doofy did have a father, didn't he? Hadn't he been planning to hitch-hike up to Scotland to live with him on the day of The Accident?

I did recall seeing an older, extremely scruffy man occasionally walking hand-in-hand with Gypsy Gwendoline through the village during my early teens. But, come to think of it, he didn't look at all like Doofy.

While Doofy was tall and dark-skinned with thick black hair, the character I remembered seeing his mother with was short – only around 5′ 5″ – with a slight frame and mousy hair.

Doofy looked nothing like him. He was much more the dark Mediterranean type ... like my father.

And me.

Of course, Doofy's mother had thrown plenty into the equation. She was an old-school gypsy type: all wispy black hair and swarthy olive skin.

But there was no mistaking it. The resemblance was there.

I shook my head wearily.

There was no one with whom I could share this. But, as my guilty conscience delighted in telling me, I had only myself to blame.

One thing was plain and simple. There was nothing to be gained by questioning my father about it. If there were even a shred of truth to the story, it could damage my family as much as the truth about The Accident would.

It was as if I was locking myself deeper and deeper into a prison complex, and throwing away the keys each time.

I was going to have to live with it.

Even Doofy's mother had gone. Everyone in the village knew that she passed away a few months after Doofy disappeared. She probably assumed he was happy with his new life in Scotland with the stepfather whom she had long lost contact with, and died bitter and heartbroken.

More for me to feel guilty about.

I gripped the steering wheel so hard I saw my knuckles turn white under the red glow of the handbrake light on the dashboard.

I wondered if my father had ever tried to make contact with his illegitimate son?

It was doubtful. He would have had too much to lose. No, my father wouldn't have told a soul. He would never have given in to his conscience and risked ruining his whole life, and that of his young family, by admitting a few, simple, damning words.

He would know that his best bet was to keep his mouth shut to all and sundry.

But I couldn't stop myself thinking about Doofy's face, as he lay there motionless next to the millpond. Stopped dead – literally – by a couple of kids with air pistols who didn't know any better, and an incredible amount of bad luck. That bullet could have gone anywhere. Why did it have to rebound straight into Doofy's face and kill him – not wound him, or render him blind in one eye – but kill him?

Despairingly, I checked the car's digital clock. It was nearing midnight. My business here in this deserted lay-by was done. I had been sitting thinking for almost three hours about Doofy, The Accident, my father and Richard.

It was time to go home.

eighteen

I let myself in quietly. The house was quiet. That was good. Silvie must have gone to bed. I was worried that if I saw her, my conscience would get the better of me and I would end up telling her everything.

I sneaked upstairs, slipped past Lily's and Giles's rooms and went into the bathroom where I splashed my face with cold water and examined myself in the mirror.

There were huge bags under my eyes, but what really struck me was the undeniable look of guilt. It was plain to see; the anxious, rabbity eyes, watery with fear, the lower jaw hanging open, ready to deny, argue, accuse.

I filled the sink and submerged my face in cold water for ten seconds.

Then I slunk into the darkness of the bedroom, and found my pyjamas on the back of a chair, hoping that Silvie didn't wake up.

Immediately after I took off my socks, I heard Giles awake in his bedroom and begin making the whimpering noises that were always the precursor to all-out wailing.

I considered carrying him down to the kitchen and warming a bottle for him, but in order to avoid the danger of confessing all to Silvie, I did what we members of the male species are occasionally wont to do, and slipped into bed and pretended to be asleep so my wife would deal with the baby.

Silvie rolled over, groaned, rubbed her eyes, got out of bed and walked to Giles's room, pulling a dressing-gown over her on the way. A few minutes later the crying stopped. I heard her walk down the stairs to the kitchen. Giles was tucking into a late-night snack.

I lay awake thinking about Jared, Nigel and Karen at the awards ceremony. Tomorrow I would be subjected to a lambasting session from them about my failure to show up. Lots to look forward to.

The bed felt deliciously warm after Silvie. I longed for her to return. I stretched out my arms behind the pillow and realized I was still wearing the tuxedo.

At that instant I heard Silvie approaching the bedroom door. I could also hear Lily whispering to her excitedly.

The door swung open and the light came on. What was this? I kept my eyes shut, pretending to be asleep.

'Daddy!'

I popped my head out from under the duvet and made a show of opening my eyes sleepily.

Silvie had the kind of look on her face you don't mess with. Her lips were pursed into an ironic smile so tight it could have been used to cut paper. 'Hello, darling,' she said. 'Would you mind getting out of bed? My private detective here has told me something rather interesting.'

'Hi Silvie, hi Lily. Sorry I came back so late. Did you have a nice dinner?'

'Out of bed, darling. Come on, out of bed you get. I'm keen to get back to sleep.'

I stood up on the bed with the duvet pulled across me so they couldn't see what I was wearing. 'I'm not decent,' I said.

'Oh, for heaven's sake!' Silvie stepped forward and snatched the duvet away.

She and Lily both began laughing hysterically. Lily pointed at me. 'That's not pyjamas, Daddy!'

'Good night at the awards?' asked Silvie.

'It was all right.'

'Are you drunk, getting into bed dressed like that? You look pretty sober, though.'

'Sober? Yes, you could say that. How did you know I wasn't wearing pyjamas, Lily?'

'I woke up. Then I watched you, Daddy,' said Lily. 'You're *funny*.'

'I'll take that as a compliment, Lily, thank you.'

Silvie said, 'Right. Back to bed everyone. Joke over.' Whilst I changed into the proper attire, she took Lily back to her bedroom. Then she switched our light off and snuggled up close to me.

'You've been a very naughty boy, haven't you?' she said, resting her cheek against my chest.

'What do you mean?'

'Hey, don't worry, it's not a big deal.'

'What's not a big deal?'

'Jumping into bed like that and leaving me to do the feed. Naughty. For that, you're on early morning duty.' She squeezed my arm.

'Oh, thanks.'

'You've also got to buy me a proper cup of coffee when we go shopping at Covent Garden on Saturday, too. I'm starved of such pleasures, you know, living out here in the sticks.'

'I'd forgotten about that shopping trip.'

She squeezed me again. 'You can afford it, and it's about time you treated us.' She kissed my cheek. 'Now, let's get to sleep. Otherwise you're going to feel truly awful in the morning.'

I tensed. It was unintentional *double entendres* such as those that would end up tipping me over the edge.

But I didn't want to sleep yet. I didn't want to go to the place where I knew Doofy and Richard would be waiting for me, I wanted to keep talking to Silvie. 'How were your parents?' I said. 'Sorry I couldn't see them.'

She yawned. 'Oh, don't worry. We had a proper family get-together while you were out living it up at your awards show. My mum and dad were fine. We were just having a cup of tea, when who should turn up? Your parents.'

'What, my ... mum and dad?'

Silvie laughed at me for sounding such a dunderhead. 'Er, yes, Duncan. Your mum and dad are usually your parents.'

'Were they all right?'

'They were fine! They were worried about you. They decided to give you a surprise visit.'

'Worried?'

'Yes, apparently you'd got very upset at your grandmother's house. I told them it must be because you've been having a rough time after what happened to Anne. They wanted to cheer you up.'

'All the in-laws together, eh? Very cosy, very civilized.'

'You're getting worked up about something,' Silvie said. 'I can hear it in your voice, but I know you're not going to tell me what it is. So let's go to sleep.'

'No, I'm fine. I really don't want to sleep yet. Did you have a nice time?'

'It was a lovely evening. It was the first time our parents have met up for a long time. Shame you couldn't be here. But you must have enjoyed yourself. Did you win anything at the awards show?'

'I don't really want to think about work.'

'OK.' Silvie drew her head away from my chest. 'Don't worry, there's always next year.'

'Next year?'

I felt her turn to look at me in the dark. 'Next year's awards. I take it you didn't win anything, otherwise you would have told me the second you got home. You would have woken me up to tell me, just like you did after last year's show.'

I sighed. 'How were your folks?'

'Touchy subject, I can see,' she said. 'My parents? Oh, they were fine. I told them how you were selling your shares for your grandmother, and they thought you were very noble.'

'Noble? Is that what they said? They didn't say The Acorns was too expensive?'

Silvie chuckled to herself. 'No, no. They've always liked you.'

'Noble,' I repeated, turning the word over in my mind. 'That's a new one.'

Over the next few minutes her breathing slowed. Just when I thought she had fallen asleep, she said, 'One thing I forgot to mention: Richard called from your office.'

Oh, God. I was thankful that Silvie couldn't see my expression in the dark.

'Really? What did he say?'

'Actually, it was intriguing. He asked me to tell you, "I hope you haven't forgotten the deal," or something like that. Do you know what he's talking about?'

'It's to do with a client. Was that all he said?'

Silvie was quiet for a few seconds as she searched her memory. 'Actually, now you mention it there was something else. He said, "Expect to see the truth on Ad-versity next week." At least, I think that's what he said. He was very friendly, asking how I was, asking how Lily was. What's Ad-versity?'

So it had started. Richard Regan had decided to turn the pressure up a notch.

'It's the name of a website I use to catch up on stuff happening in the industry. Agencies losing clients, staff fired, that sort of thing. The stuff that really makes the ad industry tick.'

'So what did he mean by "expect to see the truth"?'

'I presume he was referring to that big client we're after. The Tea Society. I think Richard's as confident as I am that we'll win the account.'

Silvie snuggled up close again. 'Oh, that's all right then.'

nineteen

All that night, I battled with the unshakeable urge to tell Silvie the truth. Although each time I moved to wake her up, the rational side of my thinking cut in and made sure my hand failed to connect with her shoulder.

There was something else, too. It was an odd, primeval feeling that seemed to well up from deep within me. Over the last couple of hours, I had become convinced that Doofy should be avenged in some way.

What was I thinking? That it was up to me to *punish* Richard for what he did?

In a word, yes. If Doofy was indeed a blood relation, then it was up to me to put the record straight.

Before Richard could destroy my life, I would somehow have to find a way to destroy his first.

I popped a pre-prepared bottle of formula milk into a mug of hot water, and changed Giles's nappy, all the time considering my strategy regarding Richard Regan. I sat the little boy on my knee and removed the cap from the bottle. He sensed the food was near and began wailing for it.

After the feed had finished, I carried him upstairs and gently laid him in his cot, then wandered back down to the kitchen, knowing that it would be pointless to try to grab any more sleep.

I made a cup of Earl Grey, dropped three teaspoons of sugar in, and sat at the kitchen table. I pulled up the blind to look at the back garden. It was covered with a thick layer of frost. It was still pitch black outside, but the light from the kitchen illuminated the lawn in a silvery-grey haze.

I wrapped my fingers around the mug and let the warmth from the hot drink flow through them.

Suddenly I heard a ringing in the study. It was where we kept the fax machine. I checked my watch: 6.30 a.m. It was a hell of a time to be sending a fax.

I went into the study and quickly closed the door behind me, hoping the noise hadn't woken the family. Whoever was sending a message at this hour had better have a good reason for doing so. Hadn't they heard of email?

I sat down and watched the fax machine as it chugged into life.

When it had finished printing, I tore the paper away from the machine and returned to the kitchen.

I hadn't even reached the table when I noticed the big black capital letters scrawled across the paper.

It read, 'WORRIED YET? YOU SHOULD BE. REMEMBER WE KILLED DOOFY.'

Signed, Richard.

Oh, shit.

His name and number were even printed at the top of the page, there for all to see. I wondered if one of these faxes had arrived when I had been out, although I doubted it. Silvie had already told me Richard had called last night, and if a fax like this had arrived, she wouldn't be asleep, she would be awake, demanding we go to the police.

Before I did anything else, I returned to the study and pulled out the power lead to the fax machine. I couldn't risk any more messages from Richard coming through while I was out.

Then I tore the paper into small pieces and dropped them into the wastepaper basket.

Torment and harassment, Richard Regan style. This was going to become the norm over the next few days. Not content with the prospect of getting his hands on my shares, he couldn't resist the chance to make life uncomfortable for me.

I flopped down in the chair.

Today was Friday. I had less than three days to solve the problem.

There wasn't time to start bluffing him. And, anyway, that was the worst thing I could do. Richard would probably leak the truth about The Accident just for the hell of it.

No, there was no point denying it. I was going to have to consider the unthinkable.

Killing him.

Was I capable of it?

I suspected not. I wasn't even the type to step on a spider, let alone end the life of another human being.

But I was rapidly coming round to the view that Richard was *not* human. How could he be? He appeared devoid of any standard human emotions. And now, by deliberately seeking to bring my family into it by sending a message to my house, he was showing the depths to which he was prepared to sink.

Perhaps doing away with him wouldn't be that difficult after all, from a moral point of view at least.

OK, so I'm a hypocrite. Here I was feeling torn apart over Doofy and The Accident, and I'm entertaining the idea of murdering Richard.

But what else could I do? He had pushed me into a corner and I had to react somehow. I had to ensure my survival. And, if my grandmother was to be believed, I had a family member to avenge. Richard had forced me to bury Doofy crudely, shamefully – and I simply couldn't allow him to go unpunished.

Just supposing that I did decide to do away with him, how would I go about it without being found out?

I had a vague idea that the place you went to for that sort of thing was the classified ads at the back of Soldier of Fortune magazine. I had once seen a TV documentary where an investigative journalist had arranged a meeting with a would-be hitman contacted via the magazine, and then turned the cameras on him.

But it really wasn't worth thinking about. I would be way out of my depth. Besides, I didn't have the spare cash I imagined would be required for such an act.

What else?

Maybe Richard could have an accident of his own? The idea was plausible, but everything depended on exactly what the accident would involve. Although I clearly knew nothing about this sort of thing, I imagined that making it *look* like an accident would be the trickiest part of all.

Causing a gas explosion, for example, would be difficult to set up and held considerable risks that others would be hurt, too.

Poisoning him?

Worse than useless. You didn't decide to poison someone if you were a new business director in an ad agency, just like that. You considered that particular scenario if you were an expert chemist with a knowledge of untraceable toxins.

I once read somewhere that a massive dose of potassium was enough to kill a grown man, and that all traces of it would disappear before an autopsy could be carried out. But what good was that? What did a massive dose of potassium measure? And where would I get it?

Get real. Come on, think, Duncan!

Ether, too, I had read about in some crime novel or other over the years. It's the stuff you see being put on handkerchiefs in movies to knock people out.

Stop it. Stop it! I had less than three days. Where was I going to get some ether in that time? Back to the brainstorming stage.

As I busied myself examining ways in which I could deal with Richard, I was suddenly aware that I felt better than I had done in days. I knew the reason why. It wasn't because I was some kind of closet psycho with a suppressed longing to murder. It was because I was finally *doing something*. Fighting back. I was just an ordinary guy who had been pushed towards the edge, and was damned if I was going to let Richard shove me over.

I knew that if I didn't face this decision now I would run out of time. So I stayed rooted to the spot, my arms folded on the desk in front of me, my mind taking off at all kinds of alarming tangents.

What about – and pardon me if I sound like a bloodthirsty lunatic here – stabbing him with a kitchen knife and running away?

OK, so it sounded like the plan of a madman – but you hear about those incidents all the time on the news. Unprovoked attacks that are never solved.

I examined the idea.

I had no doubt it would be a horrendous experience for me. For a start, I would have to make sure he was dead. That meant I would have to drive the knife deep into one of his vital organs. Was I really capable of doing something like that?

There was only one way to find out.

Assuming I had the guts to go through with it, what were the chances of pulling it off?

It depended on the circumstances. If it could be done, say, in the early hours of the morning in a street where there were no CCTV cameras, I might have a reasonable chance of getting away with it – provided I had an airtight alibi.

But where was I going to find Richard wandering around in the street in the small hours before Monday?

I had it.

Nigel's party on Saturday night.

Richard had already promised he would be there. All I had to do was find out exactly where he lived, so I could catch him on the way home.

Nigel lived in Bloomsbury. And what had Richard said on our first meeting? He lived near Old Street tube? The two areas were only thirty minutes walk from each other, and I knew the area pretty well, having consulted for a year or so at a start-up agency during the late nineties in Scrutton Street, EC2.

What time would Richard leave the party? Somewhere between 12 and 2 a.m. seemed about right. With it being November, the partygoers couldn't reasonably expect to make full use of his roof garden. So I was pretty certain they wouldn't make it an all-nighter.

Besides, none of us were in our twenties any more. These days, and I had heard Nigel agree with me on this, staying up partying past 3 or 4 a.m. at the weekend was guaranteed to wipe you out for half the following week.

I lifted my bare feet and rested them on the desk, Jared-style. The study was usually one of the warmest rooms in the house, but as it hadn't been used for several days the radiator had been turned off. It was distinctly chilly, but I didn't mind. My mind was always sharper when I was cold.

I knew Richard would take a taxi home after the party. This meant I would have to wait outside for him in my car, and when I spotted him, drive away discreetly and make sure I got to his flat before he did.

It wasn't as crazy as it sounds. At that time of night, it would take a good five or ten minutes to find a cab. And I didn't expect he would bother ordering a minicab from Nigel's flat.

So after I arrived at his flat, what then?

Well, with a bit of luck, he would have been drinking heavily, so hopefully I could creep up on him as he was unlocking his front door and attack him before he knew what was happening.

My alibi?

Silvie. Brought about by default. The only time to do this was the early hours of the morning, which meant I would have to slip out of bed in the middle of the night, travel down to London, carry out the attack, and return without her knowing.

I suddenly felt queasy about the idea. I was determined to keep my family distanced from anything to do with Richard Regan, but I was already drawing in my unsuspecting wife as an alibi. I felt cheap and shoddy. But, as I said before, what else could I do?

As I examined the idea further, I realized the timing would fall into place around Giles's feeds. I would volunteer to handle the midnight feed, and when he was safely sleeping in his cot, I would slip out of the house and drive down to London on the A1. I would then carry out the strike, and drive back home again. It was imperative that I was back in bed before Giles woke up for his early breakfast at 5 or 6 a.m.

As far as Lily was concerned, I was just going to have to step lightly, and hope to God that she didn't hear me sneaking around, or, worse, see me leaving the house.

That was the plan.

Dangerous, daft, hare-brained, risky? Of course, but it was all I had.

What I needed to do first was find out Richard's address from the files at the office, and do a quick recce by his house on Saturday afternoon whilst Silvie and the kids were shopping in Covent Garden.

What would the police make of it all? First one of the founding partners of the company is killed in a botched break-in. Then her replacement is murdered in the street. I considered this for several minutes, and concluded they'd just have to put it down to coincidence, because that's exactly what it was.

I lifted my feet off the desk and stretched my arms. I heard the joints crack.

There was a noise upstairs. Lily and Silvie were awake.

I took a last look at the confetti in the bin and made sure the fax machine was disconnected.

Time for breakfast.

If I could just stall Richard Regan for one more day …

twenty

As I expected, most people in the office arrived late with raging hangovers following the previous night's awards ceremony.

And, equally predictably, most of them were annoyed with me for not turning up.

The real surprise was Jared who, despite picking up two silvers and a gold award for his work on Jackmann Fitness and Dreem Lo-Fat Rice Pudding, was acting as if the world was about to end.

He hardly registered my presence when I wandered over to see him in his office.

'Congratulations, Jared. You've really got to do something about this habit of yours.'

'What habit?' he said, with an edge to his voice. 'Oh, hello, Duncan,' he muttered.

'This winning all the gongs. It's going to start getting embarrassing soon.'

He shrugged. 'It's OK.'

'Don't sound too excited about it,' I said. 'This is what you've been waiting for all year, isn't it?'

'I suppose. But the important thing is that I won more awards than my father's agency. Nothing else matters, really.'

'Are you sure? What about the prestige for HFPK? That's what you usually keep talking about.'

'As I said: the only thing that matters is that I beat my father's company.'

'I see.'

He screwed up a leaf of paper from his layout pad that he'd been doodling on, and threw it into the wastepaper basket. 'Where were you last night anyway?'

'Family emergency. Couldn't make it I'm afraid.'

'Whatever. Karen's really pissed off with you for not turning up, and for not even calling to say you couldn't make it. There were a ton of clients there and, seeing as we'd won some of the biggest awards of the night, all rich for the picking.'

'Well, I can't help it if family emergencies crop up, can I?'

'I suppose not. Anyway, I don't think it matters. Karen was mingling and sweet-talking the clients, fixing up appointments. Richard was helping her.'

'Enjoying himself, was he? Pretending to be me.'

Jared let out a long sigh and said, 'I'm not going to get drawn into whatever arguments you two have going, Duncan. You and Richard have never seen eye to eye since you cut him out of the deal, I know that.'

'I didn't cut him out of the deal. The reasons were simple. Anne was far better suited to the position, and Richard was a basket case.'

Jared whistled softly. 'Don't think you want to let him hear you saying stuff like that, Duncan.'

'Yeah, well. Slip of the tongue.'

'Or Rod for that matter. Rod seems like a major fan of his.'

I looked out of the door to Jared's room, and across the open-plan office towards the far corner of the building. Richard's desk was empty. Karen, however, was sitting at hers, talking on the telephone. She caught my gaze as I sat down.

'Any idea where Richard is at the moment?' I asked Jared.

'He's over at MediaWide showing Geoff Deacon the Tea Society stuff with Rod.' I could tell he wasn't happy about it.

'Didn't waste any time in kissing Geoff Deacon's arse, did he?'

He ran a hand through his shaggy curls and rubbed his eyes. 'You can say that again. Look, I think there's something I should tell you. Richard was saying some pretty damaging things about you last night.'

My heart skipped a beat. 'Like what?'

He waved his hand dismissively. 'It's probably best you don't know. Listen, just forget I mentioned it OK?'

'No, Jared. I want you to tell me what he said.'

The creative director was becoming nervous. 'Sod it. He'd had too many drinks, he—'

'*What* did he say?'

'It was probably rubbish. He has this theory.'

I was getting angrier by the second. 'What theory? Just tell me, for God's sake.'

'He thinks you might have had something to do with Anne.'

'What do you mean?'

'Anne's *murder*.'

I was knocked for six. 'Well, what the hell do you think?'

'I don't know. I really don't know what to think.'

'Come on! Think what you're saying. What is he – what are *you* – trying to accuse me of?'

'Duncan, I know it's kind of crazy. I never actually thought that—'

'No, of course you didn't. You just chose to believe what you were told. You all need someone to blame. That's right, isn't it?'

'Of course not, look—'

I pressed on. 'So what's the basis of his theory?'

'He didn't elaborate. He said things didn't seem to stack up, that's all.'

I stood up. 'What things?'

'I don't know. Control of the company. Profit sharing. He had all kinds of ideas.'

'And you believed him.'

'No! I didn't say that. Just relax for a second, will you? You know what your problem is? You're paranoid. I swear it, mate. Paranoid.'

I turned away from him to let him know the conversation was over. 'If you can't talk sense,' I said, 'then don't talk at all.'

'Fine by me. I'm feeling pretty ill anyway. Nightmare hangover. You'd have one too if you'd bothered to be there. I've got to check the studio to see if they've finished the boards for the Tea Society.'

'Yes, you do that,' I said, as he sauntered away.

I returned to my office, wondering who else Richard had spilled his drunken theories to. Rod? Karen? And why had he taken Rod over to MediaWide? The mind boggled. Why hadn't Karen gone with them? It wasn't every day that a new recruit gets to run some work-in-progress past the Chairman.

However, I couldn't allow myself to dwell on what Richard might, or might not have said. While Rod was still out, I knew I should take the opportunity to go into his office to find out Richard's address. Employee details were not stored on the intranet, except for mobile numbers and the like, and if I telephoned Nancy Cooper, the personnel director at MediaWide, it would be sure to set the alarm bells ringing come Monday.

I knew that Rod co-signed all MediaWide staff contracts, and with Richard having joined only a few days ago, I felt sure that a copy of his contract would be lying around in the managing director's office somewhere.

I took the stairs to the next floor, and was relieved to find Rod's secretary away from her desk. I went into his office.

Books, magazines, and old newspapers were scattered everywhere. In fact, there was so much waste paper around that one could be forgiven for thinking that it was a storeroom. I couldn't believe it had taken Rod only a few years to create such a mess. After MediaWide had sent him over to keep an eye on us (read: bully us into achieving our revenue targets) this former meeting room had gradually taken on the guise of being a burial ground for the dozens of publications our company subscribed to.

So, down to business. I knew I had to search quickly; if Rod or his secretary walked in, I would be in for some serious hassle.

I kneeled down behind the desk – an antique redwood piece with ornate carved legs – and began rifling through the drawers. In contrast to the rest of the room, Rod seemed to have all his documents filed perfectly. I ran my finger over the name tabs, reading the labels.

Clients? No. Reviews? No. Contracts. Yes.

I flipped through them until I found the one marked Richard Regan. I pulled it out and turned to the last page. There it was. Richard had signed the agreement and beneath his printed name was his address: Flat 3B, Bosover Court, Great Eastern Street, EC2. I committed it to memory.

I returned his file and closed the drawer quickly.

'Hey! What are you doing in here?'

I stood up.

Karen. She was dressed in jeans and a tight black sweater. And she looked extremely pissed off.

'Hi, Karen. I'm looking for the CD-Rom of the Tea Society ads. The one that Jared gave to Rod.'

'You won't find it behind there. He's taken it with him.'

'Where?'

'To MediaWide. He's gone over there with Richard. But you wouldn't know about that, as it was discussed last night at the awards.'

'I had a family emergency,' I said. 'I couldn't make it.'

'You could have at least called. How do you think we felt when we had all kinds of clients asking for our new business director's name card, and all we had to introduce them to was an empty seat?'

'Look, it was a *bad* family emergency. I didn't have time to call. I'm sorry.'

'What sort of "bad" family emergency merits you missing the most important date in your calendar?' Karen sneered.

'It was my Gran,' I said. 'She's not well. You know all about it.'

'Well, in future you'd better remember where your priorities lie. Rod's ultimatum still stands. If you don't find a major client by the middle of next week, the company is finished.'

'I'm confident the Tea Society will come through.'

'There's no guarantees in this business,' she said. 'You of all people should know that. Has it ever crossed your mind you might not win the business?'

'No. Not for a second.'

'Well, I hope for your sake you're right. Now I've got that off my chest, I think you'd better leave Rod's office before he gets back and finds you here.' She ushered me out.

She had made no mention about Richard's 'theory'. I hoped against hope that the only person he had told was Jared.

As we were walking down the stairs Karen said, 'I know you've already heard about Jared's success at the show. But you'll be pleased to hear Richard did well last night, too.'

I'll bet he did, I thought. 'Oh, in what way?'

'He showed an excellent rapport with many potential clients, and I think Rod's taken a real shine to him. In fact, he's already considering giving him a promotion.'

I almost choked.

'Promotion? To what?'

'Probably to my current job. It all depends.'

'Depends on what?'

'On whether your company survives or not. And it depends on me, also. I've been told by someone at MediaWide that Sir Geoff may want to make some big changes there soon. The right opportunity for me may arise, or it may not. We'll wait and see.' Karen tapped the side of her nose. 'Best keep that to yourself, Duncan. Think you can do that?'

'Don't I always?'

'No, Duncan, you don't always. Going to Nigel's party tomorrow night?'

'Can't make it I'm afraid.'

'Another bad family emergency?'

'Something like that.'

Karen gave me one of her quarter smiles. 'It's about what happened last time, isn't it? Well, you shouldn't worry. I don't fancy you any more. Sorry to disappoint you.'

'I've told you over and over again: nothing happened between us.'

'If nothing happened, why did your wife go so crazy about it?'

I held up my hands. 'It was a mistake. Why can't you just forget about it?'

'A mistake? I thought you just said nothing happened?'

'I'm not discussing it any more,' I said. 'We'll have a final review about the Tea Society later this afternoon. I'll send you the PowerPoint presentation at the end of the day. Agreed?'

'Agreed,' she said, trying not to laugh.

twenty-one

I slammed my office door and kicked the wastepaper bin across the room. Then I picked up a dictionary on my desk and hurled it against the wall: standard behaviour when being reminded of the second biggest mistake of my life.

OK, I guess I've got some explaining to do.

About six months before, Nigel had thrown a party at his flat to 'celebrate summer', as he put it. In true Nigel-esque style, the theme of the party was 'Teenage Kicks'. All his colleagues were invited, and the thing ended up going on right through the night until six o'clock the next morning.

I only dropped by for a quick drink after a day's shopping in London. Silvie had driven Lily home, and I assured her I would be home before midnight.

That was before I accepted a pint, and then another pint, and then another, of Jared's specially made snakebite.

I watched the creative director as he poured a glass full to the brim with a mix of Carlsberg Special Brew and Scrumpy Jack cider. He bet me the 80s designer sportsgear he was wearing – Kappa jacket, Diadora trainers, Fila tracksuit bottoms, don't ask me where he got it all from – that I couldn't down it in one. Before I knew it, I was surrounded by a group of thirtysomethings who were shouting and clapping to encourage me.

It was the most disgusting drink I had ever tasted in my life. But I didn't want to disappoint the crowd, so I raised the glass to my lips and drank it down without stopping to take a breath. I was met with an almighty cheer.

The applause doubled in volume as I extended the empty glass to the smirking, gum-chewing Jared, and ordered a refill.

It was a foolish thing to do.

I had a heavily pregnant wife at home looking after my 2-year-old daughter, and what was I doing?

Getting totally and utterly sloshed.

And, less than half an hour later, standing in Nigel's broom cupboard unbuttoning Karen's blouse.

Even now, when I think about it, I become flushed with embarrassment and regret. In truth, hardly anything did happen, as I suddenly realized my folly halfway through removing her bra, and promptly apologized and left the party. But the damage had been done. My marriage to Silvie meant everything to me and I had screwed up big time.

I told Silvie everything that had happened the moment I arrived home. Call it guilt, call it loyalty, call it selfishness, call it stupidity, but that's what I had done.

Silvie didn't take it well. But how did I expect her to take it? I guess I'd told her mainly for selfish reasons: I figured she would instantly forgive me. Instead she just cried and cried.

Whatever else it taught me, I learned that I would never, ever, lose control of myself again.

And what was I doing now? Planning to murder Richard Regan.

I opened my laptop bag and took out my A-Z map. I looked up Great Eastern Street in the index and found it on page 40.

I wondered how well lit the streets were around there, and if there were any CCTV cameras.

'Hello, stranger.'

I looked up. Richard was standing at the door, leering at me.

'Hi Richard,' I said, collecting my wits. 'Thanks for the calls and faxes. And thanks for trying to start a rumour that I murdered Anne.'

'Just a little reminder that I'm in charge, that's all.' He continued watching me. 'But I'd appreciate it if you could help me out with a little puzzle. The police speculate that Anne was killed by mindless thugs, but ... well, where are they? Why haven't they hauled any of them in for questioning? Well, I'm guessing here, but maybe it's because they have an idea of who *really* did it.'

'Meaning?'

'Meaning that, oh, I don't know, perhaps it's got a little more to do with you than you'd like to admit, that's all.' He covered his mouth. 'Oh no. I've gone and said it. I've let the cat out of the bag.'

'OK, then,' I said. 'Why? Why do you think I would have anything to do with it?' I raised my voice. 'Go on! Tell me why.'

'You tell me. Maybe you were sick of Anne being the brains of the outfit. Maybe she didn't want to sell control of the company, and you wanted to make sure she wouldn't ruin it all for you. There are many reasons why people are driven to kill, Duncan. The real question is: have you got the guts to see it through. And I think you have.'

'I never did anything to harm Anne. Why don't you take your theories and piss off? Anyway – how do I know that you didn't do it?'

It was only meant as a retort, but Richard considered this question carefully. 'Yes, I'd never thought of that. But, come on, Duncan. It's hardly worth the effort, is it? We both know that I had nothing to do with it. But neither of us is totally convinced that you aren't responsible.'

He came towards me and brought his face level with mine – close enough for me to smell his breath.

I studied the cracks in his skin, the layers of white flakes on his collar, and his dead eyes. I felt the acid of contempt swill through my veins.

He kept his face opposite mine for a few seconds to psyche me out, then said, 'But I digress. We can talk about this later. Or maybe the police will want to. Now, back to the shares you stole from me. What's your final decision?'

'I'm going to attack your skull with a golf club,' was what I felt like saying. In the event, I replied, 'I suppose I've got no option but to sign over the shares to you.'

He seemed surprised and moved his face away. 'Just like that? You're going to give up your shares as easy as that?'

'That's what you want, isn't it?'

'Yes.'

'Then what's the problem?'

Richard scratched a finger against his neck. 'Maybe I expected you to put up more of a fight,' he said. 'Disappointing, but I suppose people never change. Always were swept along by events, weren't you, Duncan?' His expression brightened. 'I'm glad you've decided not to do anything stupid. You've kept your side of the deal, so I'll keep mine. I'll bring all the paperwork on Monday. All you need to do is sign it.'

'How do I know you'll keep your word?'

'What? You don't trust me? I've kept it secret until now haven't I?'

'OK.' I wanted this to end as soon as possible.

Richard, however, did not. 'I've got to warn you again, Duncan. If you go circulating some cock-and-bull story about me stealing your shares, I'll tell everyone what happened to Doofy. I'll let your wife know first. Oh, and perhaps I'll throw in something about Anne's murder, just to make it more interesting.'

'I've said I'll give you the shares,' I said. 'That's the end of this conversation.'

Richard came towards me slowly. 'The thing is, Duncan, that's not the end of this conversation. I've been waiting years for this moment. I want you to apologize. You've still not said how sorry you are for cutting me out of the agency deal.'

He slapped my face. Not hard, but still forcefully enough to make my cheek sting.

'Hey, there's no need for that.' My first instinct was to hit him back, harder. But the little voice in the back of my mind told me to bide my time.

He slapped me again. 'I can't hear you, Duncan. Did you say sorry?'

'Sorry,' I said. 'I'm sorry I cut you out of the deal. It was wrong of me.' Just play along, said the voice, and you can even things up later.

A third slap, this time with his other hand. 'It was wrong of you. Let me hear it.'

'It was wrong of me.'

'You're a stupid little fuck. Say it.'

A fourth slap thudded against my cheek. I tasted blood running under my tongue. 'I'm a stupid little fuck.'

He stopped. 'You've got no fight in you at all,' he said. He took his mobile out of his pocket. 'Maybe I should give your wife a call and tell her about the accident. Why? Just because I can. And because maybe you deserve it for being a coward – a selfish coward.'

Just play along. 'Richard, no. She has nothing to do with this.'

He laughed dementedly. 'You're so pathetic.' He slapped me again, but this time on the shoulder. 'Remember: Monday. I take it you're not coming to Nigel's party?'

'No, I can't make it.'

'Maybe it's best you don't go. I heard what happened last time.'

'Karen told you, did she?'

'As a matter of fact, she didn't. I have my sources. I know everything about you, Duncan. Everything.'

'I'll take your word for it.'

With a long, drawn-out coughing noise, he summoned a mouthful of phlegm and spat it on my jacket. 'Hey, Duncan. No hard feelings, eh?'

I watched his spit as it rolled across the lapel. After he had left, I tore off the jacket and stuffed it in the bin.

Then I resumed examining the map, filling my head with every shortcut from Bloomsbury to Great Eastern Street.

twenty-two

I was still looking at the map about half an hour later, when the phone rang on my desk. 'I've got Detective Sergeant Tomkins waiting in reception for you,' said Hilary.

I suddenly remembered I had forgotten all about my promise of making sure no one entered Anne's office. For all I knew the cleaning ladies could have binned every document, and our IT Manager could have erased the PC's hard drive. But it was too late to do anything about that now. 'Send him up,' I said.

The policeman greeted me with a firm handshake. He had brought a colleague with him. I took this as a sign that their interest in us had taken a more serious turn. Again, I hoped that Jared had been the only one who Richard had spouted his theories to.

'This is Detective Constable Carl Stanners. He'll be working with me on this case.'

Stanners shook my hand. He was a good ten years younger than the middle-aged Tomkins, and a good five inches shorter. He wore a dark suit, and had a face that bore the pockmarks of acne from his youth. I noticed he was holding a small jotter and Biro pen and had already written some notes.

The first thing Tomkins asked me was if I had secured the room or not. I assured him that I had.

As we made our way towards Anne's office, he told me that the house-to-house calls hadn't yet produced anything.

'Typical Camden,' he said. 'No one saw or heard anything. No one noticed any suspicious characters, and no one saw the actual break-in itself. Frustrating.'

We entered the office, and I waited on tenterhooks as Stanners switched on the computer and stared at the screen. The older man pulled up a chair next to him.

After a few minutes, it became obvious that IT hadn't yet

wiped the computer. Both policemen's eyes were darting from side to side as they looked at files on the hard drive. Stanners sat in Anne's old chair controlling the mouse, and Tomkins told him what files to open. Every now and then the younger man stopped to write something down.

After a short while, Tomkins switched his attention to the desk drawers. They were all unlocked. As he rummaged through Anne's strategy documents he said, 'This may take a while, Mr Kelly.'

'OK. Would you gentlemen like a cup of tea?'

Without looking at me, both men nodded.

In the tearoom, Nigel was upset I couldn't make it to his party. 'But you've got to come,' he insisted. 'We could all do with a bit of cheering up.'

'I know, but I've got family commitments on Saturday.'

Nigel said, 'OK, I understand. You know where we are if you change your mind.'

We switched our conversation to the Tea Society pitch. Nigel had seen the presentation boards and agreed they looked sensational. All in all, the pitch seemed to be in excellent shape.

'I bumped into Rod earlier,' Nigel said. 'He was in a foul mood.'

'I hope it wasn't because of the Tea Society work. He and Richard went to MediaWide to show Geoff Deacon the work-in-progress.'

'No, it wasn't the work. Apparently, Sir Geoff loved it. I think they had some sort of disagreement or something.'

'Did Rod mention anything about the ten-day ultimatum?'

Nigel removed a tub of low-fat cream cheese from the fridge and spread a small amount on to a single slice of toast. 'Actually, he did. He said something like, "the clock is ticking", or something like that. I can't quite remember exactly.'

'Well, I'm still confident the Tea Society will come through.'

Earlier in the day I had received an email from Jane Markham saying how much she was looking forward to the presentation. I felt good about it. It was the perfect client, with the right amount of money, at the perfect time.

'There's something that concerns me,' I said. 'Jared's lost all enthusiasm for the job. It's weird. He's come up with two great ideas for the pitch, but seems less and less interested.'

I was becoming worried about Jared. Ever since Richard had muscled his way into the company, he had been on edge. It doesn't take a rocket scientist to work out that he could be the victim of a blackmail plot, too. But I was pretty sure there were no accidents buried in Jared's closet.

'It must be about Anne,' said Nigel. 'Delayed shock. You know what Jared's like. He may be a loudmouthed yobbo, but deep down inside he's just as vulnerable as the rest of us.'

'Is he going to your party tomorrow night?'

Nigel chuckled. 'Duncan, *everyone's* going. Except you. But, as you said, family calls, and family must always take priority.'

'That's right. OK, I'd better be getting these cups of tea to our visitors.'

'Have they found anything useful?' Nigel asked.

'I doubt it. Why would anything on Anne's computer be connected to her murder?'

'No idea.'

I said, 'Has Richard been talking to you?' and then wished I hadn't.

Nigel appeared confused. 'About what?'

'Forget about it. Look, I think they're just going through the motions. Covering all angles.'

I carried the tea to Anne's office. When I walked in the room the two policemen were still gazing at the screen.

Stanners spoke for the first time. 'Ms Fulton has some profit and loss spreadsheets on here,' he said. 'The figures don't look too healthy.'

'No worse than anyone else's,' I said. 'The market is up and down right now.'

Tomkins accepted the tea. He slurped it slowly, loudly. Stanners, on the other hand, raised the cup to his mouth and drank the whole lot down in one single gulp.

'We'll come and tell you when we've finished,' Tomkins said.

I told them I would be in the main boardroom. As I left, I saw Stanners grab his notebook and scribble something down.

I spent the afternoon rehearsing the presentation with Karen, Nigel and Jared. As yet, Richard hadn't managed to gatecrash his way into attending the Tea Society meeting, and I was thankful for that.

We had agreed that I would kick off the presentation with

fifteen minutes or so about HFPK. I would talk about our way of working, our history, and how we came to be a part of the MediaWide group. Then Nigel would present some case studies of our past campaigns, before handing over to Karen and Jared who would take them through the strategy and creative ideas for the proposed creative concept.

Karen insisted on giving me the cold shoulder. She avoided making eye contact with me during the rehearsals, but nevertheless executed her strategic insights speech perfectly.

Jared, however, kept mumbling to himself and staring out of the window. When it was his turn to speak, he stood up, said his piece, then sat back down and continued gazing out the window towards Long Acre in the distance.

But I couldn't hold it against him. I was having a few problems of my own keeping my mind on the job. The enormity of what I was planning to do to Richard was a huge distraction.

I asked myself the question again. Was I *seriously* planning on ending the life of another human being?

Every time I started having second thoughts, I thought what Richard was threatening to do to me – and what he had already done to Doofy.

Later, when we were finishing our rehearsals, Tomkins stuck his head round the door to tell me that he and Stanners were finished. I got up and joined him in the corridor outside the boardroom. I closed the door behind me and asked if they had found anything.

The detective was non-committal. 'Perhaps,' he said. 'There was some personal correspondence we may like to follow up on, but we'll let you know.'

When I went back to the meeting room, I noticed Jared was eyeing me suspiciously. 'Are they investigating Anne's murder?' he asked.

'Yes, why?'

'How come they're only talking to you?'

'Because Rod asked me to show them Anne's office.'

'Really? Or was it because you were arguing with Anne last Friday?'

'Of course not,' I said. 'Rod just asked me to show them her office. Anyway, it wasn't an argument.'

'I saw you both shouting at each other in your room. It looked like a pretty big argument to me.'

'It was nothing. Just a small disagreement.'

'A small disagreement? It looked pretty nasty from where I was standing.'

I noticed Karen and Nigel had stopped what they were doing and were listening.

'What are you accusing me of, Jared?'

'Stop arguing, you two,' snapped Karen, packing her notebook away. 'The police are just following procedures, that's all. They're probably just sorting through her belongings speculatively, hoping for a lead to follow.'

Jared mumbled something. Then a sudden mood of anger came over him. 'Whoever did this, I want him to rot in prison.' He went over to the window and leaned his face against it, gazing at his reflection in the glass.

After Karen and Nigel had left, he asked me for a beer at the King's Arms over the road.

'Something on your mind?' I asked.

His usual gum-chewing habits had given way to a nervous fidgeting. His hands wouldn't keep still and twitched up and down as he packed the boards away into a portfolio case.

'Yes, you could say that,' he said. 'We'll talk about it at the pub.'

'I can only manage a quick one.'

'What I've got to say will only take a half-pint.'

We exited the building and walked across the street. The area was already bustling with the Friday night crowd.

The pub was crowded, so we decided to drink outside despite the cold weather.

I went to the bar to buy the drinks, and when I returned I found Jared yelling into his mobile. I didn't get to hear whom he was shouting at, because he switched it off the instant he saw me.

'Friend of yours?' I asked.

'No,' he said.

I handed him his bottle of Newcastle Brown, and supped gently at my pint of John Smith's. 'It's been tough recently,' I sighed. 'It's really not—'

He suddenly began yelling. 'Just stop the bullshit for a while, can't you, Duncan? I'm so sick of your bullshit.'

I was taken aback. 'What's gotten into you?'

He squared up to me. 'I want you to answer one question, that's all. One question. It's not difficult. I think I already know the answer.'

I shook my head confusedly. 'What are you talking about?'

'Just listen will you? All I need to know,' he said slowly, 'is whether you're in it together.'

It had to be something to do with Richard. But I certainly couldn't jeopardize my plan. I couldn't let him know I was being blackmailed. I had to play dumb.

'In what together?' I said. 'Together with who?'

'I knew it,' Jared cried, brandishing his beer bottle at me. 'I bloody knew it! You're up to your ears in it, aren't you? And I thought I could trust you, Duncan.'

'I haven't a clue what you're talking about.'

He grabbed my neck and pushed me against the door of the pub. 'Stop talking bullshit, Duncan! All you're interested in is money, isn't it?'

'Of course I need money, but I still don't—'

I didn't manage to get any further, because at that moment Jared's fist connected with my jaw. There was a sudden white flash – the sure sign of being punched in the face; something I hadn't experienced since my schooldays.

I dabbed a finger against my mouth. Luckily there was no bleeding, my teeth were intact and, mercifully, I hadn't bitten my tongue. But the impact had caused me to spill beer all over my jacket – my only spare, as the other was stuffed into the bin in my office covered in Richard Regan's phlegm.

I stared at Jared. I didn't feel any anger, and I certainly didn't want to fight him. But I did feel genuine confusion. What the hell had he hit me for? What was he accusing me of?

Without warning, he turned and walked away. I watched him go into Shelton Street, and decided not to pursue him. The bottle of Newcastle Brown lay on the pavement, its contents emptying into the gutter.

A young man in jeans and a leather jacket who had seen the whole thing came over to me and said, 'Are you all right, mate? What did he slap you for?'

I thought for a moment and said, 'Maybe he got me confused with someone else.'

twenty-three

A broken bottle, a hammer, some rope, a baseball bat ... what was the perfect weapon?

'A saucepan set.'

... a crowbar, an ice pick ... what?

'I *said*, a saucepan set. Have you listened to a single word I've said since we came in here?'

It was midday and we were in BabyGap. I stopped pushing Giles's buggy and turned to Silvie who was ruffling through a rack of romper suits. 'Sorry, I was miles away,' I said.

'Yes, I could see that. Why don't we get the saucepan set from ToyStore as Lily's special treat? It'll go well with her mini kitchen.'

Lily nodded furiously.

'Good idea,' I said.

'Not thinking about work again, were you?'

'I suppose I was.'

Silvie popped the baby suit she had been examining back on the rack and motioned towards the exit. 'Well, you really shouldn't. It's the weekend remember? You promised you'd try not to think about work.' She smiled at her daughter. 'Let's go to ToyStore.'

'Yippee!' Lily cried, stretching both arms high into the air.

I said, 'I wish I could, but I've got to go and meet that guy from the office soon.'

Silvie sighed. 'Which guy from the office?'

'Just one of the staff. It's about the pitch on Monday. It's the most important one we've ever done.'

'Every pitch you do you say is the most important you've ever done. But I don't see why you have to keep worrying all the time. Everything's ready, isn't it?'

'I guess it is.'

'Well then,' she said, pointing towards the bright yellow

ToyStore sign that hung at the entrance to Covent Garden market in the distance, 'there's no point thinking about it then, is there?'

Lily spotted an old-fashioned sweetshop. 'I want marshmallows!'

'I don't know about that, young lady,' said Silvie, quickening the walking pace. 'There'll be nothing left of your teeth by the time we get home.'

'Want MarshMALLOWS!'

'All right then,' said Silvie, giving in. 'I suppose it is Saturday, after all.'

'I'll go and get some,' I said.

Lily did a little jig in the pushchair. 'Whooo!'

While I went into the sweetshop, my family waited on the cobblestone street outside.

It was almost time to go and see where Richard lived. Although I felt bad about lying to Silvie, I knew it could make the difference between getting away with it and getting caught.

The left side of my face still hurt from Jared's punch. It was obvious that Richard was blackmailing him too. The question was: over what?

As far as I knew, Jared's cupboard wasn't overflowing with skeletons. But then, to Jared I probably appeared the epitome of normality. The fact I had once been involved in something as sordid as The Accident would be the last thing he would expect. For all I knew, Jared could have been involved in something just as bad, or even worse.

In the shop, I surveyed the sweets through the glass-fronted display panels. There were rows of silver trays, each covered with mountains of toffees, fudge and chocolates.

'Can I help you?' said a kind-looking old lady with what looked to be a lace handkerchief knotted around her head.

I asked for marshmallows and fudge, and she removed a small quantity of them from the trays and dropped them into paper bags. I found myself thinking again about the gargantuan task that I had set for myself.

Murdering Richard Regan.

Tonight.

As to the exact type of weapon, I had initially settled on a rounders bat, before concluding that anything made of wood was more likely to cause painful injuries rather than lethal ones. After a lot of thinking, I remembered the spate of unsolved murders in the south east of the country a few months previously. They had not yet been solved although the police were fairly sure the murder weapon was a hammer.

So a hammer it was.

In addition to letting me know what type of weapon could inflict maximum damage with minimum disturbance, it could also help confuse the police. That was, providing I got away without being noticed.

I shuddered. I could hardly believe I was still planning to do this.

The shop assistant carefully weighed the two bags of sweets. I handed her some money, and looked out of the window to where my family was waiting.

And saw him talking to Silvie, with Lily peering up at him, wondering who we was.

Richard Regan.

Before I knew what I was doing, I had darted out the shop, and was sprinting across the cobblestones towards them.

'Oh, Duncan,' said Silvie as I ran up to them, 'I've just been talking to your friend Richard here. He noticed you walking into the shop, and introduced himself to me.'

Was he following me?

'Yes, you really should watch what you're up to,' said Richard, enjoying the shocked expression on my face. 'Those things will go straight on your waist.' He pointed to the bags of sweets and he and Silvie both laughed. Lily joined in, and I felt a desperate need to pick her up and carry her as far away from him as possible.

I heard a commotion behind me, and looked around to see the lady from the sweet shop running towards me waving her hand in the air. 'You forgot your change,' she gasped.

'He's got a mind like a sieve,' said Silvie conspiratorially. 'Always forgetting things.'

'I don't know about that,' replied Richard with a knowing smile in my direction. 'I always thought he had an excellent memory.'

My wife smiled. 'So you'll be taking my husband off my hands for the afternoon?' she asked Richard.

He appeared confused. 'I'm not sure what you mean.'

'I've got to meet someone,' I said.

'Someone from the office?' asked Richard.

'Yes,' said Silvie.

'Really? Who?'

'Dan,' I said, trying to think of someone whom Richard wouldn't call. 'One of the copywriters. We have to go over a few things about Monday's meeting.'

He cocked an eyebrow. 'The Tea Society? Strange. I didn't think he had much to do with that. I thought Jared had done everything.'

'No, Dan had some valuable input,' I said. 'I need to discuss some last minute points about the headlines with him. Nothing major.'

'Interesting.'

I could feel insincerity creeping its way across my face. I removed a piece of fudge from Lily's bag, rolled it into my mouth and began to chew. 'It's no big deal. I want to be totally prepared for Monday, that's all.'

Richard cocked his eyebrow again. 'Yes, Monday is a very, very important day. People to meet, documents to sign ...'

I tried to smile, but it probably came off as a grimace. 'Yes,' I said.

'So where are you meeting Dan?'

'Nowhere special,' I shrugged. 'A coffee bar in Camden.'

Richard seemed pleasantly surprised. 'Oh! I'm up at Camden this afternoon. We can go together if you like.'

'Did I say Camden? I meant Soho.'

'You see!' piped Silvie, rocking Giles's buggy gently and accepting a marshmallow from her daughter. 'A mind like a sieve.'

Richard chuckled and patted my shoulder. 'OK,' he said. 'You go and meet Dan in a Soho coffee shop and talk about work. *I'll* go and enjoy Camden. Remember to bring a nice pen on Monday for the grand signing. *Adios.*'

He said goodbye and walked off towards the tube.

I waited until he had gone, then grabbed Giles's buggy and walked briskly into Covent Garden market. I desperately wanted to make sure he couldn't follow me when I went to check his flat.

'Where are you taking us, Duncan?' said Silvie. 'ToyStore is the other way.'

'I know. I want to check one of the other shops.' I pushed the buggy around a block of shops, before stopping at a random tourist gift store. 'Excellent,' I said, pointing at the display in the window. 'That's what I'm planning on buying your mother for Christmas.'

Silvie wheeled Lily's pushchair alongside me. 'Great English windmills?' she said, studying the knitted tea cosy that I was pointing at in the window. 'How super. Can we go to ToyStore now?'

'ToyStore!' cried Lily.

'Are you all right?' asked Silvie. 'You seemed a bit uncomfortable with him.'

'Who?'

'With Richard. The guy we just met. Your *colleague*.' She stressed the last word as if I had no idea whom she was talking about.

'No, I was fine.'

Lily spotted ToyStore on the horizon and shrieked with glee.

'You looked very uncomfortable to me. Especially when he patted your shoulder; you flinched.'

'No, I was fine.'

'OK, just making an observation,' said Silvie. 'But he's a weird-looking guy, don't you think? So washed out and thin. Small head. Sucked-in cheeks. Kind of like a skeleton, don't you think?'

'Hmm. Yes, I suppose he is.'

'You've never noticed?'

'I don't make a habit of studying him closely, but I guess he could do with two weeks away in the sun without the Pot Noodles.'

Lily was holding two marshmallows. She ate one and tore the other into little pieces, which she dropped on the ground.

'Weird,' said Silvie again. 'Friendly enough, but kind of spooky. After speaking to him on the phone, he doesn't look at all like I expected him to.'

'How did you expect him to look?'

'Well, less … scary, I suppose.'

'He's harmless. I don't really know him that well.'

'What did he mean about the "grand signing"?'

'Client contracts. Nothing to worry about.'

Silvie told me she would wait with Lily and Giles in the MagicCafé in an hour's time. I packed Lily's pushchair away into a locker and kissed them all goodbye.

After they had gone, I did a quick scan of the crowd outside for Richard. He was nowhere to be seen.

I walked as fast as I could away from the market in search of a taxi, and found one on Bedford Street.

I asked the driver to take me to Old Street tube. From there, I would walk to Richard's flat. After I had decided on the best way to carry out the attack, I would catch another cab back to ToyStore.

All I could hope was that Richard wasn't planning on going home before he went to Camden.

twenty-four

I paid the cabbie and walked down City Road, taking a detour down Epworth Street. When I reached the junction with Great Eastern Street I began looking for Richard's building.

It didn't take long to find it. Bosover Court was a large Victorian warehouse building that had been converted into flats.

To the right of the front door was a panel of doorbells, each of which had a small name plaque beneath. I found the name 'Regan' under the bell for flat 3B, and then set about seeing if there were any hiding places nearby.

To the immediate right of the front door was a disused carport. It was about twenty feet long and blocked by two huge black cast iron gates. They didn't appear to be in regular use judging from the rubbish piled up in front of them.

I wondered where I should leave the car.

I was keen to avoid being seen by anyone, which meant leaving it in a car park was out of the question. So I decided to park it somewhere further west. About twenty minutes' walk away from Richard's flat should do.

Clerkenwell was ideal. There were dozens of restaurants and bars. Surely no one would take notice of another black BMW parked there on a Saturday night.

I walked past the entrance to Richard's building without stopping. Hanging around waiting to be remembered by a witness wasn't a good idea.

Then I abruptly stopped and turned round. The hairs on the back of my neck were on end. I felt sure I was being watched – although all I could see were a couple of people walking in the distance, neither of whom was Richard.

I checked my watch. Forty minutes had passed since I had left Silvie and the kids at ToyStore. It was time to be getting back. I took one final look towards Richard's building, and then walked briskly for several minutes before turning right down Shoreditch High Street. I caught a taxi five minutes later at Bishopsgate.

During the journey back to Covent Garden I noticed the cabbie kept checking me in his rear-view mirror. He seemed nervous, flicking his eyes up to the mirror when he thought I wasn't looking, and then quickly back to the road again.

I wondered: had I assumed the appearance of a murderer already?

When we got home that evening, I found a message on the answering machine from my father.

'Duncan, can you call me when you get home? Speak to you later, Dad.'

I dialled the number of my parent's house.

'Hello,' said my father.

'Hello, Dad,' I said. 'I just got your message. We've been in London for the day.'

I proceeded to tell my father about our trip to London, omitting the part about my excursion to Great Eastern Street. I could hear him breathing evenly on the other end of the line, listening with interest as I told him about our visits to the Houses of Parliament and London Aquarium.

How easy it would be to ask him about Doofy. How quick it would be to find out the truth. Even a stunned silence would tell me everything I wanted to know.

But whilst I felt a natural longing to know if Doofy was really my half-brother or not, I knew it was the last thing my parents would ever want to hear. I wasn't even sure if my mother knew about my father's supposed affair with Gwennie, or if the whole thing was a figment of Gran's imagination. Either way, mentioning it would only cause pain and distress.

'Are you sure that was that all you got up to today?' my father said with a note of disdain in his voice.

I paused. 'What do you mean?'

'Are you *absolutely positive* you didn't do anything else?'

'No! That's all we did. Silvie waited for me with the kids while I met someone from work, but that was only for an hour.' Surely he couldn't know what I had really been up to?

'Hm,' he said, unsatisfied.

'Dad, what are you getting at? I didn't do anything else, I promise you.'

'Calm down, Duncan. All I'm asking is if you found time to go to the Science Museum?'

I let out a huge sigh of relief. 'Oh! Well, I wish we could have, but time just seemed to disappear.'

'Duncan, that's terrible. How could you?'

'Dad, I like the Science Museum as much as you, but we ran out of time. I promise we'll go next time. Sorry about that.'

Dad suddenly boomed with laughter and said, 'Oh, Duncan. I'm only pulling your leg. You can go and see whatever you want to. You're not twelve years old anymore!'

'Oh. Thanks.'

My guilty conscience had got the better of me again. And I'd not even carried out the attack yet. Was I capable of living with myself after having committed such a crime?

'Now,' said Dad, 'to the nitty-gritty: Gran's place at The Acorns. Your mother was too embarrassed to phone you, that's why I called instead. We're wondering if you managed to sell the shares? You know Gran loses her place on Thursday if we can't put down the deposit.'

'Yes, but you know I can't actually sell them before Monday. That's when the year no-sell clause is up. I'll be on to the brokers first thing Monday afternoon, I promise you.'

'I'm glad to hear it, Duncan, because Gran seems to be getting worse and worse. She keeps going on and on about Beryl and Kenneth. She's convinced Kenneth visited her the other day, you know.'

'The sooner she's with Aunty Beryl the better,' I agreed.

'You know, she swears blind it was Kenneth. When actually it was you, wasn't it?'

I wasn't sure what to say. 'Yes, it was.'

'Did she tell you anything strange?'

I swallowed. 'She told me a story about someone throwing things off a bus.'

My father laughed again. 'Why, she used to tell that story all the time! The funniest thing about it is it never happened in the first place – she made it up.'

'Why would she make it up?'

'Oh, she makes things up, your grandmother. Always has done. You must know that. Of course, it's a bit of a shame. I think it has something to do with her missing Aunty Beryl. But not to worry, it's all harmless fun. You have to take it with a pinch of salt, that's all.'

'I'll bear that in mind.'

We talked about Lily and Giles, and Dad insisted we come round for Sunday lunch. 'It'll be a lovely day,' he promised.

I forced myself to agree. In less then six hours, if everything went according to plan, I would have murdered Richard Regan. Would I be able to contain myself tomorrow at the dinner table, and not turn into a gibbering wreck?

'So can we expect you tomorrow for lunch?' asked my father.

'Yes,' I replied. 'Will Gran be there?'

My father was quiet for a second, and I imagined him adjusting his half-moon glasses on the end of his nose. 'Unfortunately not. I'm afraid she can't make it. She's decided to have a quiet afternoon at home while she prepares her things for The Acorns. Your mother has been packing some boxes for her.'

'It would have been nice for her to join us before she goes in with Aunty Beryl.'

'Yes, Duncan, it would. But your mother and I thought she should take some rest tomorrow. Don't worry, there'll be plenty more weekends.'

'I suppose so.'

'Don't suppose so, Duncan; know so.' I heard my mother say something in the background. 'Your mother is asking about your job. She's wondering if everything is all right?'

'It's going well,' I said. 'We've got a big presentation on Monday for a client called the Tea Society.'

'The Tea Society?'

'Yes, they're an organization – a kind of regulatory body – that works with the major tea brands.'

There came an exasperated sigh. 'Sorry, Duncan, but you've quite lost me there. All those marketing words. I can never make sense of them.' I heard my mother say something else. 'Well, as long as they've got money to spend, Duncan. That's the main thing. Just as long as your company is in good shape.'

'The company's fine. Never been better.'

'If you ever have second thoughts, you know there's always teaching.'

'We're fine. Really. There's nothing to worry about.'

He sounded disappointed. 'I'm only pulling your leg, you daft monkey! You know what I mean.'

I assured him that I did. 'See you tomorrow.'

twenty-five

The rest of the afternoon was difficult. I felt as if my conscience was attached to a pendulum, swinging between unshakeable purpose, and the overwhelming urge to bottle out and give up to Richard's demands.

I did my best to try to take my mind off it. I offered to do the weekly shopping for Silvie, and when she pointed out that she'd already done it two days before, I concocted an impromptu list of DIY items that we urgently required.

'You *are* acting strange,' she said, arranging Giles's bottles and teats on a plastic dish to put in the microwave for sterilization. 'DIY? Since when have you been interested in DIY?'

'I've just decided it's time I fixed a few things around the house, that's all. I'm going out to *Homebase*.'

She put the sterilization kit into the microwave and set the timer for six minutes. 'Don't you think that would be a waste of money? It's quicker to pay someone to do it, that's what you usually say. I know what you're like, Duncan. You'll go down to the hardware shop and spend an arm and a leg on a load of expensive tools that you'll never use.'

'No, it's not like that at all.'

Silvie put her hands on her hips and said, 'Oh yes it is, Duncan. And I've been doing a bit of thinking. I think you should stop wasting money on things we don't need, since you're intent on giving away all your shares to house your grandmother.'

I really couldn't face this conversation.

'You're right,' I said, keen to appease. 'Maybe I'll just buy a pack of light bulbs. We can always do with some spares.'

Silvie dismissed my suggestion with a flick of the hand. 'Whatever,' she said. 'Just remember you're on night duty with Giles tonight, OK?'

'No problem,' I said, grabbing my coat and car keys. I kissed her cheek, feeling a torrent of questions flood into my mind.

Fifteen minutes later I walked into Homebase, knowing there was no way I would be purchasing the murder weapon. It was imperative to leave behind no trails of any description. Purchasing a hammer at my local DIY store would be a foolish move indeed.

But I knew where I could get a weapon that couldn't possibly be traced.

When we had purchased the house a couple of years ago, the owner had left behind a collection of old garden tools. They were stored inside the garage roof: numerous spades, a few rusty trowels, a pickaxe and a lump hammer. They were covered in cobwebs and appeared to have been there for years.

It was the lump hammer that particularly interested me. As far as I could remember, it was clean and rust-free. If forensic experts use Richard's injuries to determine what kind of weapon had been used, I doubted they would be able to trace it back to me.

Besides, by the time Sunday morning arrived, it would be lying at the bottom of the river that ran through the outskirts of my village.

I collected a box of 60-watt bulbs from the lighting department, and made my way to the checkouts.

My mobile went off in my pocket. I took it out and immediately recognized Richard Regan's number on the screen. So this would be the last time I would ever talk to him. It was important I remained composed. It would be disastrous if he sensed something was wrong and decided not to go to Nigel's party after all.

'What do you want?' I said.

'That's not a very nice reception, Duncan.' It wasn't Richard's voice at all, but Karen's. She was shouting over the background noise of a pub or bar. 'Can you hear me? It's Karen. I wanted to make sure everything's ready for the pitch on Monday.'

She spoke in a slurred voice. So Richard and her were enjoying a cosy drink together in a Camden bar, were they?

'Yes, all the boards are at the office,' I said. 'We'll meet there Monday morning and then all go over to the Tea Society together.'

'What? Wait a minute, this is useless,' she said. 'Hang on.' The noise got louder for a few seconds, and then suddenly quieter. I heard a door slam. 'That's better, I'm in the ladies. Now, what did you say again?'

'I said, everything's ready.'

Karen said, 'Good. You sound like you're looking forward to it.'

'Of course.'

'I'm happy to hear it, Duncan. But I'm worried about Jared. Do you think we should call him and ask him not to come with us? There's no point him coming if he's in one of his moods. He'll only mess it up.'

'Well, you know Jared. It's probably some kind of backlash from winning those awards. You know, an anticlimax.'

'Yes,' she said, with heavy irony, 'That's always depressing isn't it? Are you sure you can't make it to Nigel's tonight?'

'I'm absolutely positive I can't. It's too far away, and I want to spend some time at home with the family.'

She assumed a tone of sarcasm. 'Oh, how *lovely*,' she said. 'A night in with screaming children? That sounds like fun.'

'It is fun. It's my family you're talking about.'

'The next thing you'll be telling me is that they're the most important thing in the world.'

'Well, they are.'

'Oh, Duncan, please! Why don't you come out just for one night? Have some fun for a change?'

I was becoming more and more annoyed. I was witnessing the insular world of the London advertising industry's young and beautiful at work. If there's one thing they hate, it's someone with more to do with their life than spiriting away money in London's oh-so-trendy bars and clubs.

'Sorry, Karen. I can't make it to the party and that's the end of it.'

There was a short pause and then she said, 'Disappointing. I suppose I'll see you on Monday then.'

Just before I cut the call, my curiosity got the better of me and I asked if she was with Richard. 'Yes I am,' she replied. 'Nigel's here too, and a few others from the office. I'm borrowing his mobile because my battery is flat. We're just getting ourselves in the mood. Richard's an absolute hoot. He's got some very interesting stories about you, Duncan.'

Oh, God. Not again. 'Stories?'

'Yes, I almost forgot to tell you! He says you were at school together, but he's on his fourth bottle already, so Nigel and I just assumed he was drunk. He's talking rubbish, isn't he?'

'Yes,' I said. 'He's talking absolute crap. Before Jared introduced us a couple of years ago, I'd never met him in my life.'

Karen was surprised. 'Oh really? Well, he's got a very vivid
imagination then. We can't shut him up.'

'What else is he saying?'

'He's claiming that you and him were blood brothers and
signed some sort of oath – frankly I don't know what on earth
he's babbling on about – and he says there's a surprising end to
the story, but he won't tell us what it is yet. He wants us to wait
until Monday.'

I caught my breath and said, 'It's all lies. He's making it up.
Does he know you're telling me this?'

'No. I'm in the ladies, remember?'

'Then I'd be grateful if you didn't let him know.'

'You could talk to him yourself, tonight at Nigel's party if you
weren't so scared about upsetting your wife. Find out why he's
making up this stuff about you.'

'I don't think that would be a good idea.'

'Oh, come on, Duncan. You've got to come! It'll be a giggle.'

'Karen, I've really got to go now.'

She said goodbye to me and cut the call.

So it was official: Richard had absolutely no intention of
keeping his promise. It was obvious he couldn't wait to start
telling people about The Accident, whether I signed over the
shares or not.

Adrenaline pumped its way around my body, energizing me
with the vital strength I needed to even things up.

I was now ready for the task ahead.

twenty-six

Saturday evening, 11.30 p.m.

I carefully laid Giles in his cot and sneaked out of the room. I peeked in the master bedroom to check the baby monitor was on, and saw its little red light blinking lazily in the darkness next to the sleeping form of Silvie. All I could do was hope it wouldn't come into use when I was out.

It was unlikely, but if Giles did wake up between now and, say, three o'clock, there would be a lot of explaining to do in the morning – and more on Monday when Richard's face appeared on the front page of the newspapers as the victim in a brutal murder case.

I tiptoed past Lily's bedroom door towards the stairs. I was confident my daughter wouldn't suddenly come running out and lynch me. The trip to London had tired her out, and I could hear little snoring noises coming from the room as I crept past in the dark.

I moved slowly down the stairs, and let myself out of the back door. I locked it before the cat could escape. Then I opened the car door and slipped into the driver seat, running my hand under the passenger seat to check the lump hammer I had hidden earlier was still there.

Quietly as I could, I backed the car out of the drive. As luck would have it, our immediate neighbours had gone away for the week, but I still didn't want to risk waking up the old lady who lived in the cottage across the road with any unnecessary revving of the engine.

As I drove down the A1 to London, I focused on how I should handle myself at the crucial moment when Richard arrived back at his flat. Was there any right or wrong way to bring the hammer down on him? Should I do it more than once? Should I attempt to cover his mouth first?

So many questions yet so little time to prepare for any of them. I would just have to take my chances and see what the situation threw at me.

An hour and twenty minutes later, I was driving along Gray's Inn Road, near to where Nigel's flat was situated. Looking at the bumper-to-bumper parking, I realized I had forgotten how impossible it was to find a parking space in Central London. Not only that, but I needed to have an unobstructed view of Nigel's front door to stand any chance of seeing Richard leave.

I turned right into Northington Street, and drove past the Victorian building in which Nigel lived on the fourth floor. I was reflecting on what a fool I had been to risk driving so close to the flat, when I spotted a space between another BMW and a clapped-out Vauxhall with a wheel clamp.

I parked the car and turned off the engine. In the rear-view mirror, I had a perfect view of the red entrance door to his building next to the Italian restaurant on the ground floor.

Nigel's flat was a recent addition to the building, and consisted of a lot of tinted glass and polished aluminium. It was achingly modern and not really my cup of tea at all.

If I got out of the car and moved closer, I would no doubt be able to hear music playing, and the sound of laughter and chatting. But I was staying put. I knew it could be a while before Richard turned up, so I leaned back and settled down for a long wait.

After about ten minutes I watched someone arrive from the Gray's Inn Road end of the street, and stomp up to the door. The figure was dressed in a snorkel jacket with the fur-lined hood pulled up to cover his face. Even at this distance, I knew it was Jared. I could also tell he was very drunk, as he was holding a beer bottle in his hand and swaggering around as he waited. I felt a sudden pang of resentment in my gut as I remembered how he had thrown a punch at me. What had he said? That I was in it together with Richard? As he hadn't been returning my calls, there was no way of finding out exactly what he meant unless I asked him face to face. And I wasn't going to do that. I was here to deal with Richard Regan.

Then disaster struck. As I was spying on Jared talking into the intercom system, a hand rapped against my window. I turned round like a guilty schoolboy and saw Dan from the office.

Oh, God.

I lowered the window. He had a huge grin slapped across his face. There were two other people with him whom I didn't recognize. 'Mate, you are one spooky git sometimes,' he said in his rattety-tat Liverpudlian burr. 'I *thought* it was you! Why are you sitting here looking at the flat, and not in there getting pissed? Come on, let's go in.' He opened the door of the car to let me out.

'Hang on,' I spluttered, 'I wasn't planning on going in just yet.' I knew there was absolutely no chance of being able to carry out the act now.

Dan's friends burst out laughing. He looked at me, then back at them, and laughed even louder. 'I *told* you my boss was heavy on the skunk,' he said. 'Duncan, quit winding us up, it's freezing out here. Let's go.'

I had no choice. I locked the car and walked with them. 'I've got to get back soon. The baby might wake up.'

They all hooted again as if it were the funniest thing in the world. We reached the front door and Dan pressed the buzzer.

'Hello,' cackled Nigel's voice through the intercom. I looked at the speaker, and saw a small glass lens. 'Heavens! Who is that you've got with you? It's not Duncan is it?'

Dan laughed again. He was obviously stoned. I stood motionless in front of Nigel's security camera, not saying a word, feeling utterly drained and deflated. I was ruined.

The door buzzed open and I followed them up the stairs. This was definitely *not* in the script. I would have to make my excuses and leave as soon as possible.

Loud music thumped down the stairs. Depression began to set in. I really had to get away from here.

We reached the fourth floor and the door swung open, releasing the full force of the music. Nigel stepped into view. He was dressed in a tight, see-through T-shirt that looked as if it had been fashioned from cling film. Both his nipples were pierced. Two lads with shaven heads and similar clothes were standing by Nigel's side with their hands draped over his shoulders, dancing suggestively. To say I felt out of place would be the understatement of the year.

'Duncan! The pleasure is all, all mine!' shouted Nigel above the din. 'You're a cheeky so-and-so turning up like this. Let me get you a drink.'

Dan and his friends shuffled inside without saying anything and began nodding their heads to the music. All the lights were turned off, and I watched them disappear into the darkness. I suddenly rued my snap decision to tell Richard I was meeting Dan in Soho this afternoon. All I could do was hope the two wouldn't bump into each other.

'Can't stay long,' I said. 'I've just had to drive back to London to pick something up.'

Nigel didn't seem to have heard. He marched into the kitchen, and arrived back a few seconds later clutching a bottle of Becks. 'Go easy on that,' he warned. 'You know what happened last time.'

I took a very small swig. 'That was different. It was snakebite. I'm not getting into that state again.'

'Forget it. It's ancient history now.'

'I wish it were.'

'Everyone's here. Karen's dancing somewhere over there.' He pointed to the other side of the room where I could make out an assortment of bodies swaying drunkenly. 'And guess what? Jared just turned up, too. Very drunk, mind you. He's in about the same state as Richard, who's been drinking with us all afternoon. I don't know where he is now, though. But he's definitely some-where around.'

Right, that was it. I would slip into the darkness, disappear amongst the bodies for a few minutes, and then exit discreetly.

'I'll see you later,' I said to Nigel.

I walked forward, pretending to enjoy the music but desper-ately wanting to escape. How could the plan have gone so wrong?

It was so dark I could hardly see what I was doing. I was aware of people standing around the walls nodding their heads to the music or talking. Many of them seemed to be clinging to one another. Some groups were a mass of arms belonging to four people or more. The air reeked of weed, tobacco smoke, beer and sweat.

Nigel had shut the curtains to ensure the flat wasn't lit unnec-essarily by the streetlights outside. This creeping around was ridiculous. I decided that I would walk straight past Nigel and leave.

Something prodded into my side, and I realized I was standing against a door handle. It must be to the bedroom. Maybe I could slip in there for a few minutes whilst I waited for my chance to escape. I opened the door and stepped backwards through it, closing it behind me.

I fumbled around for a light switch in the pitch black. Suddenly, I heard a loud, long moan. Then I heard a mattress creaking.

This was going from bad to worse.

'Oooooooohhhhh,' moaned a woman's voice. 'No. No! No, don't stop. Keep going. Don't you *dare* stop!'

I recognized the voice immediately. It was Karen. Time to leave.

I grappled around for the door handle, and was just about to leave when a male voice said, in between grunts, 'I thought ... I heard ... someone ... come in. I'm going to see ... who it is.'

Without wasting a second more, I sneaked back into the main room, and closed the door behind me. It was then that it dawned on me: that was Richard's voice.

Was I hearing things? The first voice had most definitely been Karen's. I would know that voice anywhere. But *Richard*?

What was Karen doing having sex with ... *Richard*?

I didn't understand, and I didn't want to understand. I just wanted to leave.

I stepped further into the darkness of the body-filled living room and negotiated my way towards the stairs. Nigel stepped out in front of me.

'You naughty boy, Duncan, creeping around in the dark.' He raised his hands above his head and snaked them around in time to the music. 'I know you're up to no good.'

'Look, I'd really better be going....'

'Don't be silly! Come on. Have some fun. Cheer up and enjoy yourself. Don't feel so responsible all the time.'

'I'm not feeling responsible. Why should I feel guilty?'

He stopped dancing. 'Forget it. Come on, I'll mix you some snakebite. With your favourite scrumpy. You need it. Follow me to the kitchen.'

Suddenly there was a loud scream and the sound of glass smashing. Someone turned the music off and the dancing bodies froze. There were more screams. I looked to the centre of the room, and could just make out two figures clinging to each other, squirming around, scuffling down on the floor like a dying insect, and then back up again. I'd never seen dancing like that. It had to be the drugs.

'They're fighting,' said someone. 'Turn the bloody light on!'

The lights duly came on, and everyone, bar the two moving

figures, instinctively raised their hands to shield their eyes against the brightness.

But I kept mine open – wide open. The two people fighting were Richard and Jared.

Richard was dressed only in polka dot boxer shorts, and was bent double with his face covered in blood. Jared, his face covered in what looked to be a mixture of vomit and snot, was throwing his fists wildly, and landing a good proportion of blows in Richard's face.

A couple of people moved forward to restrain him, but he shook them off, saying, 'I'm going to kill him! I'm going to kill him!'

I didn't wait to see the rest. While everyone had their eyes on Jared, I slipped out of the flat and bolted down the stairs. No one saw me leave.

I ran down the stairs, taking them three at a time, and sprinted to the car. I unlocked the door and jumped in. I looked in the rear-view mirror and saw Jared exiting the building. He hobbled drunkenly down the street in the opposite direction.

What the hell had just happened?

I recounted the events.

First, I had heard Karen making love to the ugliest, cruelest, most disgusting man in the world. Then Jared had arrived, and began beating the crap out of him in front of everyone.

Well, whatever. I would have plenty of time to examine the whys and wherefores later, but for now I just needed to get back home. I was a fool to have even come down here.

I tried to put the key into the ignition, but my hand was shaking so much I couldn't hold it straight.

After I did finally manage to get the car going, I caught sight of someone else coming out of the building. It was Richard. He was now wearing a long coat, although I could clearly see his bare legs beneath it. He was walking slowly, unevenly, having to steady himself by running a hand along the wall.

I expected to see Karen follow him out, but the door to Nigel's building remained closed.

He walked straight past the car, holding his hand over his face and staring at the ground. I turned away and pressed myself down in my seat, but it was clear he hadn't noticed me.

He walked into John Street. I switched the ignition on. Still he didn't look up.

My mind was flooded with images of Gran, Doofy and my father. I felt every ounce of my being urge me to stamp my foot on the accelerator pedal and run him down.

But there was absolutely no chance of getting away with something like that, not in Central London.

Then I watched him enter an alleyway.

This was my chance.

Without hesitating to question my actions, I shoved my hand under the passenger seat and grabbed the lump hammer. If I was going to do this, it had to be now. Never mind it was near Nigel's flat. A chance like this might never present itself again. I would have to take my chances.

I hid it under my jacket and jumped out of the car. I ran quietly to the alley where Richard had already disappeared into the darkness.

The alley was completely unlit, the nearest streetlight being at least thirty feet away. Even though it was almost as dark as Nigel's flat, I could see Richard up ahead, struggling to put one foot in front of the other. He was mumbling something. It was obvious he didn't know I was behind him.

So this was it. The moment I been waiting for – waiting fifteen years for. I thought again of Doofy, and of Richard's determination to ruin my life.

Say your prayers, Richard Regan.

I removed the lump hammer from beneath my jacket and extended my arm high above his head.

I held my breath. I gritted my teeth tightly and tensed my outstretched arm. Still, Richard kept stumbling on.

And then I brought the weapon down.

Carefully, evenly … and slowly.

And put it back under my jacket.

I couldn't do it. No matter what he'd done in the past, no matter what he was trying to do now, I could *not* bring myself to kill him.

I walked back to the car, leaving Richard to take step after careful step towards the streetlight at the end of the alley, and to a taxi that would return him home safely.

twenty-seven

It was already the middle of Sunday afternoon, and I was lying on top of the bed at home.

Silvie was leaning against the door with a concerned expression. 'Still feeling rough, Duncan?' she said.

Lily was standing further back, holding the bedroom door, fidgeting nervously. I knew from infrequent experience that she was always unsettled when her father was ill.

'I feel like I've been trampled by a herd of elephants,' I said.

'You look like it too.'

I managed a smile.

She and Lily began to leave. I knew Giles was fast asleep in the other bedroom. Even the cat seemed unwilling to venture into my room for any length of time.

'Don't go just yet,' I said. I wanted to savour the time we could spend together before Richard made good his threat about going public about The Accident. 'Did you manage to give my parents a call to tell them we couldn't make it this afternoon?'

'Yes, I did that while you were having a snooze earlier. Your father's convinced that it's stress that's brought this on.'

'How would he know?'

'Nerves about that Tea Society thing tomorrow?'

'I don't think so. I don't know what it is.'

Silvie considered this and said, 'Yes, you never normally get this worked up about a meeting. It would have to be something pretty serious to get you into this state.'

Perhaps I should tell her now. Let her know everything. I had been lying for too long, after all.

I thought about how I had managed to slip back into the house last night undetected.

What sort of man played such games of deception with his family?

The sort that will do anything – nearly anything – to protect them from the truth, I tried telling myself for the hundredth time that day.

There was something more. I enjoyed being trusted. I loved the intimacy of it, the fact that my wife didn't view everything I did with a suspicious eye.

Would that be lost forever if I told the truth?

At least if Silvie heard about The Accident from Richard, I could still tell her I had kept it a secret to protect her.

So I kept my mouth shut. Again.

And Richard Regan was still alive.

Only because of me.

It was a small consolation.

True, I had been defeated by a more ruthless and, some would say, smarter man than me. I didn't feel surprised that it had ended the way it had. Richard had won because he was willing to damage the lives of others to get what he wanted, whereas I wasn't.

However, it wasn't Monday yet. There could still be a way out.

It was far too late to look into a bank loan for Gran's place at The Acorns. Anyway, how would I keep that one quiet from Silvie?

I closed my eyes. I simply couldn't bear to think about it any more. All this constant searching for an answer that didn't exist was getting me nowhere and only succeeded in making me exhausted.

'Daddy's tired,' observed Lily. 'Daddy wants to sleep.'

I smiled thinly at the chirpy sound of my daughter's voice. All I could hope was that, somehow, as she and her brother grew up, the shame of the next week's events would fade.

'Yes, Daddy's very tired,' said my wife. 'I think we should let him rest. He's got a big day tomorrow.' I heard the door sweep lightly across the carpet.

'A big day?' Lily questioned. 'Why?'

As they walked down the stairs together I heard Silvie saying, 'It's an important day, Lily. The kind of day you never forget. A big day is an *exciting* day.'

'I want a big day like Daddy!'

'Then you'll have to ask Daddy to tell us all about it when he gets back tomorrow evening.'

I listened to them walk down the stairs and enter the living-room. Lily was talking, and I heard the TV cabinet being opened, which meant that she was going to watch a video.

It went quiet for a short while, and I knew what was coming next. Lily let out her usual cry of delight as the cartoon started, and I heard the floorboards – the ones in the centre of the room that I had refitted in a rush last winter – creak loudly as she began to dance.

I listened for other familiar sounds and, sure enough, heard the unmistakable whoosh of Silvie's espresso machine as she made herself a cappuccino.

I imagined her sitting at the kitchen table, browsing through a book by Nigella Lawson or Nigel Slater. She would go through the recipes searching for something delicious and surprising enough for me, whilst making instant deductions of ingredients that were unsuitable for Lily.

Always thinking what was best for the family …

It was at that moment I called Silvie.

I heard a chair scrape on the kitchen floor. She said something to Lily as she passed through the living-room and made her way up the stairs. I waited on the edge of the bed. The bedroom door opened and she entered the room holding a coffee-cup.

'Silvie, I've got something to tell you.' I did my best to make it appear grave and important, but not *catastrophic*. She stirred her drink slowly, keeping her smile, and sat down in the old pine chair beneath the window. She kept the curtains closed.

'Yes,' she said. 'I know you have.'

'How?'

'Duncan, I'm not daft. You're my husband. I think I know when something's wrong.' She crossed her legs. She was wearing jeans without socks and a black top that I had bought her from Next last winter. It was all so familiar. The sheer otherworldliness of the blackmail – and The Accident – had no place here, but I had to tell her. 'And if it seems like I've been awfully nice about it so far, it's because I know it's nothing about that Karen woman.' I felt my face getting hot. 'Yes, it's more serious than that. You're not looking for forgiveness this time, but understanding.' She gave me one of her special sighs that signalled the time for messing around was over, and I loved her for that.

I started right at the beginning. The very beginning.

My first day of school, in fact.

twenty-eight

It was 9.20 on the first Monday of Goltmore Junior School in Bedford. We were all sitting at our new desks and the teacher – Mrs Evans, a fortysomething lady with a tweed jacket and mountainous beehive hairdo – was learning our names.

Whilst the other pupils were sharing desks, I was sitting by myself. It was nothing intentional, just the way things had turned out. I knew no one in the class. My parents had moved house during the holidays and all my usual friends were enjoying their first day of junior school twenty miles away.

I was feeling exposed and uncomfortable.

The classroom door opened and a pale boy with short, dark hair came in. His uniform was ill-fitting, and his blazer appeared too big for him. It looked like a hand-me-down that he had yet to grow into.

But his confidence was obvious. Why was I feeling so nervous about all this, I wondered, when someone else could look so … unaffected.

'Ah, you must be Richard Regan,' said Mrs Evans. 'Come on, it doesn't do to be late. Quick march! There's a spare chair on Duncan's desk over there.'

Richard, however, had already found the spare place and seated himself. I grinned sheepishly. The boy called Richard Regan seemed to look right through me.

Sitting behind him was a large boy with spiked hair named Jason. The cuffs on his blazer were folded up, exposing his bulky forearms, and he had a loud, piercing laugh that had already marked him out as one to watch.

Every time Mrs Evans's back was turned I saw him kicking his friends' legs under their desks. Richard had his attention on the blackboard, watching the teacher writing, with the look in his eyes that I was to become all too familiar with.

Eventually, the teacher announced that we were going to play a game to help her remember our names. She wanted us to say our name to the class followed by our favourite word. To my dismay, she decided to start from my side of the room. The boy called Jason must have noticed my expression for I heard him chuckle to himself.

Mrs Evans and the class waited.

'Yes, just your name,' she said. 'And your favourite word.'

'Duncan,' I said quietly. Followed by: 'Kelly.'

'Kelly! It's a girl's name,' Jason whispered to his friends.

'Yes, Duncan,' said Mrs Evans. 'What's your favourite word?'

I thought about this question carefully. Too carefully. My mind drew a blank. I couldn't think what to say. Favourite word? What was my favourite word? Was it to do with the way it sounded? Or was it the meaning?

Clearly not wanting to waste any more time, Mrs Evans said, 'Very well. Then perhaps one of Duncan's friends can tell me what his favourite word is? Anyone?'

I was burning up. My cheeks were on fire. I couldn't believe it. Why had she mentioned my friends? Didn't she know I was new at the school? My friends were all miles away. And here was I, alone, being labelled as someone to avoid by the rest of the class.

Jason was laughing silently behind his satchel. Why didn't Mrs Evans notice that? One of his friends clenched his hand into a fist and brandished at me under the table, then pulled a stupid face.

The class waited. The teacher waited.

She was just about to move on when suddenly I heard a voice say, 'Think.'

The teacher said, 'Pardon?'

It was Richard Regan. 'Think,' he said. '"Think" is Duncan's favourite word. It's the most important thing anybody can do. It's the most powerful thing. It's why anything ever happens, or has happened. Because we think. Duncan told me that.'

The class was stunned.

'Thank you, Richard,' said Mrs Evans. 'Are you one of Duncan's friends?'

Richard nodded twice. 'I'm his best friend.'

I continued to tell Silvie about my time in High School, and how I had nearly failed my exams, until The Accident had happened.

She listened intently as I explained to her what had happened to Doofy. When I told her the worst parts, about how I had weighed his body down in the mud, I had to close my eyes tightly. When I finally opened them, I saw that Silvie had hers closed too.

I even told her that I thought Doofy was my half-brother.

I went into the details of how Richard had joined MediaWide, and about my meeting with him when he made his threat. This was the end of the story; the blackmail. Silvie listened very carefully, not wanting to miss a thing. The only other reaction she gave was to touch a hand to her mouth when I mentioned that Richard was demanding my shares.

I finished with how we had met with him yesterday in Covent Garden. I couldn't bring myself to tell her about my plan to murder him, and I omitted to mention I had slipped out of the house last night ... some things could never be shared.

'And that's it,' I said. I could still hear the television downstairs, and knew that as Lily hadn't made an appearance, she must have fallen asleep on the sofa.

Silvie waited for a moment and then tried to speak. She stopped herself. I still wasn't sure about her reaction. Then I saw a tear slide down her cheek. I moved across to her. Still she didn't say anything. I opened my arms and she let me hold her. Her hands gripped around my shoulders so hard I thought I would lose my breath. She began sobbing; deep noises of grief that were deeply upsetting to listen to. But after a few seconds she composed herself.

'You should have told me,' she said.

'I know,' I said. 'I'm sorry.'

'It wasn't your fault. *This* isn't your fault. It's just the way things are. Sometimes you think too much, Duncan. Sometimes,' she said, 'there are no answers *worth* looking for.'

She held me there for a long time. Then she took a deep breath and kissed me on the cheek, and then on the mouth. It was a hungry, urgent, life-affirming kiss. I moved my hands up to her chest, and she broke away, pulling me down on the bed.

Neither of us said a word. We didn't need to. It was the act of love that was important. It was as if we had to prove to ourselves – and each other – that we were still truly alive.

Afterwards, as Silvie rested her head against me, I said, 'I *know* I'm feeling better now.'

Silvie said, 'I can see that,' and I immediately knew she still trusted me.

'What do you think I should do? Tell the police?'

'No,' she said firmly. 'No, no, no. You've told me. You've got it out in the open. What you've got to do is talk to Richard. Make him see sense. Tell him what you've said to me. Make him *think*.'

I stroked her hair. 'I'll do it.'

twenty-nine

Monday.

Picture the scene: a nondescript high-rise office block in Hammersmith, one polished boardroom table, five inscrutable clients, and three severely pumped up ad execs.

I emphasize the word three. Our creative director hadn't turned up.

I had met Nigel and Karen at the office an hour before. It appeared that no one had heard from Jared since Saturday night. Karen had tried to call him four times, but had only succeeded in getting through to his voicemail.

There was one small upside to this, however. Both Karen and Nigel had been so annoyed by the cowardice and incompetence shown by Jared, that neither of them had referred to my surprise visit to the party.

That suited me fine.

During the cab ride to the Tea Society's offices we discussed which of us would present the creative ideas in Jared's absence. Cancelling the meeting at the eleventh hour would be incredibly bad form. No client would hire an agency that dared to pull such a stunt.

I thought again about Richard; his threats of violence, his black, piggy eyes, his enjoyment at watching me struggle.

'Duncan?'

Jane Markham was staring at me with a bemused look on her face. The other four clients waited patiently. Nigel and Karen watched me intently.

The PowerPoint presentation, which was being beamed by projector on to the far wall, was on the screen that displayed our company logo. The blinds had been closed and the room was dark and quiet. While I'd been daydreaming, someone had dimmed the spotlights in preparation for Duncan Kelly to kick things off with his pulse-quickening set-up speech.

So what did I do?

I pulled myself together.

I got to my feet, rested my fingertips against the table for a second, then took a deep breath and pressed the space bar on the laptop. The first screen of the presentation appeared on the wall. It said: 'The Tea Society. Winning over the youth market. A presentation by Holt Fulton Powell & Kelly'.

A torrent of words began to flow. I did a little pre-rationale, recapping on what the Tea Society had achieved in their marketing operations over the past twelve months, and what they hoped to achieve in the future. I touched on their objectives and the reasoning behind repositioning their brand to appeal to the notoriously fickle youth market.

All this was done with the occasional flick of the space bar to cue another screen. I was amazed with the fluidity of the presentation. And, judging from their ever-widening smiles, so were my colleagues.

When I had finished, I handed over to Nigel.

By the time he wrapped up the presentation with a short explanation on why our client servicing abilities were second to none, I knew the clients had warmed to us.

And by the time Karen had explained the 'someone give him a cup of tea' campaign idea, I felt that we had it in the bag.

I thanked the clients for their time and attention, and asked if they had any questions. This was the acid test. In my experience, if you had made a winning presentation there was either no questions, as the client had already made up their minds, or an endless stream of the damn things as they endeavoured to check the tiniest of details of what they were about to sign up to.

The Tea Society clients fell into the latter category.

Jane Markham led the barrage, followed by the brand manager who wanted to know everything from whether our ideas could work in radio, ambient and mobile, to what other campaigns we had seen recently that we liked.

After almost one full hour of intense questions and answers, we finally left the building. Nigel could hardly contain himself, and didn't even bother to pack the boards back into the portfolio case. He stood in the elevator with them bundled under his arm, giggling excitedly to himself.

Even Karen had a spring in her step, and she ruffled my hair as we stepped out into the street. 'You did brilliantly, Duncan.'

'Thanks.'

'So now the presentation's over I can ask you the burning question. Why did you turn up to Nigel's party, and then disappear after twenty minutes?' She saw a taxi and threw her hand into the air.

'Yes,' said Nigel. 'Was it anything to do with Jared and Richard fighting?'

'Jared and Richard were fighting?'

'Don't play dumb with me,' Karen said. 'You saw it happen, and left while it was going on. Why don't you pull yourself together and stop acting like such a fool.' Then she added, 'Or are you just *jealous*?'

I didn't reply. Her comment brought back all my feelings of hopelessness. The pitch had finished, and we had performed well. But the sense of purpose I had experienced during the presentation had vanished.

I was back in reality. And it didn't feel good.

Jealous? I had felt almost every conceivable emotion over the last few days, but not jealousy. I wished I could tell Karen to go to hell, but as long as she was higher up in the MediaWide food chain than me, my hands were tied.

'Well, whatever,' she said, stepping into a taxi. 'I'm really looking forward to telling Richard how it went.'

thirty

After the taxi arrived back at our office, I let Karen and Nigel go into the building first. Then I waited on the pavement and gazed at the building for a while. Was I about to become a ruined man?

I must have waited there for at least five minutes just rooted to the spot. Eventually, I walked into the building and, guided by autopilot, into the elevator and up to my office.

I looked around for Richard, but couldn't see him.

Jared, also, was nowhere to be seen. I wondered how long it would take before he trundled into the office, shamefaced at the unbelievable recklessness at lashing out at one colleague (me), beating the crap out of another (Richard), and then not even turning up to the presentation.

It occurred to me that Richard could have taken a sick day off work to nurse the bruises from his beating. But that was just the eternal optimist in me, continuing to hope against hope.

Rod paced into my room. 'Karen told me it went well,' he said. 'I really hope so, Duncan.'

'Yes, it was good,' I said. 'We did our best.'

'We?' said Rod. 'We? You mean you and Nigel did, with a little help from Karen. When I get hold of that young fool Jared, he's going to have to convince me that he still deserves his job.'

Rod's cheeks were flushed a deep shade of crimson. His jowls twitched back and forth as he searched his jacket pocket for his cigarettes. He was extremely annoyed with Jared, but I knew he had no intention of really sacking him. Everyone knew the company wouldn't be half as good without Jared's original ideas to carry us.

'Now,' said Rod, 'I can't stay all day, I've got a client waiting for me to call him back, but I just wanted to ask if you've bumped into Richard today?'

'Not yet.'

'Damn! He must have gone out to some other meeting. I urgently need a copy of your Tea Society ideas on disc, and Karen is out with Nigel.'

'Maybe they're all somewhere together?'

Rod was flustered. 'I haven't got time to speculate, Duncan. Can you run over to Richard's office and see if it's lying around?'

'Of course.'

On the way, I saw Dan who was cutting some boards on the mounting table. He gave me a conspiratorial wink as I pushed open the door of Richard's office.

The room was in perfect character with its owner: cold, clinical, and devoid of any kind of personality. The walls were stark white and the desk was clear, except for a pad of white paper and a box of HB pencils next to it.

There was nothing else of interest in the room. In fact, there was hardly anything else there at all. No personal items, no photos of family. No post-it notes saying 'Don't forget' stuck on the edges of the desk. The room seemed devoid of not only the habitual tabletop litter common to every advertising agency, but also devoid of *life*.

There was a set of drawers next to his desk, but they were all locked.

I imagined Rod fuming with anger as his impatience overtook him. I decided I'd better not keep him waiting any longer.

Before I left I checked the drawers one more time. They were definitely locked, but a stationary drawer above them slid open. It appeared to be empty, although I could see the side of a CD case.

I slid one finger into the space between the desk and the drawer, and managed to push it out.

It was indeed a CD, but not the one Rod was after. It was *Rumours* by Fleetwood Mac.

Richard listened to music? Maybe he did have a human side to him after all.

I opened the case, but the disc didn't seem anything to do with Mick Fleetwood and Co. at all. It was blank, except for the word 'Info' scrawled in small letters with black marker pen. Better than nothing, I thought, and carried it off to my laptop to see if it was the Tea Society presentation that Rod was looking for.

When I got to my room I put the CD in the drive. Rod came back. 'Did you find anything?'

'Nothing,' I said, 'except this CD-Rom. I'm going to have a look at it now.'

He stood opposite me, waiting. The icon labelled 'Info' appeared on the screen and I double clicked on it.

The CD seemed to contain a series of Word documents, each titled with the name of someone who worked at either HFPK or MediaWide. There were probably about fifteen or twenty names in total. I clicked the file titled 'Rod Russell'. It opened and I was faced with a series of bullet points. I took in the words:

Pays frequent visits to Starlights Sauna, York Way, King's Cross.

Then I fixed my eyes on the second paragraph.

'The visits usually take place on the first and third Tuesdays of every month after 8 p.m. Judging from Rod's elaborate cover-story, his wife, Marjorie, is unaware of this. She and Rod are planning to celebrate their ruby wedding anniversary in October – this presents an opportunity'.

'Well what is it?' demanded Rod. 'Is it the Tea Society or not?'

If he walked just three steps forward to look at my screen, he would have seen for himself that it was anything but.

'No,' I said. 'It's nothing. Just a standard company creds presentation.' I closed the document. 'It's not relevant at all.'

He paced around my desk to see the display.

'Info? No, that's not it.' He turned and marched out of the room. 'If you see Richard or Jared,' he yelled back to me, 'tell them I want to see them immediately.'

I kept staring at the screen.

By sheer chance, it seemed I had discovered Richard's blackmail files.

I copied the Word files on to my desktop. Then I ejected the CD and walked quickly back to Richard's office. I had to get it back there as quickly as possible – before he came back.

Dan wasn't at his desk anymore and Richard's office door was closed. I didn't enter. Even though I doubted it was Richard himself in there (I knew the instant he arrived back at the building he would come to my office and demand my signature on his share transfer agreement), I still didn't want to take any chances.

Instead I walked away, clutching the CD in my pocket.

thirty-one

I wanted to examine the CD as soon as possible, although I strongly sensed it was the kind of information I would come to regret being party to.

In the end, however, I decided I would be a fool not to look at it, as my only chance to fight back against Richard could be contained on there.

And at this stage in the game I had to jump at every chance I got.

I peeked out of my office to see if Richard was around yet, but he was nowhere in sight. It was eerie, this prolonged waiting for disaster. It was like being forced to wait at the base of the steps to the gallows while they fixed a mechanical problem with the drop platform.

I didn't discount the fact that Richard could have planned it this way. I knew he had trailed me on Saturday afternoon in Covent Garden before presenting himself, just to let me know that he could lynch me whenever and wherever he liked. So perhaps, as a final Richard-esque tactic, he had wanted me to stew in my own anxiety until he decided to stroll into my office with a pen and share transfer document.

That was why I had to look at the CD immediately. But I didn't want to risk being caught, so I decided to go out to a coffee shop.

Quickly, I left the building via the stairs rather than the elevator. On the way out, I asked Hilary at the reception desk if she had seen Richard. She shook her head.

After five minutes' brisk walk down Endell Street and Long Acre, I came across a Caffe Nero. I ordered a medium latte, and found a seat at the back of the café.

A waiter came over to clear the table next to me, and I found myself shutting the fold-down screen on my laptop as he passed.

The computer went through the motions of its start-up

program, and I watched with trepidation as the file marked 'Info' loaded up. I ran my eyes over the list of names.

Natasha Brian
Boba Brown
Jo Craighen
Baz Drinkwater
Dan Hitchin
Jared Holt
Martin Jenkins
Duncan Kelly
Barbara Mason
Bharat Mistry
Nigel Powell
Rod Russell

The first thing that struck me was that Jared was indeed on the list. I ran my eyes over the other names.

The next thing I thought was: how could Richard have come into possession of sensitive information on so many people?

Roughly half the people worked for HFPK. The rest of them worked for MediaWide. Without doubt, the biggest name on there was Rod Russell. It would have been a little too tumultuous if Sir Geoff Deacon had been on the list.

I decided to begin with Dan. His name seemed as good a place to start as any, and I felt I wasn't yet ready to read unpleasant facts about Nigel or Jared.

NAME: Dan Hitchin
POSITION: Copy-writer, HFPK
INVESTIGATION STATUS: In progress
CLAIM: Possible neo-nazi

I moved back in the chair. What? It had to be made up. But the only way of finding out for certain was to read on so, reluctantly, I continued.

EVIDENCE: Internet history file reveals visits to a large number of neo-nazi websites, including: All Reich Jack, WebStika and Skinn!

Have been unable to determine whether or not Hitchin is a

member of any neo-nazi groups, but it is doubtful – website visits should be enough.

Have yet to confront Hitchin.

ANGLE: Hitchin's brother, Dominic, works in the City as a clerk for investment bank Golding Brothers. His boss is DAVID HOROWITZ, an American Jew.

SOURCE: Hitchin's laptop/browser history. Golding Brothers website.

RATING: 8

Needless to say, it was worse than I thought. My opinion of Dan instantly plummeted to somewhere below tarmac level. Neo-Nazi? In the London advertising industry? In my agency?

My mind went into fast-rewind mode, furiously scanning the past for possible evidence to help me dispute the claim. Unfortunately, the more I thought about it, the more it did seem to make sense.

Hadn't Dan once said the phrase 'token black' during a pre-production meeting to discuss casting for the new Jackmann Fitness commercial, with a raspy, hateful sneer? Wasn't it he whom I once noticed standing in front of the TV in reception, with gritted teeth and sweated brow, as news of another asylum-centre breakout was announced.

Come to think of it, didn't he seem awfully smug last summer when the British National Party won another by-election in Bradford?

Enough!

Don't get bogged down with insignificancies. Move on.

Nervously, I slid my finger around on the trackpad and clicked on Nigel.

NAME: Nigel Powell

POSITION: Co-founder HFPK, Client Services Director

INVESTIGATION STATUS: Completed

CLAIM: Worked as a male prostitute to pay his way through university

EVIDENCE: Powell attended North London University, formerly North London Polytechnic, located in Kentish Town

Powell worked independently, advertising his services as a 'Rent Boy' specializing in 'Full Bum Work'. He advertised himself by

placing cards in telephone boxes and on small ads boards in
newsagents.

Powell used to work two nights a week, charging between 50 and
100 pounds a session, depending on client and service required.

This was getting out of control.

I took a first, tentative mouthful of latte and considered the
information. It was shocking, but we weren't living in the 1950s
anymore. Surely Rod or Sir Geoff Deacon wouldn't be remotely
interested in it. But, as I read the file some more, I discovered that
Richard had other people in mind to reveal the information to.

ANGLE: Powell's parents, who live in the North East, still have no
knowledge of his homosexuality. His mother, in particular, is a
prominent member of the 'Village Committee', and has spoken
out publicly against Gay adoption.

SOURCE: Jordan Stanley, ex-roommate of Powell

RATING: 9

I realised that with just a few phone calls from Richard, Nigel's
relationship with his parents could become very strained indeed.
Maybe even ruined.

However, I was pretty sure that Richard hadn't yet approached
him. If he had done, I am certain Nigel wouldn't have been able
to contain the pressure. Although, judging from the 'completed'
status of the report, an initial confrontation probably wouldn't be
long in coming.

Jordan Stanley was a name I had never heard Nigel mention.
Still, the London advertising industry is an incredibly insular
place. All it took was a little chatter with a stranger in one of the
agency-frequented pubs in Soho, a spot of name-dropping, and
you had what you were looking for.

Richard truly was evil beyond belief.

Just as I was clicking on Jared's name, my mobile rang. I
checked the caller ID: my parents. No doubt it was my father,
ringing with the account number of The Acorns, so I could
transfer the funds raised from the sale of my shares.

I switched it to voicemail. I had no idea how I was going to
tackle the loss of the shares I'd promised to Gran. I guess I was
foolishly telling myself that, until I did put pen to paper and sign
over my shares to Richard, I didn't have to think about breaking

the devastating news to my parents that the funds would not be coming.

I swallowed and clicked on Jared Holt. Perhaps now his reasoning for giving Richard a good beating would come to light.

As I read the file, my reaction changed from incomprehension to shock, before finally settling on anger and disgust.

Not only had Jared put his reputation on the line by being an unethical fool, he had put the whole company's future at risk.

There was no getting away from it. Whatever strife was dealt to me over the coming week, I would *have* to confront Jared about this.

I knew that if it got out, HFPK wouldn't have a chance of winning the Tea Society business. In fact, it wouldn't have a chance of getting to the end of the week.

My mobile went off again. This time the caller ID indicated it was Rod. I would have to answer it.

'Duncan?' he said. 'Something's come up. Very, very urgent. Can you make it back to the office at once?'

So this was it. Richard had finally come back, and sent the message out via Rod that he wanted me back there. Now.

thirty-two

'Rod wants to see you in his office right away,' Hilary told me as I entered the reception five minutes later.

My worst fears were confirmed. Richard must have gone straight to Rod and blurted everything about The Accident. I hadn't even been able to reason with him as Silvie had suggested.

I groaned.

Why had Richard done this? I wondered if the next time I saw Hilary I would be out of a job.

I went into the elevator and imagined the routine.

Rod would first demand to know if Richard was telling the truth. When I answered that he was, Rod would ask me if I knew how damaging this would be, not only for the reputation of HFPK if this got out, but for MediaWide too.

I would reply that, yes, I knew full well. Then he would remark that it would be better for all parties if he 'let me go'.

My last hope would be to remind him of our certainty of winning the Tea Society account. To this, he would become flushed and irritated, and remind me that nothing was ever certain in the advertising business until after it had happened.

The elevator doors opened and I made my way towards his office. Carol was away from her desk, so I walked straight in.

The portly managing director stood up as I entered. The look on his face told me everything I had expected. His lips were slammed tightly together and his jaw was quivering, as if he were trying to speak but couldn't. I spotted Richard's brogues from the corner of my eye. He was sitting in the battered old leather chair to the side of the door. I could sense him sitting up in anticipation. He coughed, trying to get my attention, but I made sure I didn't look at him.

It was anger that dominated my feelings more than defeat. My pulse was getting quicker and my senses were becoming heightened with adrenaline. I pulled my hands out of my pockets and thrust them down by my sides. I felt cheated. But it was my own fault. I should have told Silvie about the blackmail earlier.

If I could have sat Richard down and talked to him....

My heart quickened. Maybe I should choke the life out of him with my bare hands right now.

Was this my last chance?

I had failed once before – I wouldn't make the same mistake twice.

Rod's mouth was moving, but the words passed right through me. I didn't hear anything apart from the booming voice in my head that was ordering me to attack Richard.

I turned to face my blackmailer.

But it wasn't Richard at all.

It was Detective Sergeant Tomkins. Detective Constable Stanners was sitting next to him.

I said, 'What's happening? Where's Richard?'

Rod pressed a hand on my shoulder. 'I'm sorry,' he said. 'I know this is hard to believe. But I'm afraid it's true.'

'What's true? What are you talking about?'

Rod looked sympathetic. 'It's OK, Duncan, you're in shock. That's all. You're in shock.'

'What—'

'It's OK, it's OK,' said Rod, patting a hand on my shoulder again. 'I know it's hard for you to take. It's hard for everyone. But I'm afraid it's true. Richard's body was found this morning.'

I froze. *Richard's body was found this morning.* I can't remember much about what happened next, but I do recall the room spinning round. It was Tomkins who snapped me back to life.

'Mr Kelly, are you all right? Mr Kelly!'

I considered this question carefully. 'Yes. Yes, I think I am.'

'I know it's terrible news,' he said, 'but we'd like you to answer a few questions if we may. Time is of the essence.'

Rod gestured for me to take a seat on one of the leather-bound chairs that were tucked against the opposite wall. 'Please,' he said.

My mind went completely blank. What do you think in those situations? What can you think? Your conscience engages in a tug-of-war with itself. A man is dead. No, the man who was trying to *blackmail* you is dead. It is tragic. No, it is not tragic – it is *fortunate*. Wasn't it only yesterday that you were dreaming about murdering him?

'First things first,' began Tomkins. 'Richard was found early this morning by a couple of tramps on a section of headland near Westminster Bridge. His appearance suggests he's been in the river for at least twenty-four hours.'

I noticed Stanners writing something down. I wondered what it could be. My appearance? I could feel myself starting to sweat. Did that mark me out as having a guilty conscience?

'How do you know it's really him?' I asked. Call it paranoia if you will, but something at the back of my mind made me wonder if this was one of Richard's schemes.

'There's absolutely no doubt it's Richard Regan,' said Tomkins. 'We found his wallet on him, which contained his business cards. As there was no next of kin immediately available, Mr Russell kindly lent us a member of staff to do an ID.'

Rod interrupted. 'Karen,' he said. 'She went as soon as she came back from your meeting. Nigel went with her to lend his support, but I gather he didn't participate in the ID.'

I didn't reply.

Shouldn't I be glad? After all, I hated Richard didn't I? Maybe so, but I was a civilized human being.

All I felt was a sense of liberation. I had been relieved of the burden that had been crushing me for the past week. I was a free man again, and it felt strange.

Tomkins regarded me with a menacing air. 'What are you thinking?' he demanded. 'What's that look on your face?'

'I don't know,' I replied. 'How did he end up in the Thames?'

'Can't be sure at this stage. Could have jumped, or maybe he was pushed. We'll find out soon enough, I can assure you of that. In the meantime, I'd like to build up a picture of Richard's last movements on Saturday evening. Tell me Mr Kelly, were you with him on Saturday night?'

Stanners stopped writing and listened. He was anticipating my answer. I wondered if he had already decided what it should be, and was waiting for me to trip up.

'Yes, I was with him. At least, I was at the same place as him. It was a party at Nigel Powell's flat in Bloomsbury. Nigel is our client services director.'

'Yes, we know. Go on.'

'I drove down to London and parked nearby. I only stayed a short while.'

'Did you talk to anyone?'

'Nigel, mainly. And Dan Hitchin from our creative department.'

Stanners resumed writing.

'What time did you arrive?' asked Tomkins.

'Around one o'clock.' No lies, I told myself. I would find a way to placate Silvie later if the need arose.

Tomkins creased his upper lip as if he'd just tasted something sour. 'One o'clock in the morning? Bit late to arrive at a party, wouldn't you say, Mr Kelly?'

His partner nodded in agreement.

I shrugged. 'Last time I went to a party at Nigel's flat it went on all night.' That much was true. 'I decided to make an appearance this Saturday after my wife and children had gone to bed, so as to make sure I could spend the whole day with them.'

'Fair enough,' said Tomkins. 'Do you live in London, Mr Kelly?'

'No, I live in Cambridgeshire. That's another reason I arrived so late, because I had to drive all the way down to London. There are no trains that time of night.'

'Really?'

The younger man said, 'Where were you during Saturday?'

'I was in London, shopping in Covent Garden with my family.'

'You came by car, I take it?'

'Yes.'

'Terrible waste of petrol wouldn't you say?'

'Pardon?'

'Driving all the way into London on a Saturday, then driving back to Cambridgeshire, then driving back to London again at one o'clock in the morning.'

I was worried, but he could press me all he wished. The fact was I had nothing to do with Richard ending up in the River Thames.

'Like I said, I wanted to spend all day with my family. I wanted to make sure they were at home when I went to the party. I didn't want them to have to go home on the train while I stayed in London. Two kids can be a real handful.'

'Oh, tell me about it,' said Stanners. 'I've got three. Two boys and a girl.'

'And I've got four,' added Tomkins. 'All boys. All in their teens.'

Stanners was observing me carefully. I expected him to ask me if I had had any contact with Richard during Saturday afternoon, but instead he said, 'What time did you leave Nigel Powell's flat?' This was the question I'd been dreading.

I answered, 'Around thirty minutes later.'

Tomkins, who had been momentarily looking out of the window watching a crowd of girls walking towards Long Acre, turned to stare at me. 'You leave your wife and children in the middle of the night, in Cambridgeshire, to drive down to a party in London, and you only stay for half an hour? Now why was that, Mr Kelly?'

No pauses, I told myself.

'Because Richard got into a fight with our creative director, Jared Holt.'

'A fight? What about?'

'I don't know.'

'So why should *you* leave? Why didn't you break it up and help sort it out?'

I rubbed my chin. 'I'm not sure if I should tell you this.'

Tomkins leaned one hand on the side of Rod's desk and said, 'Oh, I think you should Mr Kelly. I think you should tell me everything you can.'

'OK,' I said. 'Jared punched me in the face outside a pub on Friday night after work.'

Rod shifted uncomfortably in his seat.

Stanners said, 'Why?' His tone was one of accusation.

'I don't know. He never told me. He just said something like, "You're in it together with Richard."'

'Do you know what he meant?'

'No, I haven't any idea.'

'Are you sure about that?' probed the younger of the two policemen.

'Yes. I really don't know what he was talking about.'

Tomkins nodded slowly. 'Thank you, Mr Kelly. This is very helpful, but there's just a few things more.'

He walked back to Rod's window and gazed out of it. From this corner of the building, you could also see a fair distance west. The Centrepoint building dominated the view, and the still futuristic Telecom Tower stood imposingly towards the north-west. He decided to raise the sarcasm up a notch.

'What did you do at the party,' he asked, 'in your thirty minutes there? Drink half a bottle of lager shandy? Dance to four and a half club remixes?'

Just tell him, I thought. No point in hiding it. 'Well, it was a bit difficult. I walked into one of the rooms, and heard Richard with Karen Bennington.'

'What do you mean "with"?'

'You *know.*'

'No, Mr Kelly, I don't.'

I didn't know why I was struggling. 'Well, it sounded as if they were in bed together. I couldn't tell for sure, because the room was dark. But it was definitely Karen and Richard; I heard their voices. So I left. I didn't want to wait until one of them turned on the light.'

Tomkins raised his eyebrows and said, 'Quite.'

'I don't know if that's significant or not.'

'Thank you, Mr Kelly. It could be highly significant. Now, where did you go immediately after leaving the flat?'

'I drove home.'

'Did anyone see you?'

'I don't think so.'

'Was you wife awake when you returned?'

'No, she was sleeping. It was the middle of the night. And I didn't want to wake her.'

Tomkins nodded at his partner again, encouraging him to ask a specific question. Stanners said, 'Now, let's just return to something you said earlier. I want to get to the bottom of why Jared Holt attacked you outside the pub. Are you sure you don't know what he meant by "You're in it together with Richard"? That seems to be one of the key points here.'

'I honestly haven't got a clue.'

Stanners: 'Did you think to ask him?'

'Yes, I tried to call him numerous times on his mobile but he didn't answer.'

He tapped the pen against his chin. 'Would you mind telling me your mobile number, Mr Kelly?'

I read it out to him and he scribbled it down. Rod watched carefully. I wondered again if he had also been blackmailed by Richard and was experiencing the same clash of emotions as me – or if he was just plain suspicious.

'Is there anything else?' I said to Tomkins.

'We're almost done,' he said. 'What I really want to know is: were you and Mr Regan at odds over anything. Any disagreements between the two of you? Anything I should know about?'

'No,' I said, careful not to make it sound too defensive. 'Although I did recommend that he didn't become the fourth partner in our business when we started it three years ago.'

'Yes, we know all about that,' said the Detective Sergeant. 'Your reason?'

'I wanted someone a bit more stable. I judged Richard Regan to be something of a loose cannon. In my mind, Anne Fulton seemed far more professional and suited to the job, that's all.'

I knew that Tomkins would cross-check everything I said against the statements from Karen and Nigel. My main worries were that Karen might tell him about Richard's claims that I knew him at school, and Nigel would mention Richard's idea that I was involved in Anne's murder. Being subjected to more intensive questioning was the last thing I wanted.

'While we're on the subject of Anne Fulton,' he said, 'why didn't you tell me you had an argument with her on the Friday before her murder?'

I began scrambling for a suitable answer. Then I realized I had simply forgotten to mention it to them. 'I'm sorry, but I must have forgot.'

'Oh, you *forgot*! Well, may I ask if you can remember what the argument was about? Or have you *forgotten* that as well?'

'We had a slight disagreement about my new business strategy. I was spending a lot of time chasing after small, project-based clients, and Anne thought we should concentrate on finding large, retainer-based ones.'

'A bit like the challenge set by Mr Russell here,' quipped Stanners.

Rod didn't say anything. He kept sitting in his chair, stroking his moustache, studying my every reaction.

'Yes, that's right. Every new business director wants to get his hands on the biggest accounts he can. If they're not coming through, all you can do is carry on with the smaller ones.'

'Did you often have arguments?' continued Tomkins.

'It wasn't an argument,' I said. 'As I said, it was nothing more than a slight disagreement. A difference of opinion. It's completely normal in this business.'

'A difference of opinion,' repeated Stanners. 'I'd like to know, Mr Kelly: have you ever visited Anne Fulton at her flat in Camden.'

I said, 'My wife and I have been there for dinner on several occasions, although not recently. Perhaps not for six months, or more.'

'Have you ever visited her at her flat alone?'

'No,' I said firmly. 'Why would I have wanted to visit her alone?'

'No specific reason,' said Stanners. 'It's just that one other female member of staff mentioned that you once got a bit over zealous at a staff party.'

That grated me. 'OK. I went to a party at Nigel Powell's flat once, and I admit I did have a little too much to drink and things got a bit out of hand.'

Stanners said, 'We heard as much. You were quite ungentlemanly, apparently.'

'It's all sorted out now. I apologized to the person involved. And I admitted everything to my wife. It's all in the past now.'

'A party at Nigel Powell's flat you say? So your wife let you slip away at twelve o'clock at night this weekend for another one of Nigel Powell's wild parties, did she? After you told her what happened last time? She must be a very understanding wife, Mr Kelly.'

I couldn't think of anything to say.

'So, back to Anne Fulton. Please tell us again: why were you arguing with her on the Friday before her death?'

I was incredulous. 'You think I...?'

'Please answer the question.'

'Look, this is ridiculous. Do I have to answer these?'

Tomkins said, 'No, you don't. But we will take that as a very irregular move on your part, and we might decide to take you down to the station for more detailed questioning. If you've got nothing to hide, I suggest you answer everything Detective Constable Stanners and I ask you.'

'OK ... OK. There's no need for this to get complicated. I've got nothing to hide. Look, I'll tell you again. We had a minor disagreement about the type of clients we should be approaching. By the end of the day we'd forgotten about it and were on good terms again. That's the last time I saw her.'

Stanners referred back to some previous notes. 'We only found one item of interest on Ms Fulton's computer. A calendar entry for tomorrow's date which mentions you.'

'What did it say?'

'Rather bizarre really. All it said was, 'Tell Duncan'. Do you know what she was referring to?'

'No, I don't. It could have been anything.'

'OK, last question,' interjected Tomkins. 'Was there any bad blood between Regan and Jared Holt? Any guess as to why they came to blows?'

This would be the first white lie I had told them. Could it be enough in itself to have me brought before a jury?

I thought for a minute. 'I can't think of anything.'

Tomkins held my gaze for a short while, then said, 'Right, that'll be all, Mr Kelly. Thank you for your time. If you do see or hear from Jared Holt, do please tell him to contact us. We would very much like to speak to him.'

Stanners seemed to want to ask something else, but his superior was already putting on his coat. Rod escorted them out to the elevator.

'So would I,' I said to myself.

thirty-three

It was 4.30 in the afternoon when I put the phone down. It was done. 130,000 shares sold at 28p each. Even after the tax and broker's commission, there would still be enough left to pay the hefty deposit for my Gran's place at The Acorns.

My fingers were still shaking after my ordeal with Tomkins and Stanners, and I placed them flat on my desk in an attempt to calm myself down.

I tried to relax, but events were coming to a head. Jared may be the prime suspect in Richard's death, but I had an ominous feeling that the blame for Anne's murder might somehow be pinned on me.

I took a deep breath. I had to call my father. There were already two emails from Hilary saying that he had called, the second of which was entitled 'Urgent – Please call your father now!'

I thought again about Richard's bizarre death. Could Jared really have killed him?

It was possible. He was more compulsive than me, and much more adept at resorting to violence – as had been demonstrated outside the pub on Friday, and at Nigel's party the following night.

And after reading the information on the CD-Rom about Jared, it didn't only seem possible, but plausible, that he would be willing to murder Richard to make sure he kept his mouth shut.

Jared had been stealing his ideas.

Plagiarism.

It was the worst atrocity a creative director could commit.

I'd heard of it going on in the industry before. The creative director at my first agency, for example, would willingly recycle work from old campaigns and stick his client's logo on them.

However, there was one major difference between him and Jared: nobody minded if the former stole his ideas, because nobody had ever heard of him. He was merely a bit-player on the London advertising stage.

Jared Holt, on the other hand, had built his reputation on being the creative force behind one of the leading London hotshops. It was one of the main reasons why MediaWide had wanted to acquire the majority share in our company.

If the trade press ever heard about this, the company would be broken beyond repair. It would certainly be closed down, regardless of whether we won the Tea Society or not, and lawsuits from disgruntled and humiliated clients would follow.

Using ideas created by other agencies hadn't been difficult for Jared to do. According to Richard's evidence on the CD, he had simply lifted them out of his collection of Australian, New Zealand and Japanese ad awards annuals, reworked the headlines a bit, revisualized the layouts, and stuck our clients' logos on them.

I had seen his prized collection of awards books, which must have comprised at least fifty annuals. They were proudly displayed in a bookcase in his office. Many of them were the British D&AD books, and there were a lot of One Show and Clio annuals from the U.S. But, according to Richard's report, it was the more obscure Australian *AWARD*, Japanese *Tokyo Art Directors Club*, and the Singapore *Gong Show* annuals from the late eighties and early nineties that he had been mining for ideas – and these particular books were kept locked in a cupboard beneath the bookcase.

No wonder he had effortlessly picked up a handsome rack of industry awards over the past three years.

It hurt like hell, knowing that every pitch presentation I'd made for HFPK had been a fake. Every show I'd made of pacing around the meeting room spouting idea upon idea upon idea … it had all been *nothing*.

It was embarrassing. Of course, our clients wouldn't have the faintest idea of what Jared had been doing, not unless they made a hobby of reading obscure foreign advertising awards books in their spare time. And no one else, not even the trade press had made the connection. But they would, sooner or later.

Why had he done it? I knew he was more than capable of devising original, well-focused ideas – so why risk everything with plagiarism?

The only answer I could think of was that he was tempting

fate. Maybe he wanted to see how far he could take it before he got caught. Maybe it was his way of sticking two fingers up at the industry. Maybe it was his way of proving his father wrong.

Whatever his motivation, I desperately wanted to talk to him before Jane Markham telephoned. I needed to know if their ideas were stolen, too.

'Oh, it's terrible! Terrible!'

Karen dashed into the room in a fit of tears. She stood in front of my desk, shaking. I put my hand on her shoulder and guided her towards the two-seater.

She was inconsolable. It took me several minutes just to get her off me and into a chair. 'Try to calm down,' I said. 'It's a terrible shock.'

Karen could hardly speak. 'It was me who identified him. He … he … he looked so terrible. They asked me if it was him. I can't stop thinking about it. He was all puffed up, all bloated. His skin looked like plastic.'

'They made you look at him? At the body? Not a Polaroid? That's terrible!'

'No, no, Duncan. I *asked* to see him. It's only fair to his family. I had to know it really was him.'

'Why couldn't someone from his family do the ID?'

'Out of the country. Couldn't be contacted.'

I was lost for words. 'It must have been … pretty bad.'

But Karen didn't seem to hear. She became hysterical again, and wrapped her arms around me, digging her fingernails into my back. 'Why does this keep happening to us, Duncan? First Anne, now Richard?'

'I don't know,' I said. 'I really don't know.'

She caught her breath. 'Do you … do you think it was Jared?'

I sighed. The circumstances were indeed stacking up against him, but I didn't imagine for a second that he had murdered Anne. As far as I was concerned that was still a robbery gone wrong. It had to be.

'No, I don't,' I said. 'Why would Jared have reason to murder Richard anyway? What were they fighting about on Saturday?'

Of course, I knew full well what they'd been fighting about, but I wanted to see what Karen's reaction was.

She looked down. 'I'm afraid it could have been about me,' she whispered.

'Why do you think that?'

'I was seeing Richard,' she said, lifting her head and choking back more tears. 'Nothing serious – God, I feel awful saying that now – it had only been going on for a few weeks.'

'And you think that Jared was jealous?'

'Just a thought.'

'Why?'

'This is the first time I've told anyone, but he'd been sending me things for weeks. Flowers, presents, cards, you name it. It started off innocent enough, but got really creepy. When I told him I wasn't interested, it only seemed to make him more determined.'

'Did you tell this to Tomkins?'

'No!' she said. 'I didn't want to land Jared in any kind of trouble. Anyway, I'm engaged to Peter. I may never see him, he's hardly ever in the country – but I'm still engaged to him. That's why I didn't mention that I was involved with Richard. I don't want my engagement to be ruined because of my silly mistakes.'

'So you think Jared murdered Richard … because he found out that you were having an affair?'

She buried her face in her hands again. 'I don't know!' she cried. 'I don't know!'

I didn't want to push her too far. I said, 'What does Nigel think?'

She lowered her hands slowly. 'I haven't spoken to him about it. He's gone home. He was terribly upset and worried.'

I sat down. I wasn't at all convinced Jared had killed Richard because he was jealous over Karen. The real reason he had murdered him was because Richard had threatened to expose the plagiarism scandal.

Jared, it seemed, was made of sterner stuff than I.

'Nigel's not talking about quitting again is he?' I said.

'No, not yet. But he's very worried. He's convinced Jared has gone off the rails and wants to kill us all.'

'That's ridiculous!' I said, feeling a twinge of relief that he hadn't mentioned me.

Karen said, 'Is it? It looks as if he murdered Richard in a blind rage. Who's to say he didn't kill Anne as well?'

'Ridiculous,' I said again. 'What would his motive have been to kill Anne?'

'I don't know, but that doesn't mean he didn't do it. There could have been all kinds of things going on between them that we didn't know about.'

I put both my hands up in front of me. 'OK, OK. Just stop there. We can't pin the blame on Jared for what happened to Anne. I can't see why he would have wanted to hurt her.'

It was true – I really couldn't make a link between Jared's outburst at the party and Anne's death.

But that assumption was based on what I knew. Could Anne have somehow known about the plagiarism, too?

Again, I couldn't assume anything until I managed to talk to Jared. Although it was clear that he didn't want to talk to anyone. His mobile had been on voicemail for days.

I watched Karen as she dabbed the corners of her eyes. I wondered if Richard had confided in her about his blackmailing of me. I would have to tread extremely carefully.

'Did Richard ever say anything about me?' I asked.

Karen continued wiping her eyes. 'What does that mean?'

'When I talked to you on Saturday you said that he claimed we were at school together—'

'Yes, which you said was rubbish.'

'It is. Did he say anything else?'

'Such as what?'

'He was threatening to start spreading a rumour about me.'

'What about?'

'Something about why I'd cut him out of the original deal.'

Karen snuffled into the tissue. 'He never mentioned anything like that. Why would he want to spread a rumour about you?'

'I don't know. Jealousy maybe? He never actually told me what he wanted.'

Karen looked thoroughly gloomy. 'I know you didn't like each other, Duncan. But now he's gone and I really think you'd better stop this kind of talk. I didn't love him, but we *were* having a relationship. Why can't you be upset or depressed like everyone else? If you can't manage that, you should at least pretend you are. You can be so tactless sometimes. I hope you act with a little more dignity at Anne's funeral tomorrow.'

'Christ, I didn't mean to—'

'That's your weakness, isn't it?'

'What is?'

'You always look for an angle in everything. Why can't you just take things for what they are? Sometimes I think Rod was right about you. You're too sensitive to run a company. You question everything, but you never take a stand when it matters.'

'That's what Rod said to you?'

'On several occasions, yes.'

'So if everyone has a weakness, what's yours? Sleeping with the recent hires?'

She slapped me across the face. My cheek felt as if it was on fire. I didn't say anything. It had been a stupid comment. It was nothing more than knee-jerk reaction at hearing Karen spelling out the truth. And it had landed me in even more trouble.

She was so enraged, I almost expected her to hit me again. But the phone on my desk started ringing, and she walked out. I waited until she had gone before I answered. It was my father.

He almost cheered with relief when I told him the money was ready. He gave me the account number of The Acorns and I wrote it on a scrap of paper. I assured him that I would get the bank to transfer the money as soon as I could.

I asked how Gran was.

'Almost at the end of her tether, but she'll improve dramatically once she's with Aunty Beryl,' he said. 'How do you feel? You were a bit under the weather, weren't you?'

'Yes, I'm much better,' I said, rubbing my stinging cheek. 'Maybe I was just getting worked up.'

'Best not get worked up about anything, Duncan. It's never worth it. You can't change what's already been done.'

I wasn't sure if he was alluding to Doofy or not.

'Did you see Gran at the weekend? Did she mention Kenneth?'

'Yes, we saw her, Duncan. She was in quite good spirits, and talking about Aunty Beryl all the time. She didn't mention Kenneth. She stopped talking about him on Friday after your mother said he was dead.'

'But he's been dead since the war, hasn't he?'

'Well, he was never actually found, Duncan. Your Gran has always held on to the vague hope that one day he'd suddenly walk into the room. Since she saw you dressed up last week she's been going on about it ever since. That's why your mother had to tell her the truth.'

'Seems a bit harsh?'

'It's for the best, Duncan. Really it is. Your Gran says all kinds of things when she talks about Kenneth. All kinds of things that are simply not true. Your mother thought it was best to stop her talking about Kenneth before she went into The Acorns, just in case she upset Aunty Beryl.'

'She must have been a bit distraught.'

Dad made his characteristic humming noise.

'She was surprisingly unemotional, apparently. You know your Grandmother, Duncan. You never think she's understood what you've said, until one day she surprises you with a comment that proves she'd been listening all along.' There was a pause as he listened to the 5 o'clock chimes from the grandfather clock in the hall. 'Right, I must be going. Well done about coming through with the money, Duncan. It's very kind. Both your mother and Gran will be very pleased.' Then he added, 'You've done very well, son.'

It was the only time he had ever called me that in my life.

Five minutes later I was standing in the tearoom by myself, pouring milk into my coffee, and feeling no shame at the huge sense of relief that was surging through my veins.

I was adding the sugar when Rod walked in with Karen. He looked downbeat. She looked furious. 'Come on, Duncan,' said Rod. 'I don't know if you've checked your email or not, but I've got to make an announcement about Richard in the main boardroom in a few minutes.' He dropped his voice to a whisper. 'I want to do it before any unpleasant rumours start.'

Soon I was standing with fifty or so other advertising savvies from HFPK and MediaWide whose legs were turning to jelly. There was a huge feeling of shock, but not grief. Richard had only worked at the agency for a few days, and no one was close enough to him for it to be a catastrophic personal loss.

Having said that, several female account executives did burst into tears, and three of four buyers from the media department started hugging each other and sobbing.

Rod was wearing a face of steely resolve, and urged everyone to be strong. 'Richard was dedicated to his work,' he said. 'He was hard working, extremely driven and ambitious. We won't forget him.'

He thanked everyone for coming, and the attendees shuffled out *en masse* to an accompaniment of hushed 'That's terrible' and 'Poor guy'.

I spotted Karen a few places behind me. She caught my eye and then looked away. I wondered how much Richard had really meant to her.

After a few more minutes everyone had filtered out of the

room, but I remained behind. I leaned against a radiator on the back wall, musing over what Rod had had to say. Richard had certainly been hard working, driven and ambitious. It was just a shame that those traits had been geared solely towards trying to ruin my life.

In the end, however, he had not only lost, but paid the ultimate price.

thirty-four

I told Silvie about Richard's death the minute I arrived home that evening.

She listened wide-eyed as I explained how Rod had called me up to his office for a meeting with the two policemen. She stared at me in horror as I relayed Karen's theories that Jared could have been the murderer.

Holding back tears, she said, 'I'll never understand why people always seem intent on killing each other to get what they want.'

'We don't know if it was Jared for certain. No one's been able to find him yet. The police must be searching all over. Have you seen anything on the news?'

'Nothing,' she said.

'Probably a good thing.'

Silvie released her grip. 'How was your meeting with the tea people?'

'It went well. Let's just hope we've won the business.'

I decided not to mention that I sold the shares. It was not an appropriate time.

She carefully folded the tissue she'd been using to wipe her eyes, and dropped it into the bin. 'One thing after another, isn't it? First Anne, now this happens to Richard. It's so horrible.'

I wondered whether or not to say anything about our talk yesterday, but luckily Lily wandered in to announce that Giles was awake in his room. Then she folded her arms and said, 'Now I want cake.'

As Silvie went up to check on Giles, my daughter watched me remove a half-eaten Victoria sponge from the fridge. I cut a piece. She shook her head furiously. So I cut a little more.

'Daddy, why are you so happy?'

'Do I look happy?'

'Yes. Are you happy because you had a big day?'

'I guess so.'

She received the plate and skipped off into the living-room. 'Thank you!'

I listened to Silvie's movements upstairs as she changed Giles's nappy on his Winnie-the-Pooh changing mat. The familiar *Story Makers* theme drifted in from the TV in the living-room. How different it all would be if Richard hadn't ended up in the Thames, I thought. There was every possibility I would be jobless now.

Did I feel Richard deserved what had happened to him?

Not entirely. Although I wasn't surprised something like this had occurred. He had planted too many evil seeds. After many years, his behaviour had finally caught up with him.

'Can you give me a hand up here?' called Silvie.

I jogged up the stairs and into Giles's bedroom. She handed the baby to me, and heaved a white bag packed with spent nappies out of a plastic bin. I held my nose at the whiff, and kissed the baby's cheek. This made him snuffle. 'Oh, hungry, aren't we?'

'He is,' she said, placing the bag of nappies in my spare hand. 'Can you give him his feed? There's expressed milk in the fridge. I'm going to have a bath. I feel so grubby.'

As I was leaving the room, I said, 'I've got to drive to Anne's funeral tomorrow.'

Silvie removed her jumper. 'I know, Duncan. Don't worry. It's all taken care of. I've ironed you a white shirt. I also found you a black tie. Now, are you sure you're going to be OK tomorrow?'

'Yes,' I said. 'Thank you. I don't know what I'd do without you.'

'Oh, I think I've got an idea,' said Silvie. 'You'd probably be one of those embarrassing single men in their early thirties who stay in bed all day, but thanks to my ovaries you have a reason to get up in the morning.'

'Wow, deep. I'm going to have to have a cup of tea and a biscuit to get over that one.'

'I know. It's a quote from today's afternoon play on Radio 4. But, hey, it will keep you out of mischief, I suppose. Now, you run along and dump those nappies – no pun intended – and feed His Royal Highness. I'll lie in the bath and vegetate.'

She giggled and closed the bathroom door with a little wave.

As I held Giles against my shoulder and trotted down the

stairs, I again felt an overwhelming sense of relief that Richard hadn't been able to carry out his threat.

But I wasn't off the hook yet. I still needed to talk to Jared.

thirty-five

It was Tuesday; the day of Anne's funeral.

The morning air was crisp and only just above freezing. The sun hadn't yet managed to break its way through the clouds. There had been a frost during the night, and I had to really work at the ice on the windscreen to scrape it away.

Anne's parents lived in a small Essex village called Little Hayford to the east of the market town of Great Dunmow.

As I drove the thirty-odd miles to the Stansted Airport turn off at Bishop's Stortford on the M11, I thought about her unique character.

In contrast to her colleagues, she had always seemed happy in her work, and never complained when things didn't go her way. While the rest of us – especially Jared – were to be found vainly flicking through the pages of the trade press every week in search of our mugshots, she always treated this me-me-me obsessed business with indifference.

However, despite the enormous respect I had for her, there was a side to Anne that unnerved me as well.

She always had this knowing smile, as if she knew just a little more than you. It was never arrogant, just quietly confident. She was a woman of few words, but those she did say were often extraordinarily powerful.

Richard, on the other hand, had been quite the opposite. A thorough understanding of the power of fear, and how to use it, had formed the basis of his personality.

At school, he'd amuse himself by getting me to do crazy things like chopping frogs in half or cutting brake cables in the bike sheds: whatever it took to prove myself to him. That way, he got the laughs and I got shackled with the blame. I was completely under his control. In awe of him, even.

After about an hour of reliving the events of my school days, I arrived at Little Hayford. I found the church easily. It was at the end of a winding lane dotted with cottages, next to a pink blanc-mange-coloured manor house.

Save for a family of ducks crossing, the road was very quiet. I parked the car on one side and made my way towards the church, holding the bouquet of white lilies I'd collected earlier in the morning. There were several groups of people in dark outfits milling around outside.

I recognized Anne's parents immediately. Her mother was as tall as she had been, wore her hair up in a bun, and assumed the same posture: bolt upright with her hands clasped together in front of her. Her father had an unruly mop of hair planted atop his head, which cascaded down on to his shoulders. It was heartbreaking to see Anne so clearly in both of them. Reluctantly, I walked over to join the line of mourners offering their condolences.

When it was my turn, I simply told them how sorry I was. Not because I judged it to be the warmest, most heartfelt thing I could say, but because I was stuck for words.

I even forgot to introduce myself.

'Thank you,' said Mrs Fulton, 'and you are...?'

'Duncan Kelly,' I said. 'Anne was my business partner.'

She grasped my hand. 'Yes, of course,' she said, with a defiant sparkle in her eyes. 'Anne often spoke about you. You and the other one, what's his name?'

Mr Fulton moved on to the next griever, but Mrs Fulton waited for my answer.

'Nigel?' I ventured.

She frowned. 'I don't know him. No, what's his name? The rude one. The one that was always phoning her in the middle of the night.'

Phoning her? In the middle of the night? 'Jared?'

'No, someone else. Rob, or Bob, or someone.'

'Rod? Rod Russell?'

'Yes, that's the one. I'm sure she wouldn't have minded if I told you that she didn't think much of him. Oh, but she adored working with you!'

'Well, she was a true professional. We will all miss her very much.'

Mrs Fulton dabbed her eye. 'And so will we,' she said towards the grey, overcast sky, her voice cracking.

Her husband wrapped an arm around her shoulder and pulled her close to him.

She managed a smile. 'Maybe we'll talk after the service,' she said to me.

I walked inside the entrance to the church. There was a long line of flower bouquets to the right, and I placed mine next to them. I put the card I'd written down in front. On it was the message, 'We will miss you. Heartfelt love from all your colleagues.'

I was just about to walk away, when I noticed something on one of the other cards. I crouched down to read. It said simply, 'Why did it have to happen? Words can't express what I feel. I'm sorry'. It was left with a large bunch of white carnations. I looked closely at the writing. It was oddly familiar, but I couldn't think where I had seen it before.

Throughout the service, I couldn't stop wondering why Rod had been phoning Anne in the middle of the night, even though I should have been concentrating on what the vicar was saying.

Afterwards, the mourners were invited back to Anne's parents' house on the outskirts of the village. The house was a rambling timber-framed cottage. Set in grounds of about half an acre, it seemed the perfect place to grow up. With a wooden bridge that led across the moat at the entrance to the front garden, and a small duck pond to the side of the house, it was a world away from the Soho advertising agencies. No wonder Anne had always been so determined to remain an outsider to the London advertising party scene.

I'd been sitting in an old armchair in the conservatory for about thirty minutes or so, scratching a huge ginger cat that had invited itself on to my lap, when Mrs Fulton sat down in the spare chair beside me. She was still clasping her hands in front of her.

'How well did you know Anne?' she asked.

I considered this question. I had what could be described as an intimate working relationship, but I couldn't claim to have known her well personally.

'Professionally, very well. Privately, probably not that well at all,' I replied.

'Yes, I've gathered that.'

I reached over to my plate on the coffee-table, and took one of the salmon sandwiches. 'What do you mean?' I asked.

Mrs Fulton let out a long sigh. 'I've thought long and hard about telling you this, Duncan. But it's something you should know. Anne was meant to be moving back home this week, moving back here to Little Hayford ...' Her voice trailed off.

I said, 'What do you mean?'

'I'm sorry if this comes as a shock, Duncan, but she'd grown disillusioned with life in London, and her job in particular. She told me she'd resigned and that her employers had agreed to let her go early. She was meant to be arriving back here this week. But then that terrible break-in happened ...'

'Mrs Fulton,' I said, aware that pieces of salmon were dropping out of my mouth, 'are you telling me that Anne had resigned from the company?'

She turned her large brown eyes on me. She was nervously touching one of the collars of her black blouse. 'Yes. That's what she told us. She almost ... *almost* made it home.'

As Mrs Fulton wiped her eyes, I wondered why Anne would want to resign without telling the three other partners. She was in exactly the same situation as us: keep the company afloat for another two years, until MediaWide was obliged to buy up the remaining 49%.

'Do you know why she wanted to leave?' I asked.

'No. I wish I did. All she said was that she'd had enough of it.'

'You mentioned earlier that Rod was telephoning her in the middle of the night. Do you know what about?'

'Again, I'm sorry, but I don't,' she said. 'She mentioned it when we were chatting on the phone one evening. From the sounds of it, it wasn't a one-off occurrence.'

'I'm sorry.'

'Oh, it wasn't your fault, Duncan. She always insisted that if you didn't work with her she would have left the company a lot sooner.'

'That's nice to know. Though if that were the case, why did she eventually resign without telling me?'

Mrs Fulton used my arm to help pull herself up on to her feet. 'I suppose we'll never know for sure. What matters now is that my daughter is home. She's with us. I just want to thank you for everything you did for her. She was proud of what she achieved; *we're* proud of what she achieved.'

'I really don't think I did enough, Mrs Fulton,' I said. 'How could I have missed so much?'

She patted my hand and went back to join the other mourners.

thirty-six

After the funeral had finished, I left the car at Bishops Stortford station and caught the Stansted Express into Liverpool Street. By the time I arrived back at the office I'd already called Jared three times – but he was still on voicemail.

I was also considering what to do with the 'Info' CD. Common sense kept telling me to throw it in the nearest bin, but I was reluctant to give it up. Instead, I left it in my jacket pocket.

As soon as I got to the office, Hilary told me that Jane Markham from the Tea Society had called.

'How did she sound?' I asked.

Hilary shrugged her shoulders. 'Happy.' Then added, 'I suppose.'

A wave of anxiety hit me. I wondered about the two ideas we had presented to them, and whether they had been stolen from the awards books.

I obviously wouldn't be able to talk to Jared before I called Jane Markham back, so all I could do was hope that he didn't go confessing to anyone before I could track him down.

And there was something else I hadn't yet considered. Supposing he *had* murdered Richard? What would happen then?

Even if he was found guilty and sent to prison, we could probably still survive – if I could manage to persuade the Tea Society to keep their business with us. And if Jared could just keep his guilty secret to himself, then I figured the trade press wouldn't start leafing through the old awards books just yet.

However, I would have to convince the Tea Society, and our other clients, that Jared could be quickly replaced with another, equally talented, creative director.

Of course, I knew that Jared's conceptual prowess was a complete sham – he'd probably stolen every campaign idea we'd ever sold – but as far as Jane Markham and the Tea Society were concerned, he was a creative genius.

It would be difficult, but by no means impossible, to find a replacement. London boasted some of the best creative directors in the world. They weren't cheap, but if Jared were to be found guilty of Richard's murder and imprisoned, he would have to relinquish his stake in HFPK – and that was what I would use to attract a suitable candidate.

I arrived at my office to find Rod and Karen already there.

'We've been waiting for you,' he said. 'How was the funeral?'

I searched for a suitable word. 'Reflective.' I knew that this was a completely unsuitable moment to question Rod about his calls to Anne in the middle of the night. So I said, 'There were a lot of people there, a lot of local support for her parents.'

He said, 'Anne was truly a woman of principle.' He slapped my shoulder. 'Life goes on, Duncan. Karen tells me you put on a first-class performance yesterday.'

'It went pretty well,' I offered.

Karen said curtly: 'Credit where credit's due, Duncan. You did well.'

'When do you expect to hear from the client with the decision?' asked Rod. 'Sir Geoff's been on my back all week pressing for an answer about HFPK. If I can get back to him with positive news about the Tea Society, you'll have escaped by the skin of your teeth. That's providing Jared hasn't done anything stupid.'

'I'm sure he hasn't. What happened to Richard could have been an accident.'

Rod sighed, 'I hope so. For all our sakes.'

I said, 'I hope you weren't worried about what the police were asking me yesterday? I promise you: I did *not* see Anne during the weekend she was murdered.'

'I believe you,' said Rod, 'but you must remember there have been two tragedies in this company now. I think they see it as too much of a coincidence to be unconnected.'

'That doesn't mean it is.'

'Oh, please! Let's try and forget about all that for a minute,' said Rod, suddenly visibly upset. 'It's happened, it's a tragedy for all who knew them. Now we must move on, we really must. I don't want to hear you mention it again, unless I ask you to. Understood?' He repeated his earlier question: 'When do you expect to hear the result on the Tea Society business?'

'As a matter of fact they called me this morning and left a message. I've got to call them back.'

Karen looked at Rod in amazement. 'What are you waiting for, Duncan? You'd better call them right now.'

I removed Jane Markham's business card from my organizer and tapped the numbers into the keyboard. Please don't let it be voicemail, I thought.

She answered after a few rings.

'Hi, Jane,' I said. 'It's Duncan from HFPK. How are you?'

'Hello, Duncan. I'm fine thank you.'

'Have you managed to come to a decision?'

Jane said in a confident, assured voice, 'Yes. We have agreed on a course of action to take. I'm glad we were able to get back to you quickly.'

'That's very considerate of you,' I replied. *Come on, get the pleasantries over and give us the yes.*

'It's the least we can do. Thank you for the excellent presentation. So....'

'So?' *Please.*

'It was a first rate presentation, Duncan. Personally I think it was one of the best I've ever seen. Great creativity and the strategy was bang on.' She cleared an imaginary obstacle in her throat and said, 'However, the board has decided to review its position and put all advertising on hold for the time being.'

What?

'Jane, I think you were breaking up there. It's a bad line. I didn't catch the last bit.'

'The board has advised us they're not willing to fund any advertising activity for the rest of the year. They're going to concentrate on PR instead. I'm sorry.'

Rod and Karen were watching me intently. I could see from their still-hopeful expressions that they couldn't hear what Jane Markham was saying.

Rod tried to get my attention with hand signals. He gave me the thumbs up sign questioningly.

I couldn't bring myself to tell him that we had failed to win the business. Not after everything that had happened, not after everything I had been through with Richard.

I nodded, smiled, and pressed my ear closer to the receiver.

Rod's cheeks moved to accommodate a wide grin. Karen shook her hair and made a point of breathing a sigh of relief.

Jane continued, 'I wish the decision was mine to take, Duncan. I would have grabbed your arm off at the pitch. But it's not. And before you say it – no, the board cannot be persuaded to change their minds.'

A smile had clawed its way on to my face. It was all I could do. Putting the phone down and announcing to Rod and Karen that we'd lost the pitch would be a complete disaster. I knew what would happen: Rod would nod brusquely, his patience failing him, as I relayed the sob story from Jane Markham. After a few minutes of telling me what a useless fool I was, he would rise from the soon-to-be-relocated-elsewhere-in-the-group white leather two-seater, and announce that he had no choice but to call Sir Geoff Deacon.

I pressed the receiver harder against the side of my head. 'I see,' I said in what I hoped was a neutral voice. 'That's quite *remarkable* news.'

'You're taking it very well, Duncan, I must say. You must be very disappointed.'

More of the neutral voice. 'Oh, I am. Very much so.' Followed by a big smile.

Jane continued, 'I really am sorry, Duncan. Especially after all the effort you've made. I would offer to reimburse you for the time you spent preparing, but the board is very hard-nosed about these matters. They maintain that you understood it was only a speculative pitch, and they were under no obligation to commit to anything.'

'Amazing.' My office walls turned to a sour shade of grey. The golden warmth of the pine floorboards faded to a lifeless brown. The four corners of the room seemed to suck up any life that was left over and gag on it.

'Well, I'll have to leave it there,' concluded Jane. 'I have another meeting in five minutes. Thank you again for the presentation, and I'm sorry it didn't work out.'

'Jane, it's been a pleasure. Speak to you very soon.'

I put the phone down. 'We've got it!' Karen stood up. She was smiling. Rod leaned over and pumped my hand.

'Did they agree to the terms?' Rod blustered. 'The retainer? The fifty thousand a month?'

'They certainly did.' *I would have to backtrack on that when I had the chance.*

'Are they going to run one of the campaigns we showed them?' asked Karen.

'Yes, they've just not decided which one yet.' *That, too, would require a major spin job later.*

It was all coming out in torrents; I had no idea where from.

Rod boomed, 'Good going! Now, I'd better go and make the call to Sir Geoff Deacon. Of a rather more pleasant nature, I might add, than I'd expected.'

'Great. You do that, Rod. If you'll excuse me, I have to go out too,' I said.

I scooped up my laptop and pushed past them. 'Where are you going?' said Karen. 'I'll come too. We can talk about the Tea Society.'

'No!' I snapped.

'I beg your pardon?'

Desperation was setting in. 'It's a private appointment,' I insisted. 'A health matter. See you tomorrow.' Before I left the room, I said, 'Jane told me they're still discussing the finer points of our proposal. She asked us not to call them. They'll get back to us on Thursday. I'll see you both tomorrow.'

Ten seconds later I was into the elevator, breathing hard.

Fuck! What had I done? Why had I let it all spin out of control again?

When the elevator opened at reception, Hilary was away from her desk. I caught my breath and forced myself to count to ten.

There was only one thing I could do.

Revert to plan Z. The absolute last resort.

I would have to try to perform my own blackmail scam against Rod, using the evidence against him contained on Richard's CD-Rom.

I turned my mobile off, stuffed the laptop into my rucksack, and ran to the revolving door.

thirty-seven

It was 6 o'clock on Tuesday evening. I was sitting on the bench, gazing over the reflections in the Thames made by the stream of cars heading towards Westminster Bridge. I had come here because I knew it was the only place that I'd be able to think straight.

Most of the afternoon had been spent on my mobile trying to talk Jane Markham into changing her mind. I had broken my golden rule of never sounding desperate to a client.

But it was all to no avail. My last call had ended with Jane threatening to complain to MediaWide if I called again, and slamming her phone down.

So that was it.

I was going to have to try and blackmail Rod into him giving me his job. It was the only way I could save the company from being shut down, and the only chance of saving my career.

Rod often mentioned his coming retirement, and how he wished he could find someone to replace him. I'd always avoided putting myself forward for the job because I wanted my future to remain closely tied to HFPK.

Now, it seemed that the decision had been forced upon me. I knew there was no point in holding out and waiting to see what happened when the truth about the Tea Society came to light.

I watched the illuminated outlines of the boats as they moved up and down the river. The temperature was bitingly cold, but I was oblivious to it. The traffic on Embankment rushed past behind me in a mush of noise. I could feel my mind focusing. I had, in effect, become Richard Regan. I was going to have to make myself as ruthless as him.

The CD-Rom was in my jacket pocket. I took a sip from my take-out black coffee, and put the disc into my laptop drive.

NAME: Rod Russell

POSITION: Managing Director, MediaWide

INVESTIGATION STATUS: Completed

CLAIM: Pays frequent visits Starlights Sauna, York Way, King's Cross

EVIDENCE: Visits usually take place on the first and third Tuesdays of every month after 8 p.m. Under the cover-story of attending agency drinks, Rod visits Starlights Sauna, where he pays between one and two hundred pounds for the services of one of the girls on offer. Judging from Rod's elaborate cover-story, his wife Marjorie is unaware of this. She and Rod are planning to celebrate their ruby wedding anniversary in October – this presents an opportunity.

ANGLE: Rod's address is 43 Longford Lane, Guildford. Wheelchair-bound Marjorie is at home during the day, every day – except on Thursday afternoons when she goes out to play bridge. An envelope with a basic typewritten letter addressed directly to Marjorie should do.

SOURCE: Trish, receptionist at Starlights Sauna

RATING: 9

Given the information to hand, I had no doubt it could be done.

Yes, it was immoral. Yes, it was unethical. Yes, it was illegal. But what other options did I have?

It would require a huge amount of confidence. Whether or not I would *actually* go through with it was beside the point – the only thing that mattered was that Rod *thought* I would.

The main problem was exactly how to go about it. Confronting him at the office was totally out of the question. It wouldn't work. I wasn't ready to barge into Rod's office and threaten him.

I had it.

Starlights Sauna. Not in the sauna, you understand. I'd wait somewhere nearby and catch him on the way out.

OK, so it had a strong whiff of cop-movie stakeout about it, but I was convinced it was the best way. I'd catch him off guard and red handed. He wouldn't be able to deny a thing.

'Don't move,' said a voice behind me. 'If you touch that computer, I'll kill you.'

I could feel something jabbing into the middle of my back. I sat bolt upright, keeping my hands on the laptop. Rod's details remained on the screen. What was this? Was I being mugged?

Jared appeared and sat next to me. 'Just joking,' he said. He was holding up a marker pen. 'This,' he said, 'is a brilliant gun. It certainly had you worried, didn't it?'

I searched his expression for signs of remorse, panic or guilt, but couldn't find any. I noticed he was dressed in the same clothes as he wore on Saturday, and his hair was matted together and unwashed.

The obvious anxiety that had come over him in the days before the Tea Society pitch, however, seemed to have gone. I wondered if he was as relieved to hear about Richard's demise as I was.

'What are you doing here?' I demanded, almost shouting.

'Waiting for you. And now I've found you.'

'How?'

'Easy, I just followed you from the office. I saw you come running out of there a while ago, and followed you down here to the bench. I knew you'd come here sooner or later. Everyone needs their place to think. It's human nature.' He crossed his legs out in front of him, and dug his hands deep into the pockets of his black PVC jacket. 'I know what you're doing, and it's stupid,' he said. 'You're thinking of blackmailing Rod with Richard's CD, aren't you?'

'I don't know what you're talking about. Now, would you mind telling me where the hell you've been?'

He laughed and said, 'Oh, come on, Duncan. Don't try and change the subject. I'm not an idiot. I know everything about that CD, just as you do. I'm one of the guilty victims too.'

That one shot me in the gut. Did Jared know about The Accident? 'What do you know?'

'Richard showed me the file. You were being blackmailed by him.'

'What makes you think that?'

He shook his head and laughed again. 'Oh my, you never really change, do you? Always looking for a way out, right up until the end.'

My mouth felt dry. 'Are you going to kill me as well?' I asked him.

Jared looked away. 'I knew you were going to ask me that,' he said. 'Look, what would you say if I told you I had nothing to do with Richard falling into the river?'

'I'd say the case against you still looks pretty bad. I saw you trying to kick the crap out of him on Saturday at Nigel's, as did about thirty other people. You were shouting you were going to kill him. Not a good idea. Because, lo and behold, the next day he turns up in the Thames.'

'It wasn't me. I did want to beat him up, that much is true. After I got home that night, I panicked and have been staying in my car ever since.'

'Your car? Why?'

'Because I was worried he was going to press charges for assault. I wanted to get the CD off him, so I was planning on coming into work on Monday. But this morning I read what had happened to Richard in the paper, and decided to stay away from the office for a while.' He poked a finger at me. 'I know everyone thinks I killed him, but I *didn't*.'

'Then who did?'

Jared smiled thinly. 'Well, I was hoping you could help me with that,' he remarked. 'Because I was under the impression it was you.'

'Me!'

'Yes,' he said matter-of-factly. 'Like I said, I know Richard was trying to blackmail you as well. I also know what you did, or, at least, what Richard claimed you did. And, believe me, it was far worse than my little secret. Is it really true about the body in the millpond?'

I took a deep breath. 'Yes, it's true. Richard shot him by accident, and he forced me to help him bury the body.' *My half-brother?*

'Christ. I bet it's never stopped nagging at you, has it?'

I nodded. 'I wish I could put it right, but I can't. The longer it went on, the more difficult it became to confess.'

'I understand,' he said. 'If it's any consolation, I know the feeling. Let me tell you, Duncan, it was never my intention to keep borrowing ideas from the awards books for so long.'

'So why did you do it?'

'At first, I guess it was a way of testing the industry. You know how this business thrives on its own self-important bullshit? If you suddenly win a few awards, everyone thinks you're the best thing since sliced bread. No one ever remembers how a campaign performed anymore, only how many awards it won. I stole the ideas to prove to myself how the industry was so far up its own arse that it didn't see straight any more. The problem was, it got addictive. I didn't want to throw in the towel to a trade journalist, because I was enjoying the secret too much.'

'That was *my* company you were messing with, Jared. *My*

reputation. *My* livelihood. It's not a bloody game, you know. I've got a family to support, and you're experimenting with the future of the company?'

'Sorry, but what do you care? We won awards didn't we? And those awards helped us win extra business?'

'Don't you feel any shame?'

'No.'

'You couldn't be bothered to come up with one original idea of your own?'

'After a while, it became my way of doing things, you know? I guess I enjoyed knowing something that no one else did.'

'What do you think would have happened if Rod had found out? Or the trade press? And who knows how many people Richard told.'

'He didn't tell anyone.'

'Do you really believe him? On Saturday, he started mouthing off to Karen and Nigel that he and I were at school together.'

Jared brushed it off. 'No, he swore to me he wouldn't tell anyone. I believed him.'

'What was he asking from you?'

The creative director sniffed and said, 'Same thing as you I imagine. Your shares, right?'

So we were in exactly the same situation after all. There was one more thing I wanted to know. 'Jared, why did you punch me last Friday?'

He hunched up his shoulders and grimaced. 'Oh! I'm sorry about that, Duncan. I guess I had the wrong person. That was before Richard showed me the CD-Rom.'

'So why did you hit me?'

'Someone helped him find out I was borrowing the ideas. They must have told him which awards book to check. I assumed it was you.'

'Well, it wasn't. If I knew what you were up to, I think I would have talked to you and not Richard about it.'

He tapped a finger against the laptop. 'So I see.'

I ignored the jibe. 'OK, what about this: do you think Richard killed Anne? Or are you still convinced it was me?'

'Come on, Duncan, I was never convinced it was you.' He made it sound like it was the most ludicrous thing he'd ever heard. 'It was just something that Richard was saying, and I was curious. Who wouldn't be? I wanted to see your reaction.'

'Well, here it is again: I did not have anything to do with it. How could you even consider such a thing?'

He kept talking. 'As for Richard, well, he definitely didn't do it. I mean, what reason would he have? Anne's name wasn't on the CD, so she couldn't have had any argument with him there. No, I still think it was a screwed-up robbery.'

'Yesterday at the funeral, her mother told me that Rod had been calling in the middle of the night and shouting at her.'

'Well, there you go, then. You've caught him red handed.'

'What?'

'I'm being sarcastic. Calling someone in the middle of the night and shouting at them doesn't make you a murderer. I seem to remember Rod has called me a couple of times at home in the past. Complaining, as usual. You know what Rod's like.'

'OK, so it was a burglary gone wrong. That's what you said at the beginning. I just wish the police would hurry up and catch whoever is responsible. I'm worried they think it was me.'

'The Richard Regan theory again.' He cocked an eyebrow. 'It wasn't, was it?'

'Of course it wasn't!' I exclaimed with a burst of annoyance. 'That wasn't in good taste, Jared, and I'm getting sick and tired of hearing it. Anne was a great person and a good friend.'

'All right, I'm sorry. But what makes you think the police are trying to pin the blame on you?'

'It's the way they were asking questions,' I said. 'But I suppose I've got nothing to worry about. I was with Silvie the weekend of Anne's murder. She'll vouch for me.'

'You've got her well trained.'

'Any idea who pushed Richard into the river?'

Jared raised his eyebrows. 'What makes you so sure he was pushed? He might've decided to jump off a bridge himself.'

'Why would he do that?'

'Guilt? Remorse? Or maybe he just decided to do the world a favour. There must be all sorts of things about him that we don't know.'

I drained the drops of coffee from the cup and said, 'No, Jared. Someone must have killed him. It had to be someone on that list.'

'You still haven't proved that it wasn't *you* that murdered him.'

I flung my arms out. 'What have I got to do to convince you, Jared?' I then lowered my voice. 'OK, OK. Three days ago, I wished I did have the courage to do it. I couldn't see any other way out. But it was impossible. I simply wasn't capable of it. I was facing losing everything, and still I couldn't bring myself to harm him.'

'That's why you drove down for the party, isn't it?'

'Of course it is.'

'Well, if it's any consolation, I wanted to do him in as well, but also couldn't see it through. He insisted I meet up with him on Thursday afternoon outside the office, and when he described what he had on that CD against me, I just lost it. I was shouting and swearing. I told him I was going to kill him. That's when he showed me your file; it was a way of taunting me, I think. It showed that he held the cards over a number of people, not just me.'

'So you went along to the party specifically to beat him up?'

'No, not really. I was burning with rage all day, and just decided on the spur of the moment to go down there and kick the crap out of him. I wished I'd planned it better. My anger made me lose all sense of logic. When someone switched on the lights, I knew I had to leave.'

'So if neither of us is capable of doing it,' I mused, 'who is?'

I clicked the trackpad to close down Rod's file, and double clicked the 'Info' icon to bring up the list of names for inspection.

Natasha Brian
Boba Brown
Jo Craighen
Baz Drinkwater
Dan Hitchin
Jared Holt
Martin Jenkins
Duncan Kelly
Barbara Mason
Bharat Mistry
Nigel Powell
Rod Russell

'Have you read all the files?' asked Jared.

'Unfortunately, yes.'

'Which one's the worst?'

'Probably mine. Followed by, I would have to say, yours. Dan's was quite bad; Richard accuses him of being a neo-nazi. Boba

Brown apparently stole a harddrive from the studio. Baz Drinkwater once put potatoes up the exhaust pipe of Rod's car when he refused to sanction a pay rise. Most of the others are to do with affairs and the like.'

'I notice Nigel is on there,' Jared said. 'Can I have a look at his?'

I turned the laptop round to face him, and pushed it across the table. Still with his hands in his pockets, he leaned forward to read.

After a minute or two, he leaned back. 'You don't suppose it could be Nigel, do you?'

'Nigel? I very much doubt it. Not his style. He hates confrontations, you know that.'

'Exactly. He always bottles up his feelings. That's his problem.'

I turned the laptop round so I could read the list again. 'That's why you enjoy winding him up so much, isn't it?'

'I suppose it is. Although that's not the point. Have you ever noticed how impulsive Nigel's behaviour is? All those mood swings? One minute he's laughing at your jokes, the next he's running away in tears?'

'I thought you were the impulsive one.'

'Listen to me. Nigel's very fond of his parents, he told me once. You know he's always up there visiting them, don't you?'

'So?'

'So I just think Richard's threats could have tipped him over the edge. Pushing Richard into the Thames? It's a non-violent crime; one that even Nigel is capable of. You follow the victim, wait for the opportune moment when there's no one around, and then ...'

'We're speculating.'

'Maybe you should ask Nigel tomorrow, if he's at work.'

'Tomorrow could be a problem.'

I told Jared about my phone call to Jane Markham from the Tea Society, and how I had lied to Rod and Karen to buy more time.

'Then the company's knackered,' said Jared.

'Says the man who couldn't be bothered to turn up to the pitch.'

'I panicked,' he said. 'After I attacked Richard at the party, I was convinced he was going to let my secret out. Anyway, it doesn't matter. We failed to win the business. The company's finished. It's as simple as that.'

'Not necessarily.' I reminded him of my plan to blackmail Rod.

'Yes, but where will that leave me?'

'Providing you stop nicking other people's ideas, probably in a bigger and better position. Remember a few months ago there was talk of merging us with another MediaWide agency? If that happened, there would only be room for one creative director, and you're the one with the best reputation.'

'A reputation made from using the creativity of others, yeah.'

'No one needs to know about that,' I said. 'This CD can be destroyed. I'll wipe the information from my computer. Richard has taken his secrets with him. Nothing ever gets mentioned. But there's one condition: you have to go back to doing your own ideas. Promise?'

'OK, I promise. But what about you? How can *you* redeem yourself? What are you going to do – dig up that body?'

'No!' I couldn't bear to think about Doofy in those terms.

'Did the kid's parents know what happened to him? Isn't it time they gave him a proper burial? They must have been in torment all these years.'

'It's impossible,' I said. 'His mother died years ago.'

'And his father? What about him?'

'I'm not sure,' I said. 'I'll have to try and find out. I have an idea who it might be. I'll have to make a few subtle inquiries.'

'You do that,' said Jared. 'You can't let it go on any longer. Now that Richard's gone, it's up to you to put some poor suffering bugger out of their misery. It's the humane thing to do. Promise?'

Oh, God. This was going to be difficult.

'OK, I promise,' I said.

Jared sat up in his seat and stretched his arms. 'Good. I'm going to wander back to Charing Cross and grab a coffee,' he said. 'You look like you could use another one as well. If you're going to make a go of blackmailing Rod, it wouldn't do not to be tanked up with caffeine.'

'You're saying I should do it today?'

'Yes! Why wait? According to Rod's file, he visits the sauna on the first Tuesday of every month – which is today. So I think we should have a little trip up to King's Cross.'

'Shouldn't you visit the police? They're looking for you. You don't want to be the subject of a nationwide manhunt.'

'Let them look. Something tells me you're not capable of blackmailing Rod without my help. Once we have Rod's word, *then* I'll go and see the police. Don't forget that I want to still have a job at the end of the week. Is your wife expecting you back?'

'I called her earlier. Told her there's an emergency and I'd be working late.'

'Hah! You always were a little too liberal with the truth.'

I ejected the CD and placed it in a case in my jacket pocket. I shut down the laptop and packed it into my rucksack. 'Of course I am. I work in advertising, don't I?'

thirty-eight

We left King's Cross station and walked towards York Way. I couldn't help but notice we were continually looking around to check Rod wasn't following us.

It was almost 7.30 when we arrived outside Starlights Sauna. It was immediately striking how nondescript the place was. There was one large window with a brown curtain pulled across. Above, three light bulbs were positioned on a sign fashioned out of blue Perspex which spelt out the word 'Starlights' in a scripty, bad-taste typeface. I wondered, if the façade was anything to go by, what were the masseurs like.

However, entering the premises wasn't part of the plan. Three doors along from Starlights was a pub called The Furnold Arms from which we would keep a look out for Rod as he approached from King's Cross tube.

We stalked into the pub and grabbed two pints of Stella. Jared took a seat next to a window that looked on to the street. Luckily there was no frosted glass to obscure the view. There were, however, about two dozen small panes of brown stained glass to contend with, but it still wouldn't be enough to disguise the unmistakable rotund figure of Rod Russell.

'So what made *you* do it?' Jared asked me.

'What made me do what?'

He took a large swig from his glass. 'Oh, come on. I've told you what made me use other people's ideas. Why did you bury that body?'

I had been hoping to avoid this subject. But, with a little time to kill, a full glass of beer to drink, and his ever-curious nature, Jared was bound to dwell on such a thing.

'What made me do it? Fear. There was something in the way Richard reacted after Doofy—'

'Wait a minute – who's Doofy?'

'The guy that Richard shot.'

'What sort of a name is that?'

'It doesn't matter,' I said impatiently. 'After Doofy had been shot, and it was obvious he wasn't breathing, this expression seemed to come over Richard's face. It was almost as if he was *pleased*.'

'I don't follow.'

'It's strange. It was almost as if by accidentally shooting someone, he had achieved something he always wanted to do.'

'Kill someone?'

'I'm convinced of it. When he was ordering me around, getting me to help him hide the body, I could see he was getting a kick out of it. That's why I couldn't help but do what he said. I was worried about what he might do if I didn't.'

Jared studied his beer glass, perhaps wondering whether or not to buy a packet of crisps to accompany it. 'OK, so you went along with it because you felt you had to. Are you sure there was nothing else?'

'Like what?'

'Loyalty towards Richard? After all, he was your closest friend. Would you really have wanted to see him get in trouble with the police?'

'There was nothing like that.'

'Then did you keep quiet all these years to see if you could get away with it?'

'No, but I knew that the longer I left it, the more difficult it would be to tell anyone. The thing was, I always expected that sooner or later the grave would be discovered. Dug up by building developers, say. But it never was. I guess I'd always hoped it would be discovered so the decision to confess would be made for me.'

Jared peered at the street through the stained glass. 'No different to me I suppose.'

I remained quiet for a few moments.

'There is one other thing,' I said.

'Go on,' replied Jared, keeping his eyes fixed on the window.

'I always believed I was protecting my family by not telling anyone. Although I *did* come clean with Silvie on Sunday night. But when it first happened, I knew the truth would devastate my parents. After I got married and had children of my own, that feeling increased tenfold. Sometimes, when I'm in a cynical mood, I wonder if it was really myself I most wanted to protect. Should I feel guilty for saying that?'

'Not at all. That's the instinct of self-preservation. You can't shake it. It's programmed into you. It has to be. Whatever anyone says, it's still every man for himself. We may like to *think* we're civilized, but we're not.' He continued looking out of the window. 'All that's really changed is that we don't run around with spears or swords anymore. We use laptops and mobile phones instead. The rules haven't changed. It's still the desire to beat others that drives us along.'

'Then why do I feel guilty for saying it?'

'Because you've been taught to think otherwise. You're living in the wrong decade to be working in advertising, mate. Every industry has its time, and for ours it was the eighties. At least then you could be honest about why you worked in it. Now you have to pretend that you're a salesman in the most capitalistic of professions because you're "creative", or because you enjoy working with people, or something.'

He drained his pint.

'I know what you mean.'

'Anyway, at least you've proved you're human. If it's not the instinct for survival that makes us human, it's the ability to question ourselves. And it sounds as if you've been questioning yourself your entire life. Unlike someone like Richard, who I'm sure never thought twice about what he was doing. He was about as human as Dolly the sheep.'

I didn't reply. Instead, I decided to furnish myself with another drink. The empty pint glass had been sitting in front of me for at least a quarter of an hour.

Suddenly my attention was drawn towards the window.

'Look!' I said, pressing my nose against the glass and pointing to a portly character wearing an overcoat, walking briskly and staring at the ground. It was Rod – no doubt about it.

I ran to the entrance to the pub and peeked out in the direction of Starlights. Rod had gone in.

All we needed to do now was wait. I removed my jacket and packed it together with my laptop into my rucksack.

Jared and I began discussing how we should confront Rod. We agreed that simply spelling out the facts would work best.

The minutes crawled by. We wondered what services Rod was being treated to, blissfully unaware that a few metres away from him were two members of his staff waiting to blackmail him.

'Another animal instinct,' said Jared. 'At least Rod's honest with himself, visiting a place like that. He has a simple urge and he answers it. He doesn't let his marriage or his conscience get in the way.'

'That's no excuse,' I said.

thirty-nine

Thirty more minutes passed, and I felt my heart beating faster in anticipation. I started to become worried that Rod had left the sauna, and walked the opposite way towards Mornington Crescent tube station.

I did a little tube arithmetic. According to Richard's file, Rod lived in Guildford, which meant that he would have to take the Piccadilly and Northern lines down to Waterloo, changing at Leicester Square. And, although it was at least a ten-minute walk away, wasn't Mornington Crescent on the Northern line – ensuring an easier journey with no changes?

But Jared told me to be patient. Rod had arrived via King's Cross. The chances were that he would leave via King's Cross, too. Our boss was nothing if not a creature of habit.

Suddenly Jared shouted. 'Rod!'

Instinctively, I moved my head back to the window. I saw a hundredth of a second's-worth of Rod's overcoat moving away.

As I bolted towards the door I ran into a chair, stumbling like a drunken oaf. Jared followed. I looked back at the barmaid, and she heaved a face somewhere between a sneer and a grin.

We ran out of the pub, and I saw Rod shuffling along staring at the ground about twenty yards ahead of us. We quickly caught up with him, and Jared rapped a finger on his shoulder. Our boss spun round with a look of almost comical surprise on his face. Orange cheeks, cracked lips, bulbous nose. Yes, it was Rod all right.

'Duncan! Jared! What … wh—'

With my heart feeling as if it was going to thrash its way out of my chest, my lines kicked into play.

'You dirty sod, I know what you've been up to,' I growled, prodding him in the chest. 'I think we should have a little chat don't you?' I waited for his stutterfest to come to an end, which took some time.

'Bu-bu-bu-bu.'

'We know everything, Rod. Everything.'

'Wh-wh-wh-wh?'

'Come with us.'

The venom of my attack surprised even me. Jared was looking at me open-mouthed in amazement. I don't know quite what he had expected but, as he had said himself, if we were brazen enough to attempt to blackmail Rod, it couldn't be done in half measures.

The creative director grabbed hold of Rod's arm and we marched him like a naughty schoolboy back into The Furnold Arms. We led him to the bar. 'Two double whiskys,' I said to the barmaid.

By now our boss had composed himself and was glaring at each of us in turn. The drinks appeared and we walked him over to our seat at the front window, which remained idly vacant in the almost-dead pub.

'Take a seat.' I said. Rod sat down.

'Duncan, don't be a fool,' he growled, his cheeks becoming dark purple. 'And you!' he exclaimed to Jared. '*You're* in serious trouble!'

'Shut up,' said Jared.

The next thing that I did surprised me even more. I poured my whisky into Rod's glass, creating a quadruple. Both he and Jared looked at me as if I had three heads.

'Drink,' I commanded.

'Duncan, this is—'

'Rod, drink it.'

He raised the glass to his lips and drank half the contents. I knew that if he had a chance to speak before I'd made my pitch, the sale would be all the more difficult to close. I could see tears forming in the corners of his eyes. I didn't allow myself to feel sorry for him; I just blazed straight into my proposition.

'Rod this is all very simple. We know everything that's been going on – everything.'

The managing director began sobbing quietly. Jared sighed uncomfortably, but I was determined to see this through.

'Rod, you have been a very bad lad. You thought that—'

'OK, OK. It's all gone wrong,' he said. It was a little voice, a shaky voice.

'Listen to me, Rod. We have files, we have pictures, we have—'

'I had nothing to do with what happened to Richard.'

He lifted up his head. His cheeks were wet with tears, and puffed out. I didn't need to ask him to continue. He couldn't wait to tell me.

'Richard was murdered,' he burbled.

'Murdered?'

'I had nothing to do with it! You've got to believe me!'

'Tell me,' I said. 'And try to keep your voice down.'

'It was *them*.'

'Who? You're not making any sense.'

'*Them* ... so they would have you believe. Duncan, you've got to listen to me. I couldn't stop them.'

'Who murdered him?' asked Jared, flashing a pair of nervous eyes towards me.

'You know ... you know.'

'No I don't,' I said. 'Tell me.'

Rod checked himself and the blubbering subsided. 'Wait. How much do you know?' He saw the doubt in my face and said, 'No ... no, no, no.' He began backing away.

'Come on, Rod. Out with it.'

'No, I'm leaving.'

He slid off his chair and moved towards the door. I went after him and pushed him hard in the back. He fell down and rolled over like a barrel. I grabbed his collar, but he dodged sideways and I fell across a table. Rod ran out of the pub. Jared grabbed one of the whisky glasses and ran after him.

He hadn't gone far. His weight had made sure of that. I found him limping down a narrow side-street that ran adjacent to a building site. Jared was sprinting after him.

The street was empty save for a couple of drunks who watched us from a dimly illuminated doorstep at the far end. Jared caught up with his quarry and threw him to the ground. 'Rod!'

I watched the unfolding scene as a passive onlooker. I was aware of Jared smashing the whisky glass against a kerbstone, of pieces of broken glass bouncing on the pavement, of blood dripping from his hand.

He held the jagged remains of the glass to Rod's throat.

I caught up with them and said, 'Jared, put that down. It's not worth it.'

'Yes it is!' He pressed it against his boss's skin.

'Please, *please*. Don't hurt me,' he pleaded. 'It was Sir Geoff.'

The creative director jabbed the glass nearer to the older man's throat. Fifty per cent of me was still playing the detached onlooker, the remaining fifty was ready to move forward and pull Jared away before he did some real damage.

'Go on,' ordered Jared.

'MediaWide is going to be sold,' gagged Rod. 'You must have read about it.'

I remembered the story on the Ad-versity website. 'Jenrol,' I said. 'Jenrol is the buyer. Run by Philip Hammond. Is it definitely going ahead?'

'The MediaWide board are going to announce it tomorrow morning, just before the AGM.'

'Keep talking,' ordered Jared.

'Sir Geoff knows it's his only chance to sell up. He won't let anything scupper the deal. If he leaves it any longer the share price might fall again.' He caught his breath and swallowed. 'Richard … Richard was trying to blackmail me … it got back to Sir Geoff and …'

'Sir Geoff had him killed?'

He nodded. 'I'm sure of it. I tried to warn Richard but he didn't listen. The Jenrol deal would have been ruined. Sir Geoff would have been ruined.'

Jared continued pressing the glass to his neck, this time drawing blood.

'And Anne?' I asked. 'Did Geoff Deacon have her murdered as well?'

'Duncan, leave it,' said Jared. 'Anne doesn't come into this. You wanted Rod's job. It's our only chance, remember—'

Rod cut him off. 'Richard was threatening to go public with … with something he knew to get back at me, to get back at MediaWide. What he didn't know was it would have wrecked a two hundred million pound sale of MediaWide.'

'Plagiarism,' I said. 'Every one of our campaign concepts in the last three years has been stolen.'

Rod seemed genuinely surprised that I knew, and that was the way I wanted to keep it. It was obvious he knew nothing about the existence of the 'Info' file.

'*How do you know*? Did he tell you?' He looked at Jared, who was listening with a worried look on his face.

Jared gave me a threatening glance. 'Don't talk about it!'

Rod became even angrier. 'Has he told you the *whole* story, Duncan?'

Jared started to speak, but Rod cut him off with excited shouting.

'No, I don't believe he has! What was it you claimed, Jared? Anne's murder was a break-in gone wrong?'

'Rod, shut up—' Jared pressed the glass into his throat. A small stream of blood ran down Rod's neck. But he kept talking.

'And, yes, the murderer never got what he was looking for!'

Jared started screaming hysterically. 'Rod, I said shut up, or I'll cut you up!' But he didn't move the glass any deeper. He seemed powerless, mesmerized by what Rod was saying.

'No, *you* shut up! You see, Duncan, it was our boy Jared who killed Anne. Isn't that right, Jared? She had been keeping a record of what ideas you'd been stealing. She had it all neatly written down. You know how *organized* she was. The thing was, she had it all stored on her computer at work. Not at her flat as you imagined. But you went to her flat at the weekend all the same, didn't you? You got frustrated because you thought she was holding out on you. You didn't believe her when she said she didn't have it. That's when things get *nasty*, isn't it, Jared? With the temper we all know that you have, you lashed out. There was a scuffle. She fell and hit her head: a fatal injury. Then you ran away. Am I getting warm?'

I looked at Jared. He said, 'You stupid shit, Rod. You're lying.'

'Am I? Then how do you explain the timing, then, Jared? Anne comes to me with what she's found out about you. I tell her to go away, keep quiet, and forget it. Then she comes back to me and resigns. I call her at home – discreetly – to try and convince her not to do it. By Friday, she had reached boiling point, as Duncan here will tell you. Then on Monday we find out she is *dead*. And do you know what the last thing she said to me was?'

'What?' he said.

'She said, "I'm going to confront Jared and have him admit what he did to the others. Then I'm going public with it". Tell me, Jared, did you by any chance receive a call from Anne that weekend?'

Jared was seething. 'Who told you this?' he said. 'Richard?'

'Richard?' questioned Rod. 'No, Richard only found out you had been stealing ideas after he went through Anne's computer. And how do I know this? Because I caught him at it, that's why. That's when he tried to blackmail me. But you, Jared, I knew it was you who murdered Anne. I knew the minute I told you – I could see it written all over your face.'

'The police looked through Anne's harddrive,' I said. 'They didn't find anything.'

'That's because Jared would have erased it,' said Rod. 'And the police weren't suspicious enough to have the harddrive taken in for a forensic search.'

Jared started laughing. It was a demented, desperate laugh. It sent a chill right down to the base of my spine. 'Bullshit! You don't have any proof.'

'I don't need it,' replied the managing director. 'Because you know I'm right.'

'Rod, why the hell didn't you say anything to the police?' I demanded.

Jared turned to brandish the glass at me.

'How could I?' said Rod. 'It would be a scandal. It would end up destroying the whole company.'

'But you're going to retire!'

'Yes,' he said. 'I am. But I've worked for Sir Geoff Deacon and MediaWide for more than twenty years. Sir Geoff's done a lot for me and I owe him at least my loyalty.'

'So why are you telling me all this now?'

'I thought you already knew.'

'Of course I didn't know! You think I could live with myself, knowing something like that?'

Rod was exhausted, and lolled his head to one side. He was covered in perspiration. 'I'll tell you another thing,' he said. 'I think you'd better watch yourself. If you ask me, Jared will want to kill you next. Just the same as he did Anne.'

The creative director faltered as he tried to think what to say. I suddenly thought of the anonymous message with the carnations at Anne's funeral. 'Why did it have to happen? Words can't express what I feel. I'm sorry.' It was Jared's handwriting.

'Jared,' I said. 'The flowers for Anne. What did—'

Without warning, he threw the glass against the pavement in rage. He threw himself on top of Rod. He hauled the big man off the ground, and connected two hard blows to the side of his face. A mixture of blood and spit flew out of Rod's mouth.

Jared moved forward again, but Rod grabbed him around the waist. They struggled with each other for a few moments, in an absurd, desperate dance.

I took out my mobile and started to hit 999.

That's when it happened.

The top section of Rod's face, from the nose upwards, exploded in a freeze-frame moment of time. Then the world lurched into fast-forward as Jared was showered in a hail of blood, hair, and tiny fragments of grey matter.

I was paralyzed, completely unable to move. The mobile slid out of my hands on to the pavement.

An instant later, the side of Jared's head disappeared in a similar burst of deep red and white. Rod fell against him, and they both collapsed with a sickening thump on the pavement.

forty

I fell backwards and hit the ground hard, tearing my elbows on broken glass. I saw that one of Rod's legs was twitching, whilst the rest of his body wasn't moving at all. Jared lay flat on his back, not moving, his face – what was left of it – a picture of surprise. An instant later I heard a dull thwack and a piece of wooden fence next to me reduced to splinters.

I jumped to my feet and, expecting a scalpel of soaring pain to gouge into my back at any moment, sprinted as fast as I could towards the entrance of the building site, which – thank God – had been left open. I realized that I had dropped my mobile. It was still on the ground next to where Rod and Jared lay, but there was no way I was going back for it.

There was an excavator parked at the edge of the site adjacent to York Way. I dodged behind it and felt something whistle past my left shoulder and ricochet off the machine with a loud clang, like a spade being struck against a steel pipe.

I had still not seen which direction the killer was firing from. Pure adrenaline kept me moving. Quickly, I wrapped both hands around the top of the blue wooden fence that surrounded the building site, and locked my foot in an observation hole. I pulled myself over the top, and dropped down on to the pavement on the other side. Not waiting to check for oncoming traffic, I dashed across York Way, and then slid in between two parked cars and ran north towards Goods Way.

I knew I should try to call the police, but my overriding instinct was to try and escape from whoever was trying to kill me. Soon, I reached the intersection with Caledonian Road, and turned left. Any direction would do. I needed to find a taxi or tube station.

The pavement was filled with people going about their daily lives. No one gave me a second glance. I was just another office worker late for my bus.

I looked behind me. Nothing. But I knew I wouldn't be safe until I managed to get away from the area completely.

Taxi!

I waved my hand and shouted for a cab. One stopped and, without saying a word, I opened the back door and jumped in.

'Can you take me to Cambridgeshire?'

'Cambridgeshire? You want go to somewhere in *Cambridgeshire*?' exclaimed the driver. 'Are you mad? Why don't you bugger off and get the train?'

'I'll pay you a hundred pounds.' *Anything! Just stick your foot on the accelerator and go!*

'Oh! Now look, mate, my dinner....'

Something made me look out the rear window. I could see a man in the distance running towards me.

'I'll pay you three hundred pounds. Can we *please* go now?'

'OK, OK! I'll need a deposit first.' The cabbie pursed his lips and sniffed. His face said it all: show me the money first.

I thanked my lucky stars that I'd already visited the cash point earlier in the day. I snatched my wallet out of my back pocket and removed all the notes: five twenties. I slapped them into his waiting palm.

I looked out of the rear window again. The man was getting closer. He was tall and wide shouldered, with a shaven head. He was wearing a long black coat. His face was coming into focus. He seemed familiar but I still didn't recognize him. He got closer still.

It was Andy Flanagan: Sir Geoff Deacon's bodyguard. So it was he who had murdered Rod and Jared.

He didn't appear to be carrying a gun, which meant he must have concealed it beneath his coat. Judging from the way he held his enormous hands at his sides, outstretched and ready as he searched for a neck to squeeze the life out of, he wouldn't need one.

I slid down to the floor of the cab and looked desperately for something to use as a weapon, but there was nothing. 'Can we please, please, *please* go now?' I said.

The driver turned his attention to the road. 'Right you are.'

He pulled out into the road with only a cursory glance in his door mirror. A double-decker bus slowed to let us in. We were away.

Relief!

I sat motionless in the seat, taking deep breaths in an attempt to calm myself.

Had it really happened? Had I just seen Rod and Jared shot right in front of my eyes? It didn't seem possible.

But for two hundred million pounds, *anything* was possible.

We were now passing through Tottenham on our way to the M11. I needed to phone Silvie and warn her to get out of the house. I had no doubt that Flanagan was on his way there already. I spotted a telephone box outside a petrol station and asked the cabbie if we could stop. He swerved into the Texaco forecourt.

I got out of the taxi and ran to the phonebox. Was it vandalized? Luckily not.

My fingers pumped in Silvie's mobile number on the buttons. The number rang three times. She answered.

The important thing was not to panic her.

'Silvie, it's me.'

'Hello darling.' She sounded in a much better mood, albeit a little concerned. 'Where are you? I've been worried.'

'I'll tell you all about it when I get back. Silvie, take the kids and get out of the house. Go to the Riverside Guest House on the other side of the village. I'm on the way now.'

'What? But Giles hasn't even had his bath, and—'

'Just go. Please! I mean it, Silvie! I'll meet you there when I get back.'

The next thing I did was call Detective Sergeant Tomkins and ask him to meet me at my house.

'What the hell are you asking me to do? I was just about to leave the station and go home. And all the way up to Cambridgeshire, you say? I live in bloody Brent Cross. What's happened? Why can't you come down to the station?'

'There's no time to talk,' I said. 'Just be there.'

I gave him my address and ran back to the taxi.

forty-one

An hour and twenty minutes later we entered the village, and I asked the cabbie if he could take a detour via my house on the way to the hotel. I wanted to make sure that Silvie had left.

I groaned when I saw that Silvie's car was still parked outside. But then, the Riverside Guest House was close by. There was every chance she could have walked. I looked for signs of Flanagan. No other cars were around. I noticed that the lights in the living-room and one of the bedrooms were on. I paid the cabbie, and ran round to the back gate.

I desperately wanted to get in so I could call Silvie to check she had made it to the hotel safely, and Tomkins on his mobile to let him know what had happened to Rod and Jared.

I let myself in and rushed up the stairs, taking them three at a time. After calling out Silvie's name twice, and hearing no response, I moved towards the main bedroom. There was a phone in there I could use. I pushed the door open slowly and, seeing nothing out of the ordinary, went in.

I stopped walking, and listened. Not a sound. But I felt strange. It was as if I was somehow being watched. I couldn't be certain. The only windows in this bedroom overlooked the apple trees, and it was pitch black outside.

The number for Tomkins – where was it? Where was the card? I searched frantically in my pocket but couldn't locate it. I threw my wallet on to the bed, and shook out the contents. The card fell out. I was feeling less and less secure. All I could hear was the sound of my own breathing, but the sensation that someone was watching my every move was getting more and more intense.

I swung round to face the open door: nobody there.

Then I grabbed the phone and began to dial.

Nothing.

I shook the receiver impatiently. What was wrong with it? I pressed it to the side of my head. Nothing. It was stone dead.

I threw it down and ran to the door. I had to get to the study downstairs. I had to get to the phone.

At that instant, the lights went out.

There was a heartbeat of silence, and the burglar alarm sounded quietly and then faded away, as it always did when the main power supply was disconnected.

Now the house truly was silent. My own breathing seemed deafeningly loud.

I was momentarily blinded by the darkness. I couldn't even see my hand in front of my face, and knew I shouldn't move as I was standing right at the top of the stairs.

Everything was quiet. At the back of my mind, I began hearing the words of Richard Regan. *'Maybe I expected you to put up more of a fight ...'*

A floorboard creaked in the living-room.

'Disappointing, but I suppose people never change ...'

I lifted a foot and slowly began to retreat.

'Always were swept along by events, weren't you, Duncan...?'

I heard another floorboard creak, this time on the stairs.

Suddenly a heavy weight slammed into my stomach, knocking the wind out of me. I gasped. I could just make out the shape of someone standing in front of me. I tried to turn away.

There was a massive blow to the back of my right knee. A surge of pain darted up my leg. Unable to find anything to hang on to, I fell sideways down the stairs. I must have toppled over twice before ending up on my back in the hallway, but I couldn't be sure.

My leg felt like it was being stabbed with a dozen knives, and I screamed. My shoulder must have been twisted in the fall because it ached with a burning pain that shot through the nerves on my chest.

I looked up and saw the person who had attacked me, or at least their shape, walking slowly down the stairs in the darkness. Tall and thick-set. Flanagan. No doubt about it.

'We can get this over with much quicker,' he said. 'All you need to do is tell me where the CD-Rom is.'

'What CD-Rom?' I croaked. The pain in my shoulder was intensifying into a throbbing ache.

'What CD-Rom?' repeated Flanagan in a tone that implied I had just made a foolish mistake. 'The CD-Rom you stole from Richard Regan's office.' I saw his hand move and I heard a metallic clicking noise. Was it a gun? Was he getting ready to shoot me?

I had to play for time. Somehow I needed to slow him down while I decided what to do next.

'What if I don't have it?' I said.

'Oh dear,' he said, doing something with the gun. 'Then it will get very nasty indeed.'

My night vision was coming, and I saw him slide the gun into something attached to his side. He reached under his shirt and pulled out something that he held in front of him. It was a knife. It had a long blade – at least the length of my forearm.

I tried to push myself away, but couldn't. 'Oh yes,' said Flanagan. 'And your neighbours won't be able to hear a thing.' He brought the knife closer. 'Not after I've cut out your tongue. I'll be able to do what I like then.'

'I'll tell you,' I said. 'It's here.'

I knew that even if I did hand it over, he would probably kill me anyway. My only chance was to try and keep him talking until Tomkins arrived.

Flanagan was standing right over me. He placed his boot on my neck and began to press down. 'Where is it?' he said.

I managed to slip my hand into my jacket pocket. I could feel the CD case was broken. It must have happened when I had fallen down the stairs. I tried to find the CD, but it seemed like that, also, had been smashed. All I could feel was the sharp edges against my skin.

I heard Richard's voice again in my head.

'Think! It's the most important thing anybody can do. It's why anything ever happens, or has happened.' And then: 'I'm his best friend'.

I took hold of the largest piece of broken CD, and thrust it down as hard as I could against Flanagan's ankle. He cried out in pain as a piece of the CD broke off in his leg, and dropped the knife. I brought my hand back and jabbed the remaining shard as hard as I could into the back of his knee. Warm blood immediately soaked my hand. Flanagan swore and reached down to the source of the pain.

It was the delay I needed. I hauled myself up and grabbed the nearest object I could find – a ceramic lampshade – and threw it with both hands towards his head.

It shattered instantly.

Flanagan collapsed in a heap on the floor.

I staggered to one of the chairs next to the front door, and sat in the dark, watching him. I knew I should tie him up with something. But I was too busy trying to catch my breath.

'Hello?' said a voice from outside.

It was Tomkins. 'Here,' I said.

He walked into the hall with Stanners. The older man saw Flanagan, and ordered his sidekick to check him. 'Who's he?' he asked.

'Andy Flanagan. MediaWide. Sir Geoff Deacon's bodyguard.'

'Is he, now?'

For a second, I was filled with panic. 'I acted in self-defence.'

Tomkins was unperturbed. 'Of course,' he said. 'You're only human.'

forty-two

A giant chandelier dominated the foyer of the Capitol Hotel on Park Lane. It was suspended high above the heads of arriving guests, seemingly held by nothing more than a single, thin metal chain. Call me paranoid, but I took special care not to walk beneath it.

I folded the newspaper I had been reading under my arm, and made my way towards the ballroom. On the front page was a story detailing last night's events at King's Cross. I wasn't mentioned by name, and neither was Andy Flanagan. But the deaths of Rod and Jared were the main focus of the story, and that was enough to make many of the shareholders at the MediaWide AGM extremely unsettled.

MediaWide's share price had risen by almost 4% the previous day, but had plummeted this morning with the news about Rod and Jared.

I wasn't sure if the takeover would still go ahead or not. But one thing was for sure: this wouldn't be an easy meeting for Sir Geoff Deacon.

Especially at the end, when I knew Detective Sergeant Tomkins was planning to arrive to take him in for questioning.

When I reached the ballroom, I gave a cursory glance to the noticeboard positioned outside. It read: 'Capitol welcomes the MediaWide Annual General Shareholder's Meeting'.

As I expected, there was no one supervising the door. It was obvious why; the meeting appeared to have descended into chaos already.

The room was packed. So crowded, in fact, that there was only just enough room for me to slip in at the back. I stood on tiptoe to see a raised podium at the front, on which Sir Geoff Deacon was standing in between two glum-faced figures whom I recognized to be the group's chief accountant and chief executive.

Sir Geoff was trying to speak, but his voice was being drowned out by a number of angry questioners in the audience who were on their feet demanding answers.

Despite the noise, I could just make out what he was saying: 'Despite the downturn, our revenue remains strong and our new business prospects excellent.'

When someone stood on a chair and shouted, 'Did you have anything to do with these murders?' he momentarily shied away from the microphone, then continued reading out the financial results.

Finally, though, the audience heard what they wanted. Introducing it as an off-agenda item, Sir Geoff Deacon confirmed that a potential buyer had offered 40p a share for the Group, and that shareholders would soon be receiving their offer prospectuses in the post. A loud commotion broke out amongst the audience. That was fifty per cent more than the listed price. If I had just waited a few more days before selling my shares ...

But I didn't mind. I had kept my promise to my grandmother. My family was safe, and I was in one piece. As for my company? Well, only Sir Geoff Deacon could answer that.

I could see he was waiting for the noise to settle before handing back to his chief executive to wrap up the meeting. 'Are there any other questions?' he asked the audience.

Everyone spoke at once. I stood on the back of two chairs and addressed my question directly to the chairman himself.

'Sir Geoff Deacon! I hereby request you to stand down.'

It was drowned out in the commotion.

So I tried a different tactic.

I walked down the aisle separating the two groups of attendees. As I made my way to the stage, people sensed something extraordinary was going to happen and the noise died down. Several camera flashes went off at the sides of the room, and hotel staff stopped to watch. Even the hassled security personnel stood still and didn't try to apprehend me as I climbed on to the stage.

I spotted Philip Hammond of Jenrol, sitting in the middle of one of the front rows, watching with interest, and also Nigel who was standing against the back wall to the left. He had one of his hands clasped over his mouth in surprise.

Sir Geoff froze. I walked around the back of the table until I stood directly opposite him. 'What the hell do you think you're doing?' he barked at me.

I cleared my throat, and said what I had come to say into the microphone.

'Ladies and gentlemen. Seven days ago, this man threatened to close my company, HFPK, a subsidiary of MediaWide. This was not because we hadn't met our financial targets, but because of a cover up. He set us an impossible target that he knew we wouldn't achieve, as he desperately needed an excuse to shut us down.'

The chief executive leaned forward in his chair. I didn't know whether he was about to jump out of it and wrestle me to the floor, or put a gag on Sir Geoff to make sure he didn't interrupt me.

I continued, 'Since we started the company three years ago, our creative director, Jared Holt, had regrettably been secretly stealing the concepts of other agencies to meet our new business pitch requirements, and drive our awards success.'

I removed the newspaper from under my arm and slapped it down on the table. A thick sheath of leaflets fell out. I handed them to people in the front row who passed them along the lines of attendees.

'These documents list the exact campaigns that were stolen, the agencies where they originated, and what year they first appeared.

'It was this knowledge that led directly to the deaths of several of my colleagues. Firstly, Anne Fulton uncovered the scheme, but, when she complained to Rod Russell and Sir Geoff Deacon, was fobbed off and forced to resign. Jared Holt murdered her last weekend.

'On Saturday, another employee of MediaWide was murdered. Richard Regan. Sir Geoff personally ordered him to be drowned in the River Thames to lessen the risk of him making this knowledge public, and wrecking the sale of the group to Jenrol.'

Sir Geoff lunged forward and grabbed hold of the microphone. 'I don't know what you are talking about, young man, but I'm ordering you to leave immediately,' he hissed. 'Can somebody call security?' he shouted to a member of the hotel staff.

No one moved except for the chief executive who, gently but firmly, pushed Sir Geoff back into his seat.

I pressed on. 'Finally, both Jared Holt and Rod Russell, managing director of MediaWide, were murdered last night on the direct instruction of Sir Geoff for the same reason. The cash from the sale of the group was everything to him. If anyone got in the way, they were killed.'

There was silence in the room. People didn't know what to do. As their usual leader had fallen dumbstruck, they waited for me to make the next move.

'So I hereby request you stand down. If you care about this company and its employees, that's exactly what you will do.'

The crowd continued to watch quietly, as if weighing up the situation. Suddenly someone yelled, 'Resign!'

'Get out, Sir Geoff,' called out somebody else.

This opened the floodgates. A torrent of abuse erupted from the audience. Someone even threw a *Financial Times* newspaper at the stage in anger.

I found myself seizing his hands and pulling them behind his back.

'What are you doing? This is preposterous! Someone get him off me immediately! Why are you all acting like morons? You need me, do you hear? This company *needs* me!'

I led him off the stage and out of the room.

The truth was, I had no idea where I was taking him. I was just determined to make a stand.

When we entered the hotel reception I saw Detective Sergeant Tomkins bounding up the steps to the entrance, followed by Detective Constable Stanners, and two police constables in uniform.

'What the devil do you think you're doing?' cried Sir Geoff as I marched towards them. The reception area fell silent. Everyone was watching me.

For the first time in my life, I felt totally and utterly in control.

Tomkins sighed wearily. 'Oh, dear. Mr Kelly again. Wasn't four hours in the station last night enough for you?'

'I had to restrain him. Didn't want to let him escape. Besides, I've wanted to do that for some time. Wouldn't have been able to live with myself if I didn't.'

Tomkins was not amused. 'Release him. Now,' he said. I raised my hands from the back of Sir Geoff's jacket.

The chairman had just enough time to straighten his tie before one of the constables put a pair of cuffs on him. Then a severely disconcerted and humiliated Sir Geoff Deacon was taken outside to a waiting police car.

Tomkins didn't move. He stood opposite me, and sighed

heavily. He seemed to be wrestling with his conscience, almost as if he was psyching himself up for something he didn't really want to do. For a moment, I thought he was also going to arrest me as well. But instead, he slapped me on the shoulder with his beefy hand and said, 'Watch yourself, Duncan.' With that, he turned and left the building.

'You've left me with a bit of a problem, haven't you?'

Philip Hammond stood beside me with his arms folded. He was a small, slight man, a good three inches shorter than me.

'I guess I have,' I said.

Hammond pursed a lip and said, 'It's not a signed and sealed deal yet – but it will be. The top management may be rotten to the core, but they can be replaced. And as to whether or not clients' ideas for their campaigns have been stolen – I don't think they'll be as worried as you might think. By nature, advertising is a derivative business. It has a short memory.'

'That's your opinion.'

'It's not me, it's that of the industry as a whole. Things move on. The past gets forgotten about very quickly in this business. MediaWide has already told the City about the offer, it went on the wire this morning. Shareholders will be receiving their transfer instructions in the next couple of days. Believe me, with MediaWide in the state it's in at the moment, any shareholder would be a fool to say no. I'm offering a rescue deal for the company, Duncan. But I am faced with a problem. Losing the chairman, I can handle. As you saw yourself, the shareholders aren't going to miss him. I've got a first-rate chief executive in there who's more than capable of doing the job. That is, if he's clean.' He gestured towards the ballroom and clicked his tongue as if to help him think. 'My real problem is this: I have to find someone for a more challenging role. Someone ambitious. Someone hands-on. Driven. A thinker would be nice. I need a leader who's not afraid to take a risk once in a while to get what he wants. Yes, it's the managing director I'll have a problem finding....'

Now it was my turn to fold my arms, and turn to face him.

'… that is, if you decide to turn the job down,' he said.

He removed his spectacles and polished them with a handkerchief as he waited for my answer.

forty-three

Gran settled back in her armchair, laughing at the top of her voice at another one of Aunty Beryl's jokes.

In all honesty, they didn't make much sense to me, but it didn't matter, as Gran seemed to enjoy them. At any rate, I knew the reason she was laughing so hard was really down to the overwhelming relief and happiness she felt at getting back with the person she cared most about.

I knew how she felt.

I hugged Silvie with one arm, and Lily whom I was holding in the other. Giles was sleeping in his pram, so I left him alone.

We were with my parents and sister Julia, watching Gran and Beryl in one of the private lounges of The Acorns. It was an old manor-house that had been converted a few years ago to exacting standards. All the original features had been restored, and there were almost as many members of staff as there were residents. It stood in the centre of seven acres of private, wooded parkland. Now I could truly appreciate why the fees were so high.

Earlier, I had stood at one of the huge windows, gazing out on to the huge, snow-covered lawn, reflecting that selling my shares had definitely been worth it. I spent more than three minutes there, enjoying the sounds of Gran's uncontrollable giggling behind me.

There was still something I had to do. I hadn't yet approached my father about Doofy. Even though it had been almost four months since I had taken the job as managing director of MediaWide, I still hadn't found the courage to ask him.

Today was going to be different. I had been telling myself for days that it must be today. There was no going back. Until I did tell him, I felt sure that the guilt would always be there on my conscience. I couldn't let it wait another fifteen years.

After much thinking, I had decided to start by asking subtle questions about when he and my mother had first moved to the village. Then I would ask him if he knew Gwennie from the woods, to see what reaction he gave. Eventually I would ask him about Doofy.

I hadn't yet decided how to tell him about Doofy's whereabouts. Or how I had come into possession of this information. There was still so much I had to work out.

The dramatic orchestral theme to the news blasted out from the television in the corner of the room, and Beryl said, 'Oh, the news! You know how much I love the news!'

I tensed. It was a reaction I still experienced months after the MediaWide story had faded away. In the immediate days and weeks following the shareholders' meeting, it had been reported incessantly, until every last drop of scandal had been squeezed out of it.

Initially I had doubted that MediaWide was capable of weathering such a storm but, following the confirmation of the sale, I had met each of the major clients one by one, and somehow managed to coax them into keeping their business with us.

Nigel had insisted on leaving. The murders of Richard, Jared and Rod – in addition to Anne – proved too much for him, and rather than dragging himself into work every day for a cause he clearly didn't believe in anymore, he simply resigned.

Karen had stayed in MediaWide and, ironically enough, I was now her boss. She had insisted that she knew nothing about the plot by Sir Geoff Deacon, and the police, after much intensive questioning, had decided to believe her. She was currently in the middle of three weeks' leave, taken at my request. Although, even after all that had happened, I was looking forward to working with her again.

Andy Flanagan had already been found guilty of the murders of Jared and Rod. The evidence against him had been overwhelming. The police had recovered the bullets from the building site and matched them to the gun they had found tucked into a holster on his side. He had always protested his innocence over the killing of Richard, but a sceptical jury had thrown out his plea of not guilty, and found him guilty in a unanimous verdict. He was in Brixton Prison awaiting sentencing.

Sir Geoff Deacon was still awaiting trial in what promised to be one of the courtroom sensations of the year. I was to be a key witness, and was conversing daily with Philip Hammond and his legal team. To date, Jared and Silvie remained the only people to whom I had confessed that Richard had been blackmailing me. The only copy of the CD-Rom had been broken when I had used it to attack Flanagan. Richard's laptop had never been found, and the police had concluded that it had probably followed him into the River Thames, although Andy Flanagan vehemently denied this.

I walked over to Dad. 'Fancy going for a quick walk round the grounds?' I knew he would agree. Every time we had visited The Acorns during the past two months, he had made the same suggestion himself.

The air outside was bitingly cold. The sun was still tucked behind a thick layer of cloud, and the light had already started to fade despite it being only two o'clock in the afternoon. We walked down the stone steps on to the lawn. The grass was covered in a thin layer of yesterday's snow which felt crunchy underfoot.

We walked in silence until we were at least two hundred yards from the main building, when suddenly Dad said, 'You're going to ask me about Doofy, aren't you?'

I kept walking, but couldn't keep the surprise out of my voice. 'How do you know?'

'Ah, Duncan. We're not so different, you and I.'

'What do you mean?'

'I know about it, Duncan. I know about The Accident. I met Richard and he told me everything.'

'You met *Richard*?'

'Yes. He told me about what happened to Doofy. He told me what you did. What he *made* you do. He told me why he thought you kept it secret all these years. And he told me that he was trying to blackmail you.'

I felt a profound sadness. I desperately wanted to say something, but all I could manage was, 'How?'

'I found a fax message at your house. You were out at an awards show, or some such professional function. I went into your study to get a book for Silvie's father, and found a fax lying on the floor.' He paused to take a deep breath. 'Of course, I *wasn't* going to read it. I only wanted to pick it up off the floor. But then I saw that it mentioned … your brother.'

I swallowed. 'So you contacted Richard?'

Dad nodded. 'His numbers were on the fax paper. Seeing the message, I knew I had to.'

We reached a small wood and looked back at the grandeur of the house. We must have appeared but tiny dots against the expanse of the acres of white snow.

'So Doofy *was* my half-brother?'

'Donald was, yes.'

'He was named after your middle name?'

He nodded again. 'Yes.'

'I'm sorry,' I said. 'I've been wanting to tell you all my life about what happened, but I couldn't. I could never find the courage.'

'You're wrong,' Dad replied, though not unkindly. 'You *had* the courage, but you didn't have the cruelty. I know it was your way of protecting us.'

'Protecting myself, maybe.'

He contemplated this. 'That's not you. That's a cynic talking. It wasn't your fault.'

I leaned against the trunk of a fallen tree. 'So,' I said at last, 'aren't you disappointed with me? With the way I've turned out? Surely I'll have to make a confession to the police now. And do you know something? I deserve everything I get.'

'I don't think that will be necessary,' said Dad. 'You'll be giving me up too. And I can't imagine you want to do that.'

'I don't understand.'

He picked up a stick and ran it idly through the snow. 'Like I said, Duncan. What we do makes us who we are. And we're really the same, you and I.'

'So you keep saying.'

'Now we've got to look out for each other. Doesn't that make you feel better?'

It then dawned on me. 'You pushed Richard into the river?'

Dad turned away. 'It was an accident,' he said. 'I contacted him on Saturday afternoon, and we arranged to meet near Cleopatra's Needle early Sunday morning. It was all very strange, creeping down to London in the dark. I recognized him at once. He also looked as if he'd been in a fight ... although the unflattering glow from a streetlight will do that to anyone, I suppose. He kept threatening me with violence and I told him that wouldn't achieve anything. All I wanted to do was talk. I wanted to find out the truth about Donald.'

'What happened?'

'We walked a long way, as far as Lambeth Bridge. He became

angry and started punching me. There was an argument and, in the struggle that followed, Richard fell into the water. It all happened so fast, I didn't have time to think.' Dad turned his eyes away from the sun, and brought them to bear on me. 'I wanted to save him, but I couldn't. He just disappeared in the water. Maybe he hit his head on the way down.'

I said, 'Why didn't you say anything to the police?'

Dad didn't immediately reply. He smiled thinly, and began walking back towards the house, back to the family, his brow furrowed, his face consumed in deep thought. 'I think you already know the answer to that,' he said.